Shadmocks & Shivers

Shadmocks & Shivers

New Tales inspired by the stories of R. Chetwynd-Hayes

Edited by Dave Brzeski

Shadow Publishing

SHADMOCKS & SHIVERS

NEW TALES INSPIRED BY THE STORIES OF R. CHETWYND-HAYES

Special thanks to Stephen Jones as advisor/consultant

Special thanks to John Linwood Grant for editorial assist

ISBN: 978-0-9572962-8-2

Shadow Publishing, Apt 19 Awdry Court, 15 St Nicolas Gardens,
Kings Norton, Birmingham, B38 8BH, UK
david.sutton986@btinternet.com

Dedication

This book is dedicated with great affection to Bryn Fortey, another of those 'nicest old gentlemen one could ever hope to meet'. Bryn was published in *The Fontana Book of Great Horror Stories* series at around the same time as R. Chetwynd-Hayes was editing *The Fontana Book of Great Ghost Stories* series. One of my deepest regrets is that Bryn was unable to contribute to this volume.

CONTENTS

FOREWORD

MUCH OF WHAT you need to know about Ronald Chetwynd-Hayes is summed up in the epithet which British fandom bestowed upon him – the Prince of Chill. Neither master nor king, but prince, a worthy enough position to make him of note. His domain was indeed the chill, not the utter terror or visceral horror of some of his contemporaries (though he had his darker moments). Chetwynd-Hayes was in many ways that most underappreciated of horror writers – one of those who satisfied his many readers with everything from tales with neat little twists to the occasional true gem. In almost two hundred short stories – and ten novels – he delivered the goods.

Such a legacy is not always honoured, though it's gratifying that he did receive the Bram Stoker Award for Lifetime Achievement in 1988, and the British Fantasy Society Special Award in 1989. He deserved those awards, not only because of his long-standing service to the field, but because he was, basically, himself. Not a self-announcing, self-congratulatory celebrity of the genre, but the sort of writer who everyone said was one of the nicest people you would want to meet.

It had bothered me ever since Ron passed in 2001 that his industry and talent might be forgotten by many readers, and that we might never see more stories of some of his more memorable creations – in particular the Shadmock, from his Monster Club stories. I'd long wondered if anyone else might be allowed to add to this mythos. And then, by sheer chance I realised that 2019 would have been Ron's 100th birthday. 'What better time for someone to put together a tribute anthology to R. Chetwynd-Hayes?' I thought. At that point, I hadn't seriously considered that I might edit it myself, so I mentioned it to the man I thought in the best position to put such a project in motion. A man who knew Ron well, had worked with him and edited collections of his work in the past – Stephen

Jones.

If you've ever wondered how Steve got to be as successful and well -respected an editor as he is, it's at least partly because he's a force of nature. I'd barely mentioned the idea before he'd offered to open negotiations with the estate of R. Chetwynd-Hayes on my behalf. It turned out that Steve was already working on a Chetwynd-Hayes collection for PS Publishing, so I found that I'd volunteered myself to helm this collection of new stories.

I soon found a willing publisher in David Sutton at Shadow Publishing, an old friend of Steve's and a man with whom I had worked before, so all that was needed was authors – people who felt they had a genuine connection to Ron. Steve Jones immediately suggested John Llewelyn Probert, who is a huge fan of Ron's work, and I was soon overwhelmed by the number of well-known genre authors who wanted to be involved with the book.

The stories in this volume are split between those who directly used Ron's characters and concepts and those who were simply inspired by his writing. There are, inevitably, several that reference Ron's best known work, that being *The Monster Club*, which was also made into a film by Milton Subotsky in 1980, albeit Ron was reportedly not all that happy with the adaptation. From my personal point of view, the upside of this is we get more Shadmocks. As well as visiting the fabled Monster Club, it's worth noting that we also get to spend some time in the infamous Clavering Grange, and reacquaint ourselves with the redoubtable Madame Orloff.

The only characters the R. Chetwynd-Hayes estate denied us permission to use were Francis St Clare and Frederica Masters, his psychic investigators. There has apparently been periodic interest from television and film companies over the years (In fact the first edition of the St Clare novel, *The Psychic Detective*, actually states that it's "Soon to be a Hammer film" on the cover. Sadly that deal evidently fell through) and they thought it best not to muddy the waters with new stories by other authors at this time. To make up for this disappointment, we were given permission to reprint one of the original St Clare and Fred stories, so we open with Ron's own '*The*

Gibbering Ghoul of Gomershal'.

It seems rather apt that the first of the new stories in this anthology should be '*An Episode of Life...*' by Tina Rath. One of Tina's earliest story sales was to Ron for '*The Fetch*' which appeared in *The Nineteenth Fontana Book of Great Ghost Stories* (1983). Since her story here features a fictionalised version of a young Ron Chetwynd-Hayes, during his early days as a film extra, and an older version of Ron turns up in Stephen Laws' '*Fire Damage*', I decided it would be very fitting for them to bookend the original fiction in this volume.

I like to think that Ron would have relished the opportunity to be a character, in stories, written by other authors. He was, after all, in the acting business in his youth. As for the rest of the stories herein, they may vary in length, subject matter and style, yet each one clearly shows the genuine affection the authors hold for Ron and the influence he had on their own work. And each is offered as their tribute to our very own 'Prince of Chill'.

Dave Brzeski

MONSTER RIGHTS

By

Cardinal Cox

Lit by the sodium glare above there's
A soapbox on the corner of a street
A strange figure clambers up, starts to speak
This demagogue has cloven hooves for feet
He has done this a hundred times before
His voice is raised to be heard by the throng
He knows how to capture their attention
He has aims to correct a perceived wrong
"Did that Percy Edwards impersonate
A shadmock's notable, glorious whistle?
Would that brave slave Androcles have pulled from
A werewolf's paw a thorn from a thistle?"
Equal rights for monsters the strange throng say
They march through the town centre at midnight
They shuffle with placards and banners
Shambling, drooling, they are a frightful sight
There's a boozy party making badges
And another group printing up t-shirts
Though it's whispered in the ink they've mixed
A little pinch of cursed black graveyard dirt
A single vamgoo holds a petition
And asks everyone who passes to sign
The ignorant humans though bustle passed
No, not one of them is forming a line
A small committee has been working hard
Drawing up a list of all their demands
And first at the top of the page is that
Every silver bullet is to be banned
Holy crucifixes to be locked up

Restaurants to open where they can sup
Creations to get donated organs
Mirror-free zones declared for the Gorgon
Sea-monsters included in whaling bans
Recognition for all the sundry clans
Heating allowance for shivering mummies
Baby vampires to get stronger dummies
Cute hellish hounds to be allowed off leads
And everything to have freedom to breed

THE GIBBERING GHOUL OF GOMERSHAL

From the casebook of the world's only practising

psychic detective

By

R. Chetwynd-Hayes

M R REGINALD HAINES was a bald, ponderous man of some fifty-five years, who made a great business of smoking a pipe. He first rammed dark-brown tobacco into the bowl, then very slowly raised the stem to his mouth and inserted it between his large, white teeth. A few well-planned puffs, followed by three perfectly formed smoke rings, apparently informed him that the operation was proceeding satisfactorily and he could now – after due thought and consideration – turn his attention to more pressing concerns.

'It gibbers,' he said.

Francis St Clare, the world's only practising psychic detective, leaned back in his chair and creased his handsome face into a thoughtful smile.

'Sounds interesting. Comes out of a graveyard, you say!'

Mr Haines examined his pipe, cleared his throat, then nodded slowly.

'You must understand, Mr St Clare, when I retired last year I bought an old cottage that stands on the edge of Gomershal Burying Ground. No one's been buried there since 1854 and the place is a proper mess. Anyroad, a week or two back when I was digging 'tator patch, I hears a sort of rustling and a scraping come from the old burial ground and I says to meself – hullo, a bit of hanky-panky going on in there. Know what I mean?'

'I can guess,' Francis nodded. 'Misbehaves among the graves. Sorry.'

'Well, I climbs over the bit of wall, creeps through the trees – then I saw it. Down a pit – gibbering and when I tell you...'

St Clare raised an elegant hand. 'Don't. You've told me more than enough. It's a firm rule that I know nothing of the phenomenon, until I experience it for myself. Eye-witnesses rarely give an accurate account, and I prefer to take on a case with an open mind. Will it be possible for you to put us up?'

'Us?'

'Yes, my assistant and myself. I never go anywhere without Fred. She combs my hair.'

The pipe had called it a day and gone out. Mr Haines sighed deeply and thrust it into his pocket.

'Daresay, Jean – that's me daughter – could spend a few nights in the attic, then your assistant could have her room and you the spare. Yes, that'll be all right. I'll speak to the missus.'

Francis stared thoughtfully at his blotting pad.

'There's just one little matter. My fee. I usually charge a hundred a day, plus expenses. The first hundred in advance.'

Mr Haines said, 'Strewth!' and followed it up with an equally expressive, 'Bloody hell!'

'However,' Francis went on, 'when a case promises to be of special interest, I have been known to ask for far less. Let's leave the question of my fee in abeyance for a while. Will it be convenient if we arrive at six o'clock precisely tomorrow evening?'

'Can't be too soon for me,' his new client replied. 'Anything particular you fancy for 'igh tea? A nice piece of smoked 'addock, maybe?'

'Great. And don't worry about Fred. She eats anything. Let me see if I've got your address right – Woodbine Cottage, Copse Lane, Gomershal.'

Both men rose as Mr Haines said, 'That's right. Turn off the M6 just after you pass through Clavering. My place is on the left. You can't miss it. Three parts surrounded by tombstones.'

'Right. See you tomorrow evening then. Would you mind seeing yourself out? It's the housekeeper's day off.'

THE GIBBERING GHOUL OF GOMERSHAL

The psychic detective waited until his new client had left the room, before sitting down and calling out:

'OK, Fred – let's hear from you.'

The thick blue curtains that masked the French windows, parted and Frederica Masters stepped into the room. She was an extremely beautiful girl with ash-blonde hair and white skin, who wore a cynical expression as though her blue eyes had seen too much and forgotten too little in her short life. She wore a colourful costume that bordered on the bizarre. The bright red blouse had a dangerous split down the centre that revealed the valley between her breasts; the green mini-skirt was the stunted offspring of a broad belt, and her splendid nylon-clad legs would make any man's eyes widen with appreciation. Her voice was low and husky.

'Don't you think that one will be a complete waste of time? I ask you – a gibbering something!'

Francis fitted a cigarette into a long holder and lit it with a gold lighter.

'What about his atmosphere? Were you able to sort it out?'

Fred sank into a chair and crossed her legs,

'Suet pudding on the hoof. Not a spark of psychic awareness in his entire body. He wouldn't see a nasty if it came and sat on his lap. Don't I get a cigarette then?'

Francis pushed the box across the desk.

'That's why I think there's something 'orrible taking place down in darkest Gomershal. He's not the type to imagine a gibbering something.'

'Oh, very bright. But you underestimate the effect of late night horror films on TV. Everybody gets a free education these days.'

Francis St Clare nodded. 'The child may be stupid, but she has moments of inspiration. Well, as the eunuch said to the actress – we shall have to wait and see.'

Francis turned the car into Copse Lane and drove some hundred yards or more until he came within view of a picturesque cottage that was three-quarters surrounded by reeling tombstones and numerous skeletal trees. The psychic detective braked to a halt and after switching off the engine, examined the scene with a professional eye.

Beyond the cottage rolling hills sloped down to open moorland, that reached out green and russet clad arms to embrace the low-wall surrounded burying ground. To the extreme right stood a ruined building that had probably been a memorial chapel, but was now only two jagged walls, rearing up from a mass of weed-infested masonry.

Francis asked: 'Well?'

Fred sank back and stared thoughtfully out over the desolate countryside.

'There's the usual personality debris. I just had a glimpse of an earthbound waif. Over there by that ruined building. An old woman in a long, tattered dress. I'd say she came to a bad end some – oh, I don't know – two hundred years ago? She's no problem. Wait a sec – there's a child – I think. The head is jutting up from that mound by the large broken tombstone. Probably buried alive. They often were a century or so ago. Poor thing's trying to get out.'

Francis nodded. 'But can you see anything out of the ordinary?'

'Not so far. But one rarely does in broad daylight. Hullo – there's a nifty looking girl peering at us round the front doorway. Nothing ghostly about her. Don't you think it's about time we made ourselves known?'

'But it's only ten minutes to six.'

'So, you'll be ten minutes early! Let's get in there – I want me 'igh tea.'

The girl who stood in the open doorway was extremely pretty; an exquisite heart-shaped face that was enhanced by soft brown eyes and framed by long auburn hair. She smiled shyly and said:

'You must be Francis St Clare and Miss Masters.'

Fred ran a critical eye down the long out-of-date beige dress, then raised a slim eyebrow when she saw the cracked, down-at-heel shoes. 'You can call me Fred. And this is the genius himself. He'd be happy if you curtsied and called him sir.'

'It's one of her dafter days,' Francis explained. 'May we come in?'

The girl stood to one side and bobbed her head up and down. 'Sorry... I wasn't thinking.'

Francis – followed by Fred carrying two suitcases – entered a narrow passage, then without waiting for an invitation, turned left into what could only be the best-only-to-be-used-on-special-occasions front room. It had a faint damp smell and was equipped with fat, brocade-covered armchairs and matching sofa, a large glass -fronted cabinet that contained an assortment of china figurines, a bowl of waxed flowers and a stuffed parrot in a brass cage. Fred exclaimed: 'Knock me backwards, but never call me mother!' as Mr Haines, preceded by a plump lady, entered the room.

He rubbed his hand on the seat of his trousers, then offered it for Francis' consideration. 'Ah, Mr St Clare – so you're 'ere then? This is my lady wife – Doris.'

Mrs Haines had a pear-shaped figure, a full round face, thin lips and a pained expression that suggested she had recently eaten something very bitter and it was just beginning to play havoc with her digestion.

She nodded to Francis, and said, 'Mr St Clare – delighted I'm sure,' then shot Fred a glance of cold disapproval. 'Good evening, miss. I expect you'd like to freshen up.'

'I feel fresh enough,' Fred explained. 'But if you mean do I want to go to the...'

'Thank you, we would,' Francis raised his voice at the right moment. 'Very kind.'

'Jean will show you to your *rooms*.' Mrs Haines' voice emphasized the plural. 'We'll be sitting down to table in twenty minutes.'

The young girl led the way up a flight of narrow stairs, then first conducted Fred to a small room with a commanding view of the graveyard and Francis into a slightly larger one enhanced by a massive double-bed. He gazed upon it reflectively.

'This is the spare room,' Jean explained. 'It's usually used by my married sister and her husband when they visit us.'

'And you've been turned out of your own room to make room for Fred. I'm so sorry. But I don't suppose it'll be for long.'

The girl shrugged. 'I don't mind. I rather like the attic actually. Do you think – you'll be able to get rid of that – thing?'

Francis smiled gently and looked down into the troubled eyes.

'Is it so dreadful?'

She nodded. 'I know we're not to tell you anything about it, but I seem to see more than either of my parents. Dad thinks it's a nuisance that someone like you can explain away and Mum – well – I don't think she really believes there's anything to explain. I made them send for you.'

Francis said, 'Ah!' and waited for her to continue.

'I've read about all of your cases. At least all that that writer has recorded. *"The Headless Footman of Hadleigh"* and *"The Wailing Waif of Battersea"* – it was wonderful how you solved those.'

'The fellow dramatises dreadfully,' Francis murmured,

'So – when I heard – and saw – what I did – I knew only you and – that beautiful girl could help us.'

'I might,' Francis declared airily, 'but Fred is never much use. I only bring her along to carry the luggage.'

Jean smiled shyly and fingered the flower-patterned bedspread.

'You only say that. You must love her really.' She blushed and Francis experienced a pang of pity. 'I'm sorry, I shouldn't have said that. What must you think of me?'

He tilted her head back until he was looking straight into her eyes. 'Let's say, I tolerate her.'

Her voice was just above a whisper. 'And she must be in love with you. You're so – so handsome.'

'Francis.' Fred was leaning against the doorpost. 'Your smoked 'addock's getting cold.'

Mrs Haines watched Fred begin her third helping of baked rice-pudding, then made an utterance.

'You've got a healthy appetite, I'll say that for you. Don't pick at your food like some I could mention.'

Fred pointed her spoon at Francis. 'I need bags of grub. He wears me out. I mean to say, he might be a genius, but he's bone idle. Uses me as a packhorse.'

Mrs Haines' withering glance embraced both the psychic detective and her husband. 'They're all bone idle and use us poor women as conveniences.' She paused while Fred choked on a portion of rice-pudding. 'Which brings me to the reason for your visit, Mr St Clare...'

'Please – call me Francis.'

'In a short while there may well be some kind of disturbance. Frankly, *Mr St Clare*, I'm a plain, no-nonsense woman and have no time for ghosts, vampires and what-have-you. I think we're being pestered by some degenerate person that the local police should deal with.'

'But I've had words with Sergeant Bilkins,' Mr Haines protested, 'and he more or less told me I was off my head.'

'That's because you didn't insist that he come out here and see for himself. Well, since you're here, Mr St Clare, you might as well do what you can. Not that I've much faith...'

'Can I have a cup more tea?' Fred enquired, pushing her cup forward. 'Francis, something funny has just come in.'

St Clare took a cigarette case from his breast pocket, saw Jean's warning glance and hastily replaced it.

'Funny giggle or funny peculiar?'

'Funny nasty. There's a horrid old man dressed in a grey, monkish robe...'

'Habit,' Francis corrected. 'I think.'

'I don't know what his habits are, but he's certainly glaring at you.'

'Probably a time-image. This old place must be packed with them.'

Fred added two spoonfuls of sugar to her freshly filled cup.

'Oh, no he's not. I know a flaming time-image when I see one and this is an out and out nasty.' She suddenly shivered and looked back over one shoulder. 'Oh, no you don't! Francis, he's trying to materialise – draw power from me.'

Francis St Clare raised eyes that were suddenly alert, gleaming with interest.

'Shut down. Close your mind. Get shot of him.'

Fred momentarily lowered her head and expelled her breath as one long sigh. Presently she relaxed and looked up.

'OK. No panic. He's gone. But I had to blast him good and proper. And I'll tell you something else. He's not just an ordinary housebound. I had a glimpse of trees – moon shining on purple hills.' She smiled appealingly at Mrs Haines. 'You don't suppose I could have a slice of that chocolate cake?'

'How can you pack away all that nosh and remain reasonably slim, is beyond me,' Francis complained. 'Mrs Haines – Doris – you're not to give her so much as a crumb. It's downright greediness.'

'Don't take any notice of him. He denies himself nothing, but I'm supposed to starve so as to keep the old psychic juices running. Well...'

Too true. And I want you at your best tonight. So no cake.'

'I will have some cake.'

'You won't.'

'Pig.'

There was a loud crash as Mrs Haines slammed a fork down on to her dinner plate, thereby causing Mr Haines to spill tea into his saucer.

'Stop it this instant. You both must be mad to behave like this in someone else's house. I'm surprised and shocked.'

Instantly she was confronted by two faces that wore repentant smiles; was subjected to a combined barrage of charm that almost succeeded in erasing her forbidding frown.

'You must forgive us, but we're not really quarrelling. It's just a way of equating the fantastic with normality. Releasing the pressure if you like.'

'We have to strike sparks off each other. That makes us the perfect team.'

'That's all very well,' Mrs Haines protested. 'But what about that business of an old man in a robe?'

Francis dared to reach out and lay his hand on hers.

'I'm sorry – but you have a resident ghost. And a fully active, not very nice ghost at that.'

'Fiddlesticks!' Mrs Haines retorted. 'There's no such thing as a ghost and if there was, I would have seen it.'

'I think I once caught a glimpse of it,' Jean announced. 'The edge of a grey robe disappearing round a corner.'

'Now you've got her going,' her mother protested. 'Heaven's above knows, she's daft enough to believe anything.'

Francis stared thoughtfully at the young girl, then enquired gently: 'Well, Fred, has she got it?'

'Quite possibly, but still undeveloped. But she may well attract the attention of a powerful nasty. Even feed him.'

Even while Mrs Haines opened her mouth, prior to making yet another well – emphasised protest, there came an interruption that riveted everyone's attention and brought Jean up from her chair. Francis tried to identify the sound. A scream that came from a partially blocked throat? A screaming, bubbling howl that might have been made by a demented wolf? It rose to a high-pitched howl, then ceased.

'I say a semi-solid build-up,' Fred stated, pulling the cake-stand towards her. 'Elemental structure activated by part-human agency. It's waddling round the house now.'

'Malignant?' Francis enquired.

'As a rattlesnake. You'd better get ready for action.'

There was a kind of squelching, shuffling sound, then a soft thud as though something flabby had bumped against the front door, before a nightmare face appeared in the window-frame. Small red eyes embedded in rolls of jutting fat, curved fangs that dimpled a receding chin, wrinkled ears that resembled miniature wings – and there was a corpse-like whiteness and an obscene sheen of moisture that made the bald head glisten like a seeping skin of lard. Francis jumped to his feet.

'Quick – someone fetch a bucket of water – several buckets of water. Fred – outside. This I must see.'

'Gawd help us – must you?'

'Yes – move.'

He ran out into the passage, pulled the front door open, then stumbled over the narrow step. His head jerked round and he rejoiced that he had been permitted to witness this rare phenomenon. He spoke to a very disturbed Fred who was still reluctant to leave the doorway.

'That, my angel is yer actual, no-nonsense common or graveyard ghoul. But damn your best frilly knickers if I ever expected to see one.'

Fred made an interesting gurgling sound, but otherwise did not comment. She could only stare at the bowed shoulders, the hollow chest that surmounted the great bulging stomach, the bent, so terribly thin legs, the long arms that were equipped with two-taloned claws – and tried to disregard the sparse red hair that clung to the dead-white skin like streaks of strawberry jam. The mouth opened and closed, while a long black tongue ejected chattering – gibbering – sounds; and the thing was running forward, then retreating, like a monstrous over-grown rat that is gathering courage to take the first bite from a dying man. Francis shouted: 'Where's that bloody water?' then swore loud and clear when Mr Haines fell over the doorstep and sent the contents of a bucket flowing down the path.

The ghoul made another hair-raising shriek and leapt straight for the tall, young man who now stood with his head slightly forward, looking like a handsome leopard that is prepared to fight for its life. When the bloated face was a scarce twelve inches from Francis' own, he spat – sent a stream of saliva into one fat-embedded eye – then stepped back when the creature twisted its head round and shrieked with pain.

'Francis.' Fred's voice came from behind his left shoulder. 'Bucket.'

'Kick it. Oh, I see what you mean. About time too. Right, chuck it over howling Harry.'

'No way. I'm only the hired help.'

'Give it to me. I get no co-operation.'

He grabbed the bucket, waited until the monster had again advanced within spitting distance, then calmly poured its contents over the bald head. Water flowed down the grotesque face, over the hunched shoulders; cascaded on to the bulging stomach and formed a little pool round the claw-like feet. The immediate result was electrifying. Where water flowed, flesh bubbled – seethed – sent out spiral plumes of steam – and the ghoul began to disintegrate. The head collapsed like a deflated balloon, the stomach exploded with a muted popping sound; a taloned-claw parted company with a fast dissolving arm and landed on a clump of marigolds. Francis observed it with interest.

'Fred. Tongs and a plastic bag.'

'God help us! All right.'

Mr Haines staggered out with another bucket of water, which he placed at Francis' feet and ran back into the house, after one quick glance at what remained of the ghoul. There was really no need for further action. The psychic detective watched a cloud of steam rising from a patch of damp earth, then greeted Fred with a tired smile when she re-appeared carrying a transparent plastic bag and a pair of coal tongs.

'All over bar the screaming. But at least Howling Harry left us a souvenir.'

Fred looked from left to right, then registered a request for information.

'Where the ruddy hell has it gone?'

'Back into the womb of Mother Earth, from whence it will, as sure as God makes little things grow, rise again when the invisible nasty-man has recovered from this little caper.'

'But why hasn't that – that bit – gone as well?'

Francis sighed as he tested the tongs on a nearby stone, then shook his head in sad reproach.

'As I've had occasion to remark before, you have a brain the size of a split-pea. That dainty little mitt isn't in contact with Mother Earth – is it? It's bedded down on a bunch of marigolds – ain't it? There it remains for your delight and edification. So – you hold the bag open while I do the needful.'

'It's wriggling,' Fred protested.

'So it is. Who knows, with a bit of encouragement, it might stand up and dance the tango. Open the bag.'

The tongs gripped a fragment of flesh, without doubt the two talons did wriggle in a most alarming fashion, then that which the ghoul had left behind dropped into the bag, the top of which Francis twisted into a rope and tied a knot.

'What are you going to do with it?' Fred enquired.

'Probably put it in a glass case and charge a discerning public a pound a go to have a look. Now let us join the happy family circle and talk of things both weird and wonderful.'

Mr Haines greeted the psychic detective with a worried frown and made an announcement.

'The wife's fainted.'

Francis murmured. 'You don't say!' and Fred said, 'I don't blame her,' then everyone turned their attention to the slumped figure in an armchair, which Jean was trying to revive with a burnt feather.

'Forgot all about her,' Mr Haines said, 'what with all the excitement and all. Then when I came in here – there she was. Never thought Doris was the fainting type.'

'Neither would I,' Francis agreed, 'although a common or graveyard ghoul on the rampage might well have a fainting effect on some people. Fred was once a leading light in the girl guides, so I should let her look the poor lady over. Fred.'

Fred bent over the motionless Mrs Haines, felt her pulse, raised one eyelid, then laid a hand on the moist forehead. She looked up and addressed the psychic detective.

'Very deep faint. I doubt if Mrs Haines will be herself for some time.'

Francis nodded slowly. 'But we can expect some action in a short while?'

'Pulse is getting stronger – I'd say in about fifteen minutes.'

Mr Haines displayed all the concern that is proper to a loving husband. 'Is there anything serious? Should we call a doctor?'

Francis placed a hand on the man's bulky shoulder.

'You have my word your wife will be her old self in no time at all. Now, I think we should go into the other room. What she needs at the moment is rest.'

'What? Leave mum all by herself!' Jean exclaimed.

'Trust the young master, he knows what he's doing. We'll leave the door open.'

With reluctance father and daughter led the way across the passage and into the dining-room, where Jean turned on the ceiling light, for the sun was setting and the room already shrouded with shadows. They sat round the long table, with Francis facing the open doorway.

'Reggie,' he said quietly, 'a few questions if you don't mind. How long have you lived in this house?'

'A mite over nine months. The sale went through on September the first of last year.'

'And when did your – out of the ordinary trouble begin?'

Reginald Haines scratched his bald head. 'Must be the best part of a month ago. After I'd cleared the garden.'

'A bit of a mess, I expect. Apart from weeds, there'd be the usual collection of tins, discarded bedsteads and stuff like that?'

'Yes – there was. How'd you know that?'

Francis shrugged. 'Clearly the house was unoccupied for some time before you bought it. The new window-frames and floorboards tell me that. And people have the unpleasant habit of dumping their rubbish in the unkempt gardens of empty houses. Tell me – where did you dump your rubbish?'

Mr Haines blushed a deep red, then sent out his confession in a flurry of words. 'I dug a hole between two graves in the graveyard.

There was plenty of room – it wasn't as though I were disturbing – anything.'

'Nice deep hole, presumably? The one in which you first saw the ghoul?'

After some hesitation Mr Haines nodded. 'Yes. But I filled it in at once. And put the grass back on.'

Francis stared intently at the gaping doorway and the dimly lit room beyond, 'Disturbed soil – iron that is such a good conductor for psychic power and the presence of... It's all becoming clear. Fred, how we doing?'

The girl looked dreamily up at the ceiling, then spoke with a low voice.

'He's been standing in the passage for some little while. Now he's gone into the living-room.'

Jean half rose from her chair and appealed to the psychic detective.

'How can you leave her in there? Knowing...'

Francis took her left hand in his and raised it to his lips. He radiated soothing, irresistible confidence.

'A while back I asked you to trust me. I do actually know what to do. This is the only way I can find out why – and most important – how.'

Mr Haines looked from his daughter to St Clare, then pleaded for reassurance.

'Is Doris in some kind of danger?'

'Reggie,' Fred explained gently, 'your wife didn't faint – she's in a deep trance. This may come as a bit of a shock, but although she doesn't believe in ghosts – she's a natural medium. Not only has she been feeding old nasty with psychic essence, but helping to build-up the ghoul as well. When Francis dissolved it with water, her psycho was knocked into limbo and now...'

'She's an empty house waiting for a temporary tenant,' Francis completed the explanation.

The sound of the body rising from a chair came from the room across the passage, followed almost immediately by a slow, heavy tread that gradually approached the open doorway. Francis raised his right hand and spoke with uncharacteristic seriousness.

'No one is to move or speak. I will do whatever talking that is necessary. Above all try not to show fear. Remember the thing which now inhabits Mrs Haines' body can do you no harm, and I will ensure that its tenancy is of short duration. Fred, are you shut down?'

'Tighter than a miser's money box,' she replied. 'I've no intention of being taken over.'

Mrs Haines' body crossed the passage and slowly entered the room. The face might have been that of a corpse; white, without so much as a blinked eyelid to betray the existence of life or intelligence. One foot was raised very slowly, then lowered carefully, before the other was moved. The effect was a strange lumbering motion, that created the impression that the body might fall over at any time. Francis was reminded of a novice trying to manipulate a pair of stilts.

The body came to a halt to the left of Mr Haines' chair, where it stood and stared blankly at a picture over the fireplace. Francis crossed his left hand over his right.

'Fred.'

'Present.'

'What's going on?'

The girl closed her eyes and appeared to be listening.

'He's trying to make audible contact, which is not easy for a tired out old wanderer. A matter of getting Mrs H's brain to control the vocal cords. He's in a bit of a tizz-wazz too and is sending out hate-waves like nobody's business.'

Mrs Haines' mouth opened and Francis could see the tip of her tongue twisting as though it were trying to form words, and he nodded encouragingly when honest endeavour was rewarded by a long, drawn out croaking sound.

'Keep at it,' he instructed. 'Spit it out.'

'Give him a chance,' Fred protested. 'I mean to say – it's not his body.'

The mouth was wide open now, the tongue curled back and the eyes half closed. Mangled words were manufactured by a harsh voice.

'I...a...m...c...m...b...l...l...l...'

'Who?'

'C...a...a...a...a...a...b...b...lllll ...'

Francis expressed his impatience.

'For Pete's sake, we'll never get anywhere at this rate. Fred, give him a hand.'

'Not on your nelly. I'm not parting with any of my essence.'

'What are you saving it up for? Now, stop mucking about and get tuned in. I want this case settled by daybreak.'

After some further hesitation Fred took Mrs Haines' limp right hand into her own, then closed her eyes and appeared to fall into a deep sleep. Almost at once it seemed as if the lady had returned to normal life; with her free hand she pulled a chair back and sat down, then looked at the psychic detective with a faint smile.

'You are indeed a clever fellow,' the voice was deep and not unpleasant, 'and I'm obliged to you for this temporary return to flesh and blood life.'

Francis shrugged. 'I try to spread a little sunshine as I trot through life. I take it you are an earthbound?'

Mrs Haines' head nodded. 'For nigh on three hundred years I have wandered far and wide, looking for the miracle that I could scarce believe would ever happen. Then that fool,' there was a nod in Mr Haines' direction, 'dug into polluted ground and provided the iron which is essential – and that which can never die was once again able to obey my command.'

'How were you able to raise a ghoul?'

'With blood – well shed. With words spoken in a certain way. For I, Sir Charles Campbell was well versed in such matters and found no difficulty in obtaining various members of the local peasantry, whose worthless bodies provided all that I needed. I fed the creature to excess and thus enabled it to take on corporeal form and bring fear to those who would thwart my will.'

'But alas,' the psychic detective murmured, 'I would imagine that the ill-bred peasantry did not appreciate the estimable use to which their worthless bodies were being put and demonstrated their ingratitude.'

The voice spat out anger-tinted words.

'They came with the accursed priest at their head and put both me and my house to the flame. My ashes they buried in the graveyard, wrongly assuming that concentrated ground would ensure that my soul would not walk.'

Francis sighed deeply and gave the unconscious Fred an anxious glance.

'And now – with your pet given a new lease of life – you doubtless intend to start up business again. Send the ghoul out to feed on the quick and the dead, then use it as a milking cow. Build yourself a secondary body. Become a buck-vampire.'

Mrs Haines' body jerked forward and her face was transformed by a menacing frown.

'Too much knowledge will choke the man of little wisdom, I will send my pet to you again, but this time put not your faith in the cleansing power of water, for I will surround it by a black barricade.'

'Will cost you a mighty lot of power,' Francis stated. 'Drain you drier than an anaemic girl at a vampire's picnic.'

'It will be a worthwhile investment and I can recharge from this gifted girl afterwards. But hark you well. Before this night is done, the black hounds will chase your screaming soul across the mist-shrouded plains of Hades.'

'And you will slither in the dark alley that runs between fire-tipped mountains,' Francis countered. And now,' he raised his right hand with the first three fingers extended, 'in the name of the Light Lords I command you to leave this woman and enter her no more.'

Mrs Haines jerked violently, swayed back and forth like a wind-swept tree, then looked round the room with an air of bewilderment. It was not long before she expressed indignation.

'What on earth is going on? Why are you all sitting here looking at me like that?'

'I haven't time to explain now,' Francis said abruptly. 'But I must ask you to follow my instructions to the letter. I want you, Mr Haines and Jean to go upstairs and shut yourselves in the front bedroom and not come out until I say so. Form a circle and hold hands. Under no circumstances break the circle. Do you understand?'

'What I want to know...' Mrs Haines began, but was quickly interrupted by her daughter.

'I will see that they do what you say,' Jean promised. 'But will you be all right?'

He gave her a reassuring smile. 'Fred and I are the experts and it's our job to take risks. It will do no harm to pray for our success, for prayer is a certain way to concentrate mental energy into a desirable channel. Now, off with you.'

'Here,' Mr Haines leant across the table, 'is the missus all right now? I don't fancy being shut up with – what she was a while back.'

'Doris is, without any possible doubt, her old self again.'

Francis waited until he could hear the three pairs of feet ascending the stairs, before turning his attention to Fred. She was pale, but her eyes were still lit by the customary mischievous gleam.

'Well,' he enquired, 'all fit and ready for the fray?'

'No, I'm bloody well not. I gave my all so you could have a heart-to-heart with old nasty. What I fancy now is a nice underdone rump steak, surrounded by some roast potatoes, followed by a rum-baba with bags of cream.'

'When all this is over, you'll have just that.'

'Promise?'

'Cross my heart and hope to live.'

Fred released a sigh of intense pleasure.

'OK. What shall I do?'

'Fetch the gear.'

The dining-room had been cleared. All the furniture was piled against one wall, the carpet rolled back and what appeared to be a steel cage, erected in the centre of the room. It was indeed an awesome contraption, being constructed of metal rods, each one slotting into the other, with a large opening facing the door and a smaller one in the rear. Long wires ran from various points to a control panel which lay on the mantelshelf.

'The phantocage,' Francis announced, 'has never been known to fail. Designed by me, how could it? My genius is a truly terrifying phenomenon.'

'We've only used it once before,' Fred pointed out. 'And that was to trap a miserable old handel-monster. How do you know it will work with a ghoul?'

'Have you no faith in the young master?'

'No.'

The psychic detective shook his head sadly. 'You really must learn to use that under-developed organ you call a brain and try to think logically. Now, to lure any creature into a trap, we must have bait...'

'No.' Fred shook her head violently. 'I won't do it. I'm not sitting in that thing waiting for a corpse nibbler...'

'Will you let me finish?'

'It's always the same. Whenever a thingy-goat is needed, it's me that has to bleat me heart out in some crazy contraption you've dreamt up.'

'The hand,' Francis shouted. 'Nasty man seems unaware his pet is minus one little mitt. When he calls it up, the ruddy thing will do its nut and come looking for that which is lost. And where will it be? In the phantocage.'

'Oh.'

'Having said all that,' Francis went on, 'I will admit, it might be an added advantage if someone with a lot of lovely psychic energy were actually in the cage – sort of holding...'

'Not a hope. Dismiss the idea from your great mind. You do it.'

'I'd love to. You know that. But alas, I haven't got your natural attributes – apart from which I'd never be able to belt out of the cage in time.'

'Good. Then just chuck that hand-thing in and we'll both watch from the side-lines.'

'But, Angel, if ghoulie grabs it before I can get the power working...'

'For the last time – I won't do it.'

Fred was standing in the phantocage with a taloned-claw on a dinner-plate, which she held out to the furthermost extent that her arms would allow. She groaned when a bubbling-shriek came from the direction of the graveyard.

'Not much longer now,' Francis comforted her. 'I've left the front door open.'

'Oh, my Gawd! You would.'

Horror that had been created from the debris of the human mind; a creature drawn up from that dark country where those that have never breathed, slither in fire-tinted gloom, came howling across Mr Haines' well-kept garden, round the house – and finally in through the open front-doorway. Once in the passage it paused, emitted a rasping snort, then moved forward again, knocking a hall-stand to one side, brushing a picture from the wall, then making an unexplainable scratching sound.

With a dog-like bound it was in the doorway; bloated, slug-like, waving a white, ragged stump, where two jutting wrist-bones glittered like moist ivory in the lamp light.

'Come and get your little mitty,' Francis invited. 'Held by a pretty lady who's got lots of lovely essence.'

'I wish you'd shut up,' Fred protested. 'The damn thing's dribbling.'

The ghoul blinked and seemed momentarily disconcerted by the bright light, then it went down upon its one hand – and raced towards the psychic detective. Francis ran to the far side of the phantocage and there watched the monster, which had crashed into the piled-up furniture and was now engaged in pulling a table out into the room.

'The light,' Francis whispered. 'It can't see well in this light. It probably thinks I'm hidden behind the furniture.'

'Why the hell has it gone for you?' Fred demanded. 'I've got its bloody hand.'

'Nasty man is in the driving seat and has planted an auto-suggestion that I'm the answer to a ghoulish dream. Look out – here it comes again.'

The ghoul moved slowly now, peering from left to right, then gave a howl of triumph when Francis darted round the phantocage and in through the front entrance. This action appeared to bewilder the creature, for it tugged at the bars and shrieked with frustrated rage. Fred voiced her disapproval.

'Fine old muck up. This thing is supposed to trap the ghoul, instead we're both inside. What happens if Howling Harry decides to join us?'

'That's the idea. Give me that plate.'

'With pleasure.'

'Now you get ready to bolt out through the back when it comes in through the front. Wait until I'm clear, then pull the switch. But you'll have to time it just right.'

'Francis, I'm not all that happy. Not really.'

The ghoul was sidling round the cage, feeling its way from bar to bar; its red eyes watching the psychic detective with unblinking intensity.

'Get ready,' Francis warned, holding the dinner-plate well out before him.

Suddenly, after a blur of movement, the ghoul was blocking the doorway, its one hand reaching out, the talons slightly curved, the mouth a gaping cavern, flanked by the fearsome, dripping fangs.

'Out,' Francis breathed. 'Down on your hands and knees and crawl to that fireplace and...'

The ghoul was in the phantocage and the psychic detective found himself face to face with a nightmare; staring into the red eyes, aware of the overwhelming stench – knowing he was a few seconds away from a terrible death and only a miracle could save him.

Then he dropped the plate.

The ensuing crash made the ghoul recoil, then look down as though to see what had caused the disturbance. Francis took full advantage of this moment of distraction; he was out through the back entrance, crouching on his haunches and shouting, 'Fred – now!' before the monster had time to realise that its ordained victim had gone.

It bent down and was reaching out for its missing member, when the phantocage became a network of flashing light. Pencil thin streaks of white fire leapt across both entrances, and the cage resembled a set piece in a firework display. The ghoul screamed and for a moment – just before it disintegrated into a writhing mass of black mist – it changed into a lean old man with a long, grey beard, who glared his fear and rage at the psychic detective. Then the mist seeped down through the floorboards and there was only the stomach-heaving smell and a blob of grey jelly that fell from the cage roof on to Francis' lap

He jumped up and shook himself violently. The viscous mess slipped to the floor with an obscene squelch, where it seethed for a few moments before disappearing.

'Ugh!' Fred had switched off the phantocage and was now standing by her employer's side. 'What the hell was that?'

'All that remained of the hand,' Francis replied with some regret. 'Pity, I was hoping to keep it and possibly let you play with it sometimes. Never mind.'

'You're revolting. Can I go to bed now?'

After we've informed the Haines clan that all is well and the world's only practising psychic detective has scored again.'

Fred made a rude noise.

Francis St Clare was seated behind the steering wheel, with Frederica Masters by his side. The Haines family were clustered round the off-side window.

'I've definitely decided to move,' Mr Haines said. 'I mean to say, if the missus is what you say she is – anything might come out of that graveyard.'

'Very true,' Francis agreed. 'I should settle for a nice semi-detached in Wimbledon.'

'A lot of poppy-cock,' Mrs Haines stated with deep conviction. 'I didn't see anything and I don't think anyone else did either. But I do know someone made a fine old mess of my dining-room table.'

'I'm going to work in town,' Jean announced shyly. 'Share a flat with a friend. Perhaps we might run into one another sometime.'

The car glided away to a chorus of goodbyes and presently was braked to a halt at the end of the lane. Francis waited until a stream of traffic had passed and allowed him to turn on to the main road. Then he spoke.

'Why didn't you come out with some biting remark when the wench suggested we might get together?'

Fred nestled her head on his shoulder.

'I was too busy watching old nasty who was waving to us from the doorway. Or not so much waving as jerking two fingers in an upward direction.'

Francis swore and changed gear.

'But I thought I'd cooked his goose. Good job they're moving.'

'Yes, isn't it? Only, I wonder – do you suppose he'll move too? It might be wise to keep away from little Jeannie. Never know what she might have with her.'

She had scarcely finished speaking when a suitcase which was laying on the back seat, rose up and crashed against the roof. Fred glanced back over one shoulder, then proclaimed her concern.

'Francis... you've mucked it up again... we've got company...'

AN EPISODE IN THE LIFE...

By

Tina Rath

This story is not real. Ronald Chetwynd-Hayes did do some extra work, but it was not at the studios described here which did not exist until I wrote about them. Some may recognise details from Bray, or from Pinewood, which does in reality have a convent close by – although none of the nuns, to the best of my knowledge ever rode a motorbike. And you will not find a British, silent version of Wuthering Heights, *or* Bulldog Drummond Meets Fu Manchu *listed on IMDB (Yet – who knows what might be to come?). But now the studios and the motorbike riding nun do exist here, on paper perhaps, or electronically. And a version of Chetwynd-Hayes – and whatever else – is here, too.*

T HE YOUNG MAN had slipped out for quiet smoke. He wanted to rest his eyes from the harsh lights and occasional unnatural darknesses of the film set and his ears from the shrill complaints of an actress who had decided her costume was too tight and made her look like a sausage. Wardrobe had been brought in to mediate, but was adding fuel to the flames by suggesting that she had either falsified her measurements, or put on weight since her fitting, and it was hardly the fault of the costume or of Wardrobe that she did indeed look like a sausage – without putting it in so many words.

It was summer, but there was no sunlight. The sky was filled with that mild grey light, which, in England could mean any time of year. He stood in the middle of a devastated landscape which might have reminded him of a building site, and later – not yet, though, not quite yet – of a bomb site, but to him it was as familiar as his own home. He saw, without really registering them, temporary buildings featuring a great deal of corrugated iron, walls shored up by balks of wood, odd brick paths going nowhere, big barn-like structures with no windows, and on the far edge of the field, in the remnants of a garden, a white house that might once have been rather stately, but had lost caste, and now stood like a dowager wearing the remnants of her finery, ill at ease in the raffish world where she found herself.

She would have been teasingly familiar to the regular cinema-goer – and there were a lot of them in those days. If they walked round to the back they could glimpse, through the double glass doors leading onto the terrace, the ballroom of half a dozen romantically inaccurate re-creations of Victorian novels, or Regency love stories. Through those very windows had come the pale and panting courier with the message that warned the Iron Duke that Napoleon was on the move, and broke up the Duchess of Richmond's ball on the eve of Waterloo. On that terrace in the little known silent version of *Wuthering Heights*, which had never made much of an impact here in its country of origin, but had been a surprise hit in Japan, Young Kati and Young Onimaru, as Cathy and Heathcliffe had become in the subtitles, had lurked gazing at the unfamiliar luxury within. The flight of steps up to the main door at the front of the house had featured as several gentlemen's clubs, where once the villain of the piece was horse-whipped by an infuriated Papa, in defence of his daughter's honour; as the entry to any number of offices belonging to gentlemen in the legal profession, including those of Dodson and Fogg, Jarndyce and Jarndyce, and the solitary Mr Jaggers; and at least once as part of the façade of the London Law Courts. Now, according to the board set up on the lawn outside, it was playing the part of a private school for the sons of gentlemen.

The young man, surveying the scene through a haze of cigarette smoke which transformed it for a moment to a black and white landscape, a film within a film, suddenly became aware of a movement, a small window at the side of the house opening and a figure emerging. One of those gentleman's sons was making an illicit exit. He let the figure get clear of the building then shouted.

'Oy! You boy! Where are you going?'

The boy hesitated as if thinking about making a run for it, then trotted up to him. As he came closer he saw he was older than his costume suggested. Not really a school boy, but certainly able to pass for one. And about to play up the role of innocent for all he was worth.

'I'm an SA on the school film. We've been in the holding area for hours 'n hours and I need to go to the bog,' he said, 'your oppo said I could. We can't shoot till the sherrybangs come.'

'Charabancs,' the young man corrected automatically. 'Busses.'

'Oh, *busses,*' he sounded disappointed by this information. The exotic sounding sherrybangs, carrying suggestions of strong drink and explosions were only busses then. Hardly worth the wait.

'You're young Ron, aren't you? you've worked here a lot, you're pretty well a professional. You should know you can't go wandering about the place.'

'I won't *be* wandering. Just going to the bog – we've been told not to use the back wall any more,' he added, with conscious virtue.

'I should think not. Filthy habit'

'And they said Sparks has fixed up an electric cable through the bricks that'll burn your whatsit off if you try it.'

This was improbable, not because Sparks, who harboured a deep hatred of humanity in general and young humanity in particular wouldn't have done such a thing, but because if it were scientifically possible he certainly would have done it long ago. It wouldn't hurt if the extras believed it though, so he didn't argue with that one, but there *was* that unusual mode of exit.

'If you've got permission, why did you come through the window?'

'It's quicker.'

It was just possible... he could drag him back to the holding area, and demand of the AD in charge if he had given him leave of absence, but he would look a fool if it turned out that he *had.* Possibly he was telling the truth, and even if he wasn't he couldn't really get into much mischief. Probably he didn't want to. He hadn't been exaggerating when he called young Ron a near professional. More than likely all he wanted to do was have a quick smoke himself.

And he'd finished his own cigarette, and he himself might be missed… technically he had no more business out here than young Ron. But there was still a faint niggle. Ron was playing the gormless youth a bit too blatantly. And he had to assert his authority somehow if only because he was uneasily aware that they were pretty much the same age. He was doing a gap year before such a thing had been thought of, getting a taste of the film industry before he went on to University. Ron, serious and professional, had probably been working in films longer than he had.

'Well, don't climb through any more windows. Think about your costume.'

'Doesn't matter. It's meant to be scruffy. I'm on the call sheet. "Scruffy Boy". I'll probably get a credit.'

Rendered almost speechless by this piece of hubris, the young man still managed to say, 'Were you here yesterday?'

' 'Course I was. We've been doing this film all week.'

'Then,' he said, realising even as he spoke that he was scoring a very cheap triumph, 'your costume mustn't get scruffier. Continuity you know.'

'Well, it won't then,' Ron shuffled artistically from foot to foot. 'I've really got to go.'

'Off you trot then. Keep away from the dressing-rooms, all right?'

There had recently been complaints from the actresses that someone had been peering through their windows, along with demands for proper blinds, instead of the pages of newsprint currently pinned over the panes.

'Not going anywhere *near* the dressing rooms,' Ron said in tones of outraged virtue.

'And don't dilly dally on the way. Those busses are due any time now.'

'Could have been there and back by now if you hadn't stopped me,' Ron pointed out, not unreasonably.

And they went their separate ways. The young man returned to the set of *Bull Dog Drummond Meets Fu Manchu,* where the actress playing Fah Lo Suee was still having a strop about her costume. She was indeed, hysterically attempting to rip open the side seam of her cheongsam, to the considerable detriment of the long finger nails so painstakingly glued on by makeup. This was the most excitement they had had all week and he forgot about his encounter with young Ron.

Meanwhile young Ron made his way by a devious route, taking full advantage of the cover offered by a large stand of buddleia, towards the jerry-built block which housed the dressing-rooms. He was as interested in seeing ladies in their camis as any young man of his age, but peering through windows at them was not his style at all. Besides, there was quite enough to fire a young man's fantasies in the troupe of dancing girls who could be seen on occasion running to the set of the Bulldog film, bangles, belled anklets and girlish giggles chiming as they went. Rumour had it that their costumes were a job lot hired from a London theatre and had never seen the light of day since they were retired from the Great War production of *Chu Chin Chow* at the request of the Lord Chamberlain, shocked by their naughtiness (his Lordship's actual word).

The young ladies had been heard to complain that they certainly smelled like that, and their veils wafted not the perfumes of the Orient, but the scents of must, mould, possibly embalming fluid, and definitely industrial strength moth killer. He had never been close enough to them to find out if that was true, but he didn't think it would put him off. Possibly vampire ladies, who were also very fanciable, would smell a bit like that, considering the amount of time they spend in their coffins. Although probably not of moth killer. Who knew what effect that might have on a vampire? They were a bit like moths, after all. Fluttering about at night... a story teased at him, a young chap walking out with a girl who says she works funny shifts at the jam factory so they can only meet at night. And when he gets to know her well enough to give her a good-night kiss, not knowing she's just about to fix her teeth in his neck she gets a whiff of the jacket he's wearing for the first time this year, which was put away for the summer, pockets filled with mothballs and...collapses into moth shape, and flutters to the ground dead? Or... or something... perhaps she gets a nip in before she expires. Moths were notorious for chewing wool. They must have teeth of sorts and sharp ones too...

But he had other priorities just now. A rumour was going round that the studios were about to make a horror film which would feature a truly horrendous werewolf, and the make-up was being trialled that day.

He wanted to see that werewolf.

He strolled out of the buddleia, radiating the aura of a lad who had been sent, as he very well might have been, on a legitimate errand. No scurrying. No slinking. It wasn't the first time he had slipped away to explore the studios and he knew his way about. All he had to do was to wait until he was quite sure no one was watching, then dive into an alley created by two huts, walk casually through, and there he was on the blind side of the dressing rooms. The real problem came with getting a look through such windows as were not covered in newsprint. And he thought he might have found a way round that one. It all depended on whether the tree had been lopped...

In the distant past, years before he was born, there might have been woodland here. Most of the trees were long gone, but one had been retained due to the studios making an ill-judged foray into Westerns, for which a Hanging Tree was considered indispensable. The tree was big, and for some reason, possibly connected with amateur attempts to cut it back in the past, it had one long, thick branch projecting from the rest at just the right height to make it a very plausible gallows. Studio chippies had reinforced it discreetly so it could bear a considerable weight, and although the Western phase didn't last there never seemed to be any pressing reason to remove the tree, so it had stayed, inevitably acquiring its own folklore.

Now it was known for a fact that the tree was kept as a memorial because the screen hanging had gone horribly wrong and a well-known actor had been hanged for real and the film was shown, with his genuine death struggles, because under the circumstances a re-take was out of the question. Another, or perhaps an additional, story involved a young actress who had failed to get the lead part she so desperately wanted, (or, the whispers said, been *promised* in return for certain services) and had hanged herself in despair from that convenient branch when she was let down. People crossing the lot alone at night had heard her, whispering from her perch in the tree, trying to persuade someone to join her. A further refinement on this story was that during a night-shoot a young girl had decided to play a trick on her boyfriend by impersonating the "Lonely Lady" as the ghost had come to be called. She climbed the tree – only to feel a chill breath on her cheek and hear a voice whisper in her ear 'Oh, now you have come, I can go,' upon which she fell off the branch in shock, and broke her neck. Or she had impersonated the ghost so successfully that her boyfriend had gone raving mad and she had gone into a convent. The fact that there was indeed a Convent just down the road was put forward as absolute proof of this version.

Ron found both stories a little unsatisfactory. He liked the chill breath and the ominous whisper in the first one, but you didn't have to be very sharp to wonder how, if the ghost impersonator had broken her neck, she'd been able to *tell* anyone about them. He felt, too, that the presence of actual Convent didn't help the second version at all. The nuns he had seen out and about were just not sinister, most of them being stout, middle-aged and bespectacled. The Convent also offered Bed and Breakfast, which according to those studio personnel who needed to take advantage of it occasionally, was good but pricey, and though you couldn't have bacon for breakfast if you were there on a Friday, you got kippers instead, which made a nice change. And one of the lay-sisters rode a motorbike. It was *wrong, wrong, wrong.* He was working, mentally, on a version of his own, in which the Lonely Lady had a habit of dropping out of her tree onto the shoulders of lone men, wrapping her lean clawed fingers round their necks and riding them, emitting banshee shrieks until they dropped dead or went mad. That would be more like it. But the success of that story and that of his whole enterprise this afternoon depended on that branch still being in place.

There had been talk of taking it down, to stop what the Studio Office described as "silliness" involving some people refusing to go to the dressing-room block alone, in the dark, and others hiding behind the tree and jumping out at their friends – and sometimes making a very unfortunate mistake. (One of the executives had been jumped out at, which was bad enough. The fact that he had "screamed like a girl" made it a disaster.) But the chippies had done such solid work on the branch that it would probably just be easier to get an expert in to cut the whole thing down. The screaming executive was said to be so much in favour of that that he had offered to pay for it himself. Ron disapproved of this. It wasn't the tree's fault after all.

He slid cautiously out of the alley – one glance told him that the branch was still there and the coast was clear. A quick dash across open ground, a leap to a low-hanging branch and he was up the trunk like a scruffy squirrel and installed on the deadly branch, from where, behind a screen of leaves, he had a reasonable view of the dressing room windows. The men had loftily refused to protect their modesty with newsprint, expressing the opinion that anyone who did peer in to see them in vest and pants could be dealt with by themselves in a way he would long remember, so he had a clear view. Of course if he were spotted he faced the risk of being "dealt with" but he was confident an agile youth in plimsolls could outrun a group of fat actors who hadn't had time to put their shoes on and who didn't know the territory anything like as well as he did. Of course he would be recognised, and never allowed near the studios again, but it would be a spectacular way to end his career. Face facts, it was going to end anyway soon enough. Life as a ten shilling SA wasn't really a career. It wasn't even a viable method of earning a living. Life was real, life was earnest and beginning to close in on him.

He had a fondness for drama and he ran that final scene across his mental screen: it became a wild chase – the actors in their underwear were joined by the cast of the Bulldog film, Fu Manchu's henchmen in their improbable Oriental costumes, the dancing girls, the crew, the ADs, the sparks and chippies, the Director – and as he fled for open country the nuns joined the chase (would the censor put up with nuns *and* men in underwear? probably not but this was *his* version and he could do what he liked) and he leaped on the lay sister's motor bike and vanished over the horizon, THE END filled the screen and the credits rolled – "Featuring RONALD CHETWYND-HAYES as THE SCRUFFY BOY... the first in a series..."

The door to the men's dressing room opened... he tensed, leaning forward as far as he dared – and was disappointed. It wasn't the werewolf, just a perfectly ordinary chap, probably an actor, someone he didn't recognise anyway. Possibly a cleaner... but no, he was sitting down at one of the mirrors. Could it be that his luck was in and he was about to see the makeup applied? It would be worth the bollocking he would get from the AD if he missed the sherrybang scene, worth it... but there was nothing to support this hopeful theory. No heap of crepe hair or sticks of grease-paint, nothing but a roll of cotton wool, and a bottle of something unidentifiable which the man unscrewed – had he just slipped in for quick gin? but no, he didn't drink from the bottle. He soaked some cotton wool and dabbed his face, the typical action of an actor taking make up *off* except that he hadn't, as far as Ron could see, been wearing any. Just a few quick dabs...

And his face came away.

It wasn't that his skin came off, revealing a flayed head with raw flesh and starting veins, or even a *Phantom of the Opera* skull. If it had been either of those Ron would have felt disgust probably, terror certainly, but not this jolt of horror, the sudden knowledge that such things could happen. A man, a girl, your own mother perhaps might one day slip off a familiar, perhaps a loved face and reveal *nothing*. An emptiness, but an emptiness that could see, could be aware...

He clung to the branch, trying not to think it was sliding from under him, leaving him adrift in a day-light darkness where everything he knew and trusted was *wrong,* a film set to hide horrors behind it that might vanish at any time and leave you with them. The creature at the mirror gave a weary shrug, like someone picking up a heavy garment after a brief rest, raised his hands to his head, and again there *was* a face, but not the same as the one he had

had before. This was younger, more like the chap who had caught him sneaking off the set. But not the same, no he hadn't stood talking to something like *that* in open daylight, he hadn't, he hadn't... whatever it was stood up, stretched, went out. And young Ron slid down the tree, and careless of who might see him, ran back to the Holding Area, back to reality.

If there was such a thing as reality. He was never to be quite certain of that again.

THE MURDER MACHINES

By

Simon Clark

RACHEL TILAINEY WAS in love with money.
But, strangely enough, not purely her own money. Rachel yearned for the cash that slumbered in other people's banks accounts. She longed to sink her beautifully manicured claws into the mounds of lovely, silky tenners that weren't hers to spend. It must be said from the very start that Rachel Tilainey was a villain, a thief, a dirty crook. Yes, she was beautiful. Her blonde hair tumbled down her back in gorgeous waves; her full lips were so enticing that many a man, and woman, believed that one kiss would transport them to heaven's shining gate. However, shrewder individuals declared that though Rachel might have the face and body of a beautiful young woman she had the vicious mind of a thoroughly unpleasant ogre.

Rachel was also a widow. Her husband of five years had died ten months ago in a particularly nasty accident. Rachel coped well with bereavement. After all, there she was: slipping off her red satin bra in front of her late husband's business partner... oh, yes indeed, the business partner had pots of money, too, though he had no intention of spending much of it on Rachel, the gorgeous blond who shyly (she was good at feigning shyness) lowered her large blue eyes before his very interested gaze.

Rachel dropped the bra onto the bed before embracing Jason Telford with breath-taking passion.

'Wait,' Jason panted. 'Wait... Rachel, wait.'

All round-eyed and demure, she drew her head back, leaving a blaze of kiss-coral lipstick trails across his face. 'Don't worry, the others on the board will never find out about us.'

'It's not that, Rachel, dear. But here in your cottage... in your bedroom, where you and Bernie... slept together.'

'What of it, Jason? I've changed the sheets since, and turned the mattress.'

'Look, I don't want you to feel pressured. After all, it's ten months since... well... it doesn't seem that long ago.'

'Jason, that's so sweet of you.' She kissed him on the lips, her naked breasts brushing against his own bare chest. 'The thing is, Bernie wouldn't want me to stop enjoying myself. He would want me to live life to the full.'

'Is that one of Bernie's hairs on the pillow?'

'No.'

'It's a red hair. Bernie was pure carrot.'

'It's just a piece of thread.' She brushed the pillow. Her false nails, aflame with scarlet varnish, despatched the offending thread... or, possibly, a hair. 'These pillowcases are brand new.' Okay, she lied about that, but she found housework so dreary. Rachel had been born too beautiful to lead the life of a drudge (or so she frequently told herself).

Jason stared at her gorgeous body in such a way she could tell that sexual arousal flared up within those finely-toned loins of his.

'I want to make love, Jason.' Her eyes turned downward again in a way that was so demure. 'Love-making will help ease this terrible grief I feel for Bernie.'

A perfectly timed tear rolled poignantly down her kitten-soft cheek.

'If you are sure that this is what you want?'

'I am, Jason. I am.'

In less than three seconds his trousers were around his ankles, and her eager fingers explored the most sensitive part of his body.

She licked his cheek. 'You taste of money,' she said.

'Pardon?'

'You taste of honey... lovely, sweet honey.'

Jason made love to her with a hot urgency, making the bedsprings creak in such a way that they sounded like handfuls of coins being thrown into a bucket.

Then, somewhere out in the forest, came the sound. A rising

drone of a motorcycle engine, indicating all too clearly that the bike was slowly drawing closer and closer to the cottage.

Rachel sat at her late husband's desk in the cottage, while upstairs, worn out by love-making that had burned up more calories than a marathon run, Jason slept, dead to the world.

Rachel carefully practised Jason Telford's signature – a cocksure, strutting dandy of a signature that was all swirls, extravagant loops, finally embellished with an awesome underscore that resembled a warrior's spear in flight. Her pen danced across the paper, recreating that distinctive moniker, while outside a November breeze tugged at the dark and spiky shapes of trees that grew close to the house: those trees resembling a sinister army that had slowly, but surely, surrounded the cottage with the intention of laying siege to its two occupants.

The breeze blew across the roof, sending eerie whispers down the chimney. The branch of a bush tapped the window with a hard sound, conjuring an image of a skeleton, risen from its black void of a tomb, tapping a finger of cold, white bone against the pane.

And then, from far away, the low note of a motorcycle engine. The sound was somehow dreary, lethargic, a suggestion that the machine crept slowly along woodland paths. That mournful sounding engine didn't intrude on her senses too persistently at first. In fact, it was only as the sound faded, as if the motorcyclist rode away from the cottage that she seemed to notice it fully.

'Damn.' Rachel looked down at the signature she'd just inscribed. *Jason Teflord.* She'd spelt his name wrong. 'Never mind,' she whispered. 'This is only the rehearsal, not the actual performance.'

Rachel pulled a document across the desk towards her, the partnership agreement that Jason and his partners had signed when they formed the company. She stared hard at Jason's signature, mentally absorbing its loops, flourishes, the way the T in Telford was suggestive of a tall tree with branches projecting outward at the top. Then she practised the signature once again.

The drone of the motorcycle returned once more, a little louder now, hinting that the rider approached the cottage in a slow, roundabout way, as if following random forest trails that only gradually brought that two-wheeled conveyance in this direction. As before, the dirge of the engine slowly rose and fell in that dreary way. For all the world, the sound made her think of a greedy child that had eaten a full bar of chocolate, given itself a horrible tummy ache, and now insisted on moaning to let the rest of the family know how much the spoilt little so-and-so suffered.

Rachel paused, pen in hand, her pretty face turning into quite an ugly scowl. That infuriating engine noise. The sound was beginning to haunt her. Suddenly, she found mental concentration hard to come by. The motor's drone distracted her from what was very important work indeed.

Taking a deep breath, she sat up straight and spoke very firmly to herself. 'Come, come, Rachel. You have a living to earn.' Briskly, she pulled another document towards her, then she forged Jason Telford's signature on the bottom, complete with that amazing flourish that resembled a spear hurtling towards its target. She smiled as she read the grave, black print at the top of the document:

LAST WILL AND TESTAMENT OF JASON TELFORD.

The plan's taking shape nicely. Oh, the will required the signature of two witnesses, and this delightfully adroit forgery must replace the original, currently residing at Jason's lawyer's office, but they were trivial details that Rachel could handle with the help of one of the law firm's junior partners, who had visibly salivated that erotically-charged evening when she disrobed in front of him in her bedroom.

After locking the will in one of the desk drawers she rose to her feet before going to the study door where she called upstairs.

'Jason... Jason? Are you awake? I've got something to show you.'

Rachel led Jason from the cottage to the garage, which was actually larger than the cottage itself. Still yawning and sleepy after that humdinger of a love-making session earlier in the day, he moved like the proverbial lamb to the slaughter – uncomplaining, incognisant. Rachel was pleased. Her plan was running smoothly, indeed relentlessly, towards the destination she intended it to reach.

Jason yawned again so widely she could see the gold teeth in the back of his jaw. She wondered what would happen to the gold teeth – you know, when the inevitable happened. *I mean,* she asked herself, *who sends valuable gold to the crematorium, even if it is embedded in the jaw of the deceased?*

'What did you want to show me?' Jason asked, shivering as cold air gusted through the forest to ripple his top-quality yellow shirt and muss his expensively styled hair.

Rachel smiled her warmest smile. 'They're all still here.'

'What's all here?'

Her thumb touched the screen of the phone she held in her hand. 'This,' she said as electronics affixed to the garage door responded to her command and the door purred upwards. 'This,' she repeated. 'Bernie's collection.'

Jason's eyes widened, surprise dispelling rosy mists of post-coital drowsiness. 'Wow,' he breathed. 'How many motorbikes did Bernie own?'

'Forty-seven. He was a bike man, Bernie was. He told me that when he was twelve he kept a moped under his bed, because he was afraid his brothers would steal it. A Honda Graddy, that's what he called the moped. Such a ridiculous name.'

The pair moved into the brilliantly lit garage, which accommodated machines that would make any biker's heart throb with delight, while inflicting a vivid green streak of envy across their soul.

'It's not just bikes,' Rachel told Jason. 'Machines obsessed Bernie. As well as motorbikes, there are water pumps, generators, mechanical hoists – all of them driven by internal combustion engines. Bernie had a passion for pistons, spark plugs, drive-shafts: all things like that drove him crazy with... well, love, I suppose.'

Jason walked along a line of motorbikes that had been kept in pristine condition until a few months ago. Now, with handlebars, wheels and seats wearing a shroud of dusty cobwebs, there was a powerful hint that this place was in danger of becoming a tomb for these valuable mechanised thoroughbreds. A moment later, Jason noticed an oddity at the back of the garage, back in the furthest recess, where shadows gathered to clothe the area in despondent gloom.

Jason stared in amazement. 'Rachel, will you look at that? A lawnmower. But the size of that thing! It's the biggest mower I've ever seen.'

Rachel watched as astonishment and admiration flashed across her lover's face as if he'd discovered a chest of pirate treasure. *Perhaps Jason is smitten by mechanical things too,* she thought. *Maybe he will become as obsessed with motors as Bernie was?* Not that she was concerned he would transfer his affections from her to pistons and oily crankshafts. *After all, I've decided that Jason will be dead before the weekend's out.*

Rachel observed Jason's adoration of the lawnmower with a slight sense of disgust. He ran his hands over the huge hopper that served as a grass collection box. He oohed and aahed over the five-foot-wide cylindrical arrangement of blades that cut the grass.

'It must be seventy years old if it's a day,' he cooed. And then he climbed onto the mower to sit on its metal seat, which resembled one of those old fashioned tractor seats, moulded from iron to fit the curve of the buttocks. He fiddled with switches, swung the steering lever in front of him, and pressed the foot pedals.

'I wonder if I can get it started,' he said, peering down at the motor that was encrusted with ancient oil and dirt.

'You won't have time,' she declared somewhat shortly.

'Oh?'

She smiled sweetly. 'You won't have time for me if you start fiddling with that old contraption.'

'It's huge,' he simpered. 'It's a monster. Look at the thickness of the chain that drives the blades.'

Rachel decided to change the subject, otherwise he'd be rolling up his sleeves and starting work on the mower's engine before she knew it. 'This garage... this is where I spoke to Bernie for the last time.'

'Do you want to go back to the house?' Jason's voice was the essence of sympathy as he climbed off the grass-cutter's metal seat.

'No. It's time I talked about what happened... you know, to deal with the grief, and not to continue to repress the sadness. That's what I should do, isn't it?'

'But only if you feel ready to do so.'

'Bernie called me into the garage to show me the latest bike he'd bought. A big Honda, with a hugely powerful engine... too powerful, really.'

Jason put a sympathetic arm around her shoulders.

She continued: 'Bernie stood beside the bike, just over there, near the opening to the garage. He wore his leathers and his helmet. He said he'd take the bike out along the lanes that run through the forest. They're just dirt tracks, really, not suitable for a powerful motorcycle like that Honda.' She wiped away a carefully manufactured tear. 'I stood in the garage, watching him ride away. Before he reached the end of the drive he stopped and blew me a kiss. He'd never done that before... it was like he knew something would happen.'

'I'm so sorry, Rachel.'

'Well... he rode away into the forest, going way too fast. He never noticed that someone had strung a length of wire between two trees on the old lane up near the quarry. Probably just kids playing around, but Bernie rode into the wire so fast that...' She shook her head. 'Whatever the result, it was so dreadful they wouldn't let me see the body.'

Her gaze strayed to the wall cupboard where she'd kept the roll of steel wire that she'd tied to the two trees in such a way the wire ran from one side of the lane to the other – as sharp as a cheese wire. As devastating as a madman's axe.

'Come on,' Jason said gently. 'Let's go back to the cottage.'

As she nodded, wiping away another tear, she heard the sorrowful drone again in the distance.

'Oh, *that* sound.' Her voice hardened. 'It's really starting to get on my nerves.'

'What sound?'

'Surely you can hear it?'

'Hear what?'

'Someone's riding a motorbike out in the forest.'

'A motorbike.' Jason tilted his head, listening. 'No, I can't hear anything. Nothing at all.'

That annoying melody continued throughout the afternoon as they drank wine on the sofa. Jason insisted he could hear nothing, yet to Rachel it seemed that the motorbike orbited the cottage at a distance of a two or three hundred yards, sometimes getting a little closer, the dreary tone of the motorbike engine would then become louder, more intrusive – more annoying! Although she switched on the television to watch a nature documentary, which included grisly shots of a female praying mantis devouring its mate (the green head was munched up first), she found it hard to concentrate with that infernal motorbike sound nibbling its way into her consciousness.

Jason still heard nothing. She'd asked several times but all he did was shrug and suggest that the sound she heard might be nothing more than the breeze.

Jason, meanwhile, read a local guide book as he sipped his Riesling. 'Says here,' he began, 'that this woodland dates back to the last Ice Age. In Medieval times, this entire area was supposed to be the haunt of witches, who were drawn here by the occult power of the landscape. They declared that there was "magick in every graine of soil" and a local bishop insisted that "Muddleback Forest is a unique terrain where, inevitably, the impossible becomes possible".'

Jason's becoming a bore, she told herself. *I will kill him tonight.*

Television drama makes doing away with people look easy – the flash of a savage blade, the bang of the gun, the remorseless tightening of the garrotte around the victim's neck. But to murder someone in such a way that it looks like an accident... well, that's an altogether different art form. And much more difficult.

That evening Jason bounded downstairs, towelling his hair dry, and saying, 'Be careful if you take a bath Rachel, the bottom of the tub is really slippery.'

Ah... so much for spending a tiring half hour polishing the bath enamel in the hope he'd slip, knock himself out, then conveniently drown in the bathwater.

Now for plan B.

'Hmm, rump steak: just how I like it. Nice and bloody.' Jason beamed at her as they sat down to supper. Hungrily, he ran his tongue across his enamel-bright teeth.

'Tuck in.' She smiled as they clinked wine glasses.

'Rachel, don't think me ungrateful, but I'll leave the mushrooms.' He patted his stomach. 'Mushrooms give me frightful indigestion.'

Outwardly, she smiled – inside, she was raging. She'd spent ages foraging in the woods for toxic fungi – a rare species that would have sent Jason into fits of foam-at-the-mouth insanity before the poison ended his life. She'd even concocted a heartfelt speech she would make to the police when they came to examine the body after she'd phoned the emergency services: *'I begged Jason not to eat the mushrooms he'd found. You just can't be certain they're safe to eat, can you?'* Alas, a speech she would never make.

Jason wolfed down the steak. The fungi, however, lay in a dark, glistening mound on his side plate, their potent toxins destined for the kitchen bin, not Jason's stomach. She thought about the Last Will & Testament bearing Jason's (ahem) signature and she almost said the words out loud: *Now for Plan C.* She didn't, of course. Even under pressure, Rachel always remained as cool as the coolest of cucumbers.

From far away came the sound of the motorcycle, the engine note rising and falling in such a mournful way. A lost soul of a sound, crying out there in the forest... out in the cold... out in the darkness.

'I've had an idea,' she said. 'Tomorrow, why don't we see if we can make that old lawnmower work?'

The sound of the distant motorcycle engine suddenly rose into an agonized scream.

Jason heard nothing. He just opened another bottle of wine.

Rachel launched Plan C early the next day, a bright, cold morning, with frost adding diamond-bright gems of ice to the lawns. Jason had to die today; she must not fail because he would leave tomorrow for the airport. Jason intended to jet off to Australia to oversee the setting up of a Melbourne branch of the company. With Jason in Australia, there would be little she could do to despatch him into the eternal bliss of paradise, in order to inherit all that lovely cash that filled his bank accounts.

'Today's the day,' she whispered to herself as she entered the garage where Jason was already hard at work on the old lawnmower.

Jason leaned over the big contraption with an oil can. 'I'm just lubing her up,' he said, pleased with his oily endeavours. 'I've also poured in a nice, fresh gallon of petrol I found in a can back there.'

'Do you think you can get the engine started?'

'I'm not sure. I haven't checked the spark plug yet.'

Smiling, she purred, 'Starting the engine would be a fitting tribute to Bernie's memory.' A tear formed in her eye. 'After all, I do still treasure the times that Bernie and I shared together.'

Rachel then used one of her late husband's M&S T-Shirts, his favourite purple one, to wipe dirt away from the mower's grass collection box that was big enough to accommodate a full grown man. Her cleaning revealed the mower's name in chunky gold letters against a background of green paint and crispy scabs of rust.

Jason marvelled at the name, grinning. 'The Sprottforth Fearless... isn't that a fantastic name for a mower?'

She kissed him on the cheek. 'I'm so proud of you, bringing the mower back to life. It's what Bernie would have wanted.'

Flushed by such praise from his lover, Jason rubbed his hands together in an okay-let's-do-it kind of way, and enthusiastically grabbed hold of the D handle attached to the starter cord. 'Let's give it a go, eh?' He smiled at her. 'This is for Bernie, God rest his soul.'

Jason tugged at the handle. There was a rattle, a chug, a throaty cough, then – bingo!

The Sprottforth Fearless engine roared into life. Immediately, the cylinder blades began to turn: faster, faster, faster! Soon they spun so rapidly they were just a blur. This monster of a mower must have cropped entire football fields back in its day, with the groundkeeper sitting as proudly as a conquering warrior in the mower's saddle, decapitating innocent grass-stalks by the thousand.

Rachel stared at the rotating blades – the entire cylindrical structure of blades was the size of a beer barrel. Blue fumes spewed from the exhaust. The entire garage vibrated before the power of the Sprottforth Fearless.

Jason shouted above the thunder of the engine: 'Fantastic, isn't it? Just fantastic?'

Rachel adopted an expression of profound concern as she pointed down at the cutting gear that now hungrily chomped fresh air, not lush, green grass.

Rachel called out, 'Should it be doing that?'

'Is there a problem?'

'Look for yourself.'

Jason did look, his blue eyes all large with concern, fearing that some destructive malfunction had presented itself.

'I can't see the problem,' he called over the roar of the motor.

'Look closer... there, lower down...'

Jason bent over the mower. That's when Rachel pushed him, and pushed him hard. As he toppled forward, losing his balance, he glanced back with such an expression of horror, his eyes screaming: *What did I ever do to you that was so wrong that you want to hurt me?*

Then Jason fell into the flashing blades.

When Rachel crossed the yard to the cottage, in order to call the emergency services and report the dreadful accident, she heard a sound coming from the forest. The motorbike was back. Though, this time the note of its engine was different: harder, louder – threatening.

Ten days after the tragic incident, which lead to Jason Telford's untimely death, Rachel lay alone in bed. The police believed the story she'd told them in a beautifully teary performance as the forensic officer, clad in a white coverall, meticulously photographed the bloody remnants of Jason. It must be said that the mower's blades had chopped Jason into little pieces. In fact, finely diced he was. Then several plastic bags had been required to gather up his remains. Thereafter, police officers had kindly set to work with mops, buckets and lashings of hot water to erase the bloodstains that adorned the garage. Indeed, Rachel overheard one of the police murmur to another, 'And you know something, Jim? One of the poor bastard's eyeballs had been flung into the air so hard it had stuck to the garage roof. I had to scrape it off with a shovel.'

Now, alone in the cottage, she closed her eyes. However, the unseen motorcyclist plagued her, robbing her of her beauty sleep, as the inconsiderate yobbo rode the bike through the forest that surrounded the house. They didn't ride the bike particularly fast, as far as she could tell; no, the motor emitted a mournful drone that rose slowly before falling, the sound receding before returning again. It was as if the biker rode their metal steed aimlessly along woodland paths. By now it was two o'clock in the morning. Rachel had not slept a wink.

Anger tore down the fragile temple of rational thought, for she leapt out of bed in her little silk nightie. Quickly, she pulled on a kimono-style dressing gown in black and gold, and growled, 'That's it. I'm going to find that idiot and give him what for.'

Pausing only to tug on a pair of over-the-knee boots in the glossiest of black leathers, she ran out of the cottage into the cold night air. The moon shone brightly on trees, which now lacked their summer plumage of green. Branches were black, spiky; as sharp as a carnivore's claws. Impetuously, she rushed along the drive between lawns crusted with frost. Her breath, illuminated by moonlight, left her beautiful red lips in vast clouds of white vapour.

Homing in on the sound of the bike, Rachel moved swiftly, torrents of hot fury granting her legs the strength to move without tiring. Indeed, so angry was the woman, she didn't even notice the viciously cold air that wrapped its chill arms around her.

'When I get my hands on you!' Her head was full of vengeful acts that would be as painful as they were spectacular. 'You and that bloody bike have driven me up the wall!'

Most people wouldn't relish the notion of confronting a mystery biker in a lonely wood at night, but, remember, Rachel had killed two men. She had a strong conviction of her own power, as well as an absolute certainty that there was no man alive who could frighten her.

Rachel moved further from the cottage, penetrating deep into the forest, where witches, generations ago, had assembled to practice their necromantic arts. She glided along an ancient grove of oak trees that had once been sacred to those who worshipped the Sulphurous One, the Lord of the Flies, the Horned Genius. In the gloom, beneath spreading branches, she glimpsed a moss-shrouded granite slab where, unknown to her, blood sacrifices had taken place, and still beating hearts had been cut from screaming victims.

The motorcyclist now seemed to be aware of her presence, even though she hadn't so much as glimpsed him, the bike, or even a trace of a tyre track in the dirt. He seemed to know that the beautiful woman followed him, because he deliberately teased her by riding slowly (so the note of the engine suggested) just a short distance from her, only to accelerate away mere seconds before she caught sight of him.

'Playing hide and seek, are we?' The furnace that was her fury burned ever brighter. 'Well, I'll show you, pal. You'll wish you'd never been born.'

A twig caught the delicate fabric of her kimono, pulling it open; however, she was gripped by the hunting spirit and didn't pause to re-fasten the garment, leaving it flap in the breeze. Like a panther slinking through the bushes, she knew she closed in on her prey. Rachel prowled beneath a dense canopy of branches that blocked out the moonlight. The scents of a forest in winter became more pungent. The cold breeze blew against her hot face. Meanwhile, the sound of the motorcycle became louder.

Then the machine stopped. She could tell the engine idled – a low, burbling sound.

'I've got you now,' she hissed, padding towards a clearing where moonlight cast its silver radiance on a sandy lane that ran through the forest.

Rachel Tilainey glided with predatory grace from shadow into moonlight. The bike was close now. The motor remained at the same constant note, hinting that the rider sat astride his twin-wheeled stallion, one foot on the ground, waiting... waiting for what? The heels of her boots knifed deeply into the lane's sandy surface as she approached where she believed the bike to be.

'Show yourself! I'm not afraid of you! Come out where I can see you!'

The note of the engine changed. The unseen rider had turned the throttle, increasing revs, then a shape appeared in the shadows. Indistinct at first, the bike moved towards her – a second later, the bike passed from deep gloom into moonlight, and that's when her mouth dropped open at the sight that appeared in front of her.

Suddenly, she did feel the cold. Icy air stroked fingers that were chillier than the grave across her skin. Then those fingers became talons that clutched at her throat, or so it seemed to her. Her eyes watered, and shivers cascaded down her spine, as she finally saw what moved from darkness into light.

The first thing she recognized was the face. Bernie's face. She'd recognize her late husband's features and almond-shaped eyes anywhere. The strong nose was unmistakable. And as for those pink lips? She had kissed them a thousand times before. Yes, that *was* Bernie's face. A living face with moving eyes that fixed on her eyes, and a red tongue that emerged to lick those pink lips. But the face wasn't attached to a head. The face appeared to be glued to the headlamp of the bike.

And what an extraordinary bike. She realized that instead of being made from metal the machine had been fashioned from human bone and from human flesh. Arm and leg bones formed the frame. The wheels consisted of spinal vertebrae that had somehow been fused into a loop before being fixed into forks of rib bone, while what looked like pink intestine had been stretched over those curving back bones, resulting in the gut now serving as tyres. And was that a human lung that had been inflated into the shape of a fuel tank? And was that a gleaming, white pelvic bone that now acted as a bike seat? A complex arrangement of interwoven finger, hand, foot and toe bones connected the bizarre structure together. And there at the front, pasted to the headlamp between handle bars formed from thigh bones, was Bernie's face.

He smiled. 'Rachel. I wondered how long it would be before you ventured out here to find me.'

'Go to hell!' she howled. Because Hell is surely where that evil-looking machine had been spawned.

Despite the bike having no rider, she saw the hand-throttle, fashioned from knuckle bones, rotate; this caused the engine (wrought from an unholy conglomeration of internal organs) to roar loudly. The bike lurched forwards, moving swiftly towards her.

Bernie – or, rather, Bernie's face cried out, 'Climb onto my saddle, Rachel! Come ride with me!'

'Go to hell!' she shouted again before sprinting back along the lane. However, the stiletto heels of her boots dug so deeply down into the earth they acted like anchors, slowing her down. More than once she had to fully stop, grab her knee, then uproot her stiletto from the ground. The ache in her calves blossomed into agony, while the cocksure certainty of her immunity to harm was brutally sacrificed on the altar of vulnerability. Yes, indeed, Rachel now was cognisant of her own fragility. In short, she feared for her life.

The macabre bike followed. Bernie's face, affixed where the headlamp should be, smiled... smiled almost lustfully.

Rachel darted through the trees, trying to lose the machine. Sometimes she was almost successful – especially where trees grew so closely together the evil bike, which appeared to be constructed from Bernie's recycled remains, had to stop and find another route where trees were more widely spaced, and the bike could pass between tree trunks.

At last, she glimpsed the cottage. Almost there! Moonlight glinted on its windows. The welcoming door was still ajar, just as she had left it. All she need do was plunge into the security of the house, lock the door, and wait until daylight. No doubt dawn's welcome light would dispel the evil magic that animated the Bernie-Bike-Thing. She'd jump into her car, drive away, and instruct an estate agent to sell the cottage. She never need set foot in this accursed forest again.

Fortuitously, the lane grew firmer underfoot, the compacted soil resisting the heel of her boot to penetrate its crust. Rachel could run faster. The cottage grew closer and closer. Glancing back over her shoulder, she saw the bike, that gruesome conglomeration of bones, human offal and Bernie's dreadful face – a face that had been dead for ten months, yet now aped the appearance and movements of living, mortal features.

Rachel laughed as she ran up the drive towards the cottage and safety. That hideous bike was too far away to catch her now. She was just fifty yards from the welcoming doorway.

'Get inside! Lock the door! You'll be safe!' She shouted the words to herself in triumph as she covered the last few yards. Then she couldn't resist pausing to yell harshly back at the Bernie-Bike-Thing, with backbone wheels, an inflated lung for a fuel tank, and flatulent-sounding motor. 'Bernie! I could run rings around you whenever I wanted! And now I'm going to outrun you!'

Indeed, the monstrosity machine trundled too slowly to catch her. Yes, it was HORROR on wheels... but it lacked speed. She raced towards the door. However, a shape glided across the yard in front of her, coming to a stop between her and the salvation of the yawning doorway.

'What the—'

At first, she couldn't make out what had blocked her way. Finally, the penny dropped.

'It's the mower!'

Yes, there it was, moving without a rider too. That hulking, great mower that had claimed Jason's life. She stared at the machine, The

Sprottforth Fearless. It squatted there, engine *put-put-putting*. Suddenly, her eyes focussed on the mower properly. Dear God, there were no metal parts – it, too, was constructed from flesh and bone, and those moist internal organs that are always so unpleasant to see in medical books. When she looked more closely at the huge grass collection box at the front, she saw that a face had been massively stretched over it. Yes, there were eyes (closed eyes), a nose, a mouth, but all pulled out of shape, all hideously distorted. The mower blades, formed from rib bones, began to spin. The mower's seat was a human heart and now it began to pulsate.

The eyes in that hideously overstretched face suddenly opened and she knew who was looking at her.

'Jason.'

The mower engine roared with undeniable power as Jason's voice rang out: 'You murdered us, Rachel. It is time to pay the price!'

Even though she tried to side-step the machine, so she could rush to the safety of the cottage, she found her way blocked. Every time she took a step to the left or a step to the right The Fearless lurched forward, that awful offal motor bellowing, bone blades spinning. The threat was clear – if she attempted to run for the door, the machine would leap forward and strike her down.

She realized that her attention had been so focussed on The Fearless, the machine built from bone and all manner of body parts, that she'd not checked on the progress of the thing that Bernie had become. When she did look back over her shoulder the monstrosity was right behind her.

Suddenly, the bike lunged forwards, striking the woman – not a huge blow, but she found herself flipped back onto the machine, so she lay there, supine, balancing on the inflated lung, which substituted the fuel tank, and the pelvic bone that was the seat. In order to dismount, she realized she needed to sit up first. However, before she could make her move, the bike lunged forward again, its rear wheel spitting out driveway gravel like machine bullets. Rachel had to throw herself forward in order to grab hold of the bone handlebars to prevent herself from being flung from the skeleton machine.

Then, dreadfully, Bernie's headlamp face twisted around to look at her with a gloating smile. He murmured in a way that was loving and stomach-churningly horrific at the same time:—

'Sweetheart, it's been a long time since you sat on top of me. Now... let's go for a ride – just you and me.' Bernie laughed, the cruel sound merging with the roar of the motor as the bike accelerated away.

Rachel, in a blaze of panic, faced an onslaught of questions from her own whirling mind: *What will Bernie do to me? What are his plans? Where will he take me?* That was when the cold and cruel hand of absolute terror gripped her heart in its crushing grasp.

With Rachel clinging tight to the bone handlebars, too afraid to leap off, lest her own bones be broken, the bike sped along the driveway, out into the night, and into the ancient domain of the magic forest – a fear-haunted place where things that never "can be" quite often "are"...

SHADMOCKS ONLY WHISTLE

By

Adrian Cole

WHAT I AM about to tell you is, of course, preposterous. Pour as much scorn on it as you will, but I'd urge you to treat it as a warning, or at least, a cautionary tale. There are more things in Heaven and Earth, and all that stuff. I don't imagine that many of you chaps have ever visited that insalubrious, outrageous den of iniquity commonly referred to as the Monster Club. Those of you who have heard of it are probably labouring under the illusion that it's the product of a fevered mind, a colourful work of fiction. Not so. Never mind how I came to know it. Take it from me, it's as real as Whitechapel or Madame Tussaud's.

Suffice it to say, I have visited the Club myself and am witness to its extraordinary membership and its even more unspeakable perversities. I may have come away physically unscathed, but I'm not so sure my mental state will ever be quite what it was. No matter, I am well out of it and hope to remain so until the good, clean earth claims me. Forgive me if I shudder as I utilise that particular image.

Someone less fortunate than me in that respect was Nigel Portly-Belgrave, a man who was blessed enough to have been born with a large silver spoon in his mouth, namely an exorbitant bequest from his parents, whose vast estate passed to Nigel prematurely on the unexpected occasion of their death in a motor accident. That is, according to the approved press releases, the formal documentation of the police and other official channels. Nigel tells a very different tale, but only to a very select audience. I daresay its members, of which I am one, preferred the less colourful version.

I'd always known there was something rather odd about Nigel, right back to the time we were chums at public school. Perhaps it was the extraordinary paleness of his skin, or the way his eyes had a way of beaming right through you in the early hours, or then again the way he positively drooled over his meat, eaten practically raw and bloody. He was, as he explained one night, having imbibed far too much strong drink, a raddy. For those of you unfamiliar with the biological implications of the co-mingling of monsters, a note of explanation is necessary here. I have a rudimentary understanding of the ancestral intricacies of monsterdom, but will content myself here in saying that raddies are descended from the inter-breeding of the three primate monsters, namely vampires, werewolves and ghouls. Raddies are almost at the bottom of a gradually diluting process of miscegenation.

Nigel had been relatively fond of his (regrettably) monster parents, especially his doting mother, who forever clung to an unshakable belief that her dear boy would one day make his mark on the world, most likely along a political route, at the very least at Cabinet level. She was, after all, an eccentric and not very well informed soul. Nigel quickly recovered from his mollycoddled existence under his mater's wing and wasted little time in indulging some of his new wealth, whooping it up in the city's wildest night spots, painting the town red, as it were, and generally wreaking mayhem. He gave a new depth of meaning to the expression, Hooray Henry. Lady Penelope Portly-Belgrave would have turned in her grave – several dozen times.

Given the nature of Nigel's exploits, it seems inevitable that his drive to find new, wilder experiences led him to the door of the Monster Club. The place is, understandably, a perfect breeding ground for every kind of licentiousness, debauchery and self-indulgence. In short, where better for a monster to spend its time making whoopee? Naturally it welcomed Nigel and his sycophantic companions with open arms. Nigel was such a useful provider for the Club that he was held rather high in the estimation of its gruesome management.

One of the most popular entertainments, if I can be permitted to use such a term, among the clientele of the Monster Club is their dalliance with members of the opposite sex, on various levels of intensity. I will leave the details of these pursuits to your imagination, but I will say that variety being the spice of life, this ranges from the briefest of liaisons to more lasting bonding, or indeed, bondage. There are those who subscribe to Miss Austen's famous comment that single chaps with a lot of money need a good wife – presumably in order to facilitate the fulfilment of their existence (not a view I have ever personally subscribed to). There are also those wealthy fellows who perceive all feminine attention as driven by a powerful desire to gain access to the family silver and a goodly stock of diamonds.

I believe Nigel Portly-Belgrave was a member of neither of these male camps. At least, not when it came to his fascination for Drusilla. (If she had a surname, it has never emerged from the murkier depths of this tale. I suspect this is for good reason.) As a seventeen year old budding hostess at the Club, she was a slip of a thing, pale-skinned, dark-haired, very red-lipped and, according to Nigel, quite the most beautiful, intelligent, witty, alluring... well, you get the picture. He was smitten, so of course, she was perfection in his eyes, and indeed, to all his remaining senses. Others have commented on her thinness, her gaunt features and general inexpertise at the art of good conversation, but where love is concerned such things are necessarily immaterial.

In the interests of brevity, let me simply say, nature took its implacable course.

The love-lorn Nigel realised, with a shock, that his past way of life must end, and with it all links with monsterdom. It was that bestial side of his nature that had made him what he had been. No more! Love would work its alchemy. It was thus, in a state of misery and confusion, that he confessed to me his true nature, that he was not human, but a raddy.

He assured me that he was as embarrassed by his situation as I was horrified by it, and there was nothing he desired more than to behave like a human, repressing his monster genes to as close a point of eradication as possible. Indeed, he thereafter devoted every possible energy to becoming human, and I admired him for that.

I should have said that although Nigel was determined to make himself as human as possible, his beloved Drusilla was also a monster. She was in fact, a mock, offspring of raddy/maddy parents. The shadowy powers that control the Monster Club would not have scorned such a coupling under normal circumstances. After all, the Club benefited hugely from such conjugal bliss. Indeed, there were murmurs of real approval when Nigel announced one night that it was his intention to marry Drusilla, murmurs which swelled to outbursts of delight when Nigel and Drusilla became formerly engaged, with a date duly set for the nuptials.

When Nigel married Drusilla and removed her to his stately pile, the authorities overseeing the Monster Club were not perturbed. Nigel, so proud of his conquest, was never more delighted than when showing her off, and continued to visit the Club regularly, with the positively glowing mock on his arm.

Biology is, of course, a law unto itself, and most of us are its slaves. Nigel and Drusilla were no exceptions. The consequences of their union delivered into the world a child, a beautiful girl creature and, naturally, being the offspring of a raddy and a mock, baby Lucinda was a shadmock. A rare beauty, too, as is often the case with those creatures. Year by year she grew into a slender, elfin girl, with alabaster skin and tumbling, silken hair, her features magically striking.

By sixteen, Lucinda, a reticent, studious girl, drew the appreciative eye wherever she went, which was never far from her stately home. Her doting parents were understandably protective of her and, as an insular person, she remained close to them and preferred the confines of the estate to the ruder environs beyond it. This latter included the Monster Club. Neither Nigel nor his wife wanted Lucinda anywhere near the place. It was impossible, however, for them to obscure the fact of their darling's existence. Nigel was expected to parade his daughter.

However, he had other plans. He had become even more determined to shed his monsterdom, and had ceased to visit the Monster Club, breaking off all ties with his former associates there. He was determined to wed Lucinda, on her next birthday, to an earl, a fully human gentleman, with powerful connections, as far from monsterdom as it was possible to get. When it became clear to the authorities at the Club that Nigel had no intention of ever taking Lucinda to mingle with them, trouble brewed dangerously.

'Are you ashamed of your relatives?' Nigel was asked. 'Does you daughter not recognise the monster element in her blood? She is a shadmock! She should come to us happily and dance with us, and celebrate her heritage! Why has she been hidden from us?'

Nigel made numerous excuses, none of which washed with the Club. While shopping in the local village, Drusilla was also accosted, so much so that she and Nigel withdrew themselves completely from any monstrous company altogether and made their stand.

Matters reached a head one bleak wintry night, shortly after Lucinda's seventeenth birthday. During a storm of uncommon violence, Nigel received a visitor – no less than a senior vampire in the monster community, Vladimir Kazar. Nigel took the tall, aristocratic creature into his main living room while Drusilla quickly spirited her daughter away to a remote corner of the house. She knew well enough what the bloodsucker had come for.

While Kazar sipped the glass of rich red liquid provided by his host, he eyed him coldly. 'This will not do, Nigel,' he said in a commanding voice.

Nigel knew better than to look him in the eye and risk being mesmerised. 'I mean no insult to you or your companions,' he said. 'You know well enough that I've served you generously over the years. How much fresh blood have I brought you?'

'And we have elevated you, made you one of our most respected members. A seat on the Inner Committee beckons! Have you any idea what a privilege that is?'

'I am deeply honoured.'

'And yet you repay us with your scorn! We are not good enough for your daughter. Satan's teeth, Nigel, she is a shadmock. The lowest of our kind. For her to shun us is an insult.'

'She is not worthy of your company.'

'Ridiculous! Blood will out. There are certain rituals to be performed! For her good. Do not resist me in these matters, or it will not go well for you, or your wife. In three days, at midnight, you will come with Lucinda to the Monster Club.'

'And if we do not?'

Kazar rose like the threat of disaster, scarlet eyes ablaze. 'I will pretend I did not hear that! Three days, Nigel.' He swept out of the room, down the hall and out into the night, where he melted into the storm like one of its many brutal gusts.

Nigel and Drusilla had another reason for not wanting their daughter to mingle with the higher orders of monsterdom. She was a shadmock, yes, but she was not cast in the same mould as such beings usually were. Physically, as I have recorded, she was possessed of great beauty and the faerie-like qualities of the shadmock that make one so much more human-like than other monsters. Indeed, many shadmocks would very easily be mistaken for humans.

Lucinda was not a normal shadmock.

'I fear for our daughter,' Drusilla whispered to her husband one night when they were tucked up in bed, while the wind whistled around the gables outside. 'She should be showing signs of possessing normal shadmock powers. Yet I can detect none.'

'Perhaps she is a late developer,' said Nigel, hopefully.

'As a mock, I am far more perceptive than you, my darling. Certainly in these matters. She appears to be almost human in some ways. Perhaps our deep desire to be human has somehow been bred into her development. She is so like you.'

'Her beauty stems from you, dear heart.'

'That's very sweet of you, Nigel, but beside the point. Shadmocks may be at the lowest end of monsterdom, the most diluted blood it has, but they have the greatest powers – usually. They do not rend or feed or suck blood, they only whistle. Yet had you ever seen the results of a shadmock whistling, you would know the implications.'

Nigel shuddered and drew the bed sheets closer around him, even more mindful of the gusts buffeting the house beyond the window. He had heard whispers at the Monster Club – a shadmock's whistle could strip flesh from bone and turn it to cinders.

Drusilla snuggled up to him. 'Lucinda, an ironic name, has not perfected the shadmock whistle. It's an instinctive thing, but I am sure she has not even attempted it. It may be a physical impediment, an almost human fault in her.'

'A blessing.'

'Not when it deprives her of a strong defence against creatures such as Vladimir Kazar.'

'All the more reason to keep her out of his clutches!'

'Quite.'

'And firm up the arrangements for her marriage to The Right Honourable Lord Humphrey.'

'Exactly so.'

'Then we must secrete her somewhere far away from here. Our failure to present her to the Monster Club will have repercussions. The vampire lord's wrath will be severe.'

At about the time this conversation was taking place, there was another, entirely pertinent one happening in the murky interior of the Monster Club. I have said that I have visited the place – invariably some of my colleagues go there, too. The place is like a magnet, given the nature of its shameless activities. Naturally enough, said colleagues enjoy indulging in gossip, and Nigel and I have both been the recipients of many a tidbit of news from those shadowy corridors.

One of the servants in the Club, Jakob, a simple fellow and a mock to boot, literally, as many of the elite monsters were wont to do just that if he got under their feet, was a cleaner. I introduce him into this narrative for two reasons: the aforementioned fact that he was an unwitting party to conversations, and also the fact that he had developed an adoration for Drusilla when she had been a hostess. An adoration bordering on obsession and which had never dimmed.

As he shuffled to and fro in the Club one night, a shadow among shadows, sweeping as he went, Jakob overheard a group of werevamps and vamgoos talking more loudly than discretion should have dictated, a result, doubtless, of the amount of alcohol they had imbibed.

'The word is,' said one of them, 'Drusilla Portly-Belgrave won't allow her daughter anywhere near this place because she has an impediment. As a shadmock, she should be able to whistle up a fire storm. Well, she can't. She can purse her lips and emit a puff of air or two, but that's all.'

'Devil's horns, does Kazar know of this?'

'He should do. He's planning to abduct the shadmock girl soon. I imagine such information would delight him. The Portly-Belgraves won't be able to mount much of a defence without Lucinda at full blast.'

The group rose as one, jostling each other in their push for the quarters of the vampire lord, eager to cash in on their nugget of information. Jakob, unnoticed as usual, hunched over his broom in despair. He must warn Lucinda's parents!

Thus began a brief chain of messages, from the club, via my colleagues to Nigel. He was understandably crestfallen. 'We really must get Lucinda away,' he told his wife. 'Now that Vladimir Kazar knows her frailty, he won't wait another day. He'll be here this very night, knowing our defences will be all but useless against his own dreadful powers.'

Drusilla agreed and Lucinda was duly summoned.

'You must go north, my darling, far to the north. Your great uncle Fotherwick—'

However, Lucinda was having none of it. 'I'll not run away,' she said. 'I refuse to leave you in the lurch. No, I won't hear of it. We will stand together.'

Nigel was agitated beyond words. 'But, but, but—'

'When is he coming?' asked Lucinda.

'Now that he knows you lack the shadmock art of whistling up a fire storm, I fear it will be this very night,' said Nigel.

'If I am so pale an imitation of a shadmock,' Lucinda replied, 'why should he be interested in me?'

'Vanity!' said her mother, her voice laden with scorn. 'A vampire likes nothing more than to lord it over his subjects and strut pompously about his domain. Anyone who as much as hints at disobedience or insubordination is brought to heel. Kazar hates the idea of you marrying a *man* and divorcing yourself even more from monsterdom. He sees it as diminishing his authority. Satan forbid such a thing!'

'Nevertheless,' Lucinda insisted, 'I will not go to him willingly. Nor will I allow him to use you as pawns in his obnoxious game.'

'Pawns?' said Nigel. 'Whatever do you mean?'

'There is no doubt in my mind that he will attempt to overpower you both and then threaten me with your torment, probably death. It's how such a contemptible monster as he operates. I suggest father, mother, that *you* remove yourselves to the north and great uncle Fotherwick.'

Both Nigel and his good lady were aghast. 'That's absolutely out of the question,' gasped Nigel. 'Your mother and I would never dream of leaving you here, defenceless. Together we have some hope of defying Kazar.'

'I'm not afraid,' said the girl pluckily. For all her fragility, she did appear to have an iron backbone.

'It pains me to say it,' muttered Nigel, 'but I think we all need to be afraid. Very well, let us see to what defences we have.'

'What about your coterie of friends?' said Drusilla. 'Or are they all of the fair weather variety?'

Nigel nodded. 'Some are, but there are a few that I can depend on. I'll start ringing round. Canon Copely for one. He's a dab hand at exorcism, although I'm not sure how he stands on the excommunication of vampires.'

'Put him to the test, then.'

Thus it was that a group of some dozen of us, myself included, was politely but anxiously asked if we would assist Nigel and his family in the defence of their home, and specifically their daughter. Very few of us refused, otherwise we stood prepared, although, like me, the rest of the company undoubtedly trembled at the prospect of the coming contretemps. Not one of us had had occasion to clash with a vampire previously, our tactical know-how mainly confined to our readings of such works as Mr Stoker's famed novel, *Dracula*.

We gathered that very afternoon and quickly set about draping the rooms with garlands of garlic. Canon Copely liberally sprinkled holy water over the external door and window lintels as well as setting up as many crucifixes as he could gather from the local church. Nigel had similarly spread the family silver. It was a protracted business and the sun had dipped down to the edge of twilight by the time we had completed the work.

I spoke briefly to Lucinda, whose expression suggested she was not altogether impressed by our heroic efforts.

'Surely this will hold him off,' I said.

'Perhaps,' she said, nodding thoughtfully and I wondered what she knew that we didn't. However, I had no desire to alarm Nigel or his wife, who were already like two cats on a hot tin roof.

By the time the sun had set and twilight had melted into night's darkness, clouds scudded across the late January moon, drawing a veil over the proceedings. A solitary car was approaching along the straight road out to the distant gates of the estate. It was a black Rolls Royce Silver Wraith, a monarch among cars, the personal vehicle of the vampire lord. It reached the large gravelled turning area in front of the main doors and pulled up as silently as the ghost it was named for.

Two sinister shapes emerged, tall beings clad in long black capes, with upturned collars which kept their faces in darkness. Each carried a long cane. They parted and stood like two sentinels, facing the doors as if they would blast them aside with one sweeping pass of their canes. Vladimir Kazar then climbed out of the Rolls and stood between them. He, too, was tall, his black-clad frame exuding power, like an electrical force. Around him the wind had died, the air stiffening, the silence total.

'Nigel Portly-Belgrave,' said Kazar. 'You know why I am here.' The voice rang back from the walls of the stately old house. 'Send out your daughter and we'll forget this entire business.'

Nigel and the rest of us were all staring from various windows. I was close to Nigel and I could see that he had no intention of complying, nor indeed, of uttering a reply. Not to the vampire, though he did mutter under his breath, 'Do your worst.'

Kazar waited for a while, his scarlet eyes ablaze, his anger visibly seething. He then waved his two companions forward and both approached the doors. However, our preparations against them had not been in vain, for no sooner had the two vampires reached the steps than they shied away, arms held up across their lower faces. They had sensed the garlic, holy water and so forth. Slowly they stepped back, the ugliest of snarls on their faces, their pointed fangs gleaming in a slanting beam of moonlight.

'Hah!' I said, slapping Nigel on the shoulder. 'Yah boo sucks to these freaks.'

Nigel was watching Kazar, who alone seemed unmoved. He waited while his two servants stepped back beside him and then snapped his fingers. We heard the sound clearly in the still air.

There were trees not far from the gravelled area and from shrubs at their base, more shapes came forward. Low and streamlined, a pack of several huge hounds loped towards the house. Yelping and slavering, they were unmoved by the presence of the garlic and our other defences. They hurled themselves like missiles at the two big doors. It was a matter of moments before the doors burst inwards, showering the immediate hall in splinters. Any plans we had had for a protracted defence were shattered along with those doors. Our castle had become a trap!

There then began what I can only describe as a battle, not only of wits but also of unrestricted physical endeavour, as the hounds tore into the building, along corridors, up stairs, into rooms, snapping and snarling like the very winds of Hell itself. Our defenders used whatever came to hand to batter them back, guns, knives, heavy metal objects where nothing else was available. These were no ordinary hounds, but huge, brutish monsters, although their weakness was their aversion to the silver, garlic and holy water we had prepared. We seared them and bloodied them, keeping them at bay, but they herded us upwards into the building's higher floors.

Behind them came Vladimir Kazar and his two vampire

henchmen, treading softly and slowly through the debris, held in check by our defences, but we knew it would not be for long. I stood with Drusilla and her daughter, my nerve barely holding. I knew that if we succumbed to the onslaught, none of us would be spared a lingering and horrible death.

Nigel's resolve was extraordinary. He was truly a man possessed. Wielding a heavy brass crucifix as if it were a battle ax, he stood in the doorway of one of the larger bedrooms, framed like a latter day Horatius holding the bridge. I noticed he was wearing a very heavy pair of gloves and there was a real look of pain on his face: of course, ironically, the crucifix must have caused him serious discomfort. 'There's a fire escape!' he shouted back to us. 'Try and get the women away. It's our only hope.'

While he swung his weapon and struck aside one of the hounds – it snarled its fury as sudden flames engulfed it – I helped Drusilla. As a mock, with an element of monster blood in her veins, she, too was subject to the agonies that our defences inflicted on the vampires, though to a lesser extent. Lucinda seemed unaffected, so between us we helped her mother to the tall window.

There was a small balcony beyond and I saw in the vague night light the steel structure of the fire escape running from one side of it down into the grounds. All the cars were parked around at the front of the great house, so it would mean a mad dash to reach them. Somehow, I have no idea how, the three of us got on to the balcony and down the fire escape, while all hell broke loose up in the bedroom. Nigel and the other defenders were embroiled in a blazing, thundering conflict, the shrieks issuing from it tearing at our ears. Drusilla would have stayed by her husband's side, but was too weak to resist Lucinda and I as we manhandled her down on to the lawn.

For now we had evaded the monstrous attack and there were no hounds or other dark servants of Kazar in the immediate vicinity. However, as we began our cautious escape around the side of the building, we heard the sounds of pursuit as something in the house, several dark, misshapen creatures, caught our scent and came for us.

Lucinda shook me by the arm. 'Get to the cars. Take my mother to safety and wait for the dawn.'

'What are you going to do?' I gasped, by now my breath ragged and raw in my throat.

'I'll lead them away,' said the girl.

Drusilla tried to protest, but clearly she had become so weakened that she could do nothing to hold Lucinda back. It was all I could do to keep Drusilla on her feet.

Glass shattered behind us as the first of the windows collapsed under the fresh efforts of the things inside. A number of their shadow-shapes emerged. Lucinda ran across the lawn, crying out something I couldn't interpret. It snared the attention of the hunters, though, for as one they whirled and went for her, ignoring me and Drusilla.

Terror drove me on, for the things that had gathered were ghastly. Hideous, freakish, they were some kind of hybrid humans, their twisted faces snarling just as the hounds snarled, their gleaming teeth snapping, mouths slavering.

Drusilla was rooted. I couldn't move her. I had to push her up against the shadows of the house beside a tall bush, where she slumped to her knees. Mercifully the monstrous assailants had eyes only for Lucinda, who had crested a rise in the wide lawn, where she turned and waited. I cried out in horror – surely that frightful tide would engulf her.

Moonlight broke through the wintry cloud banks, daubing Lucinda in its garish hue.

I saw her face, an odd smile fixed to her features. And her lips.

She was trying to whistle! To do what she had never previously achieved. Whistle as shadmocks whistle.

It was no use. No sound issued from those pursed lips. Even so, the nightmarish pursuit halted in its tracks. Perhaps the creatures were wary, knowing what a shadmock could do. They cowered back like beaten curs. I knew, however, that their sudden terror would not grip them for long. Once they realised that Lucinda's powers were impotent, they would attack again and bring her down.

Behind the girl another hill rose up, shrouded in night, like a wide, black shoulder. She, meanwhile, yet had her lips pursed. If she was whistling, it was a silent sound. Silent in the way that some whistles, fashioned by human hunters, can only be heard by dogs.

Dogs – or some other creature.

The low hill blurred in my sight, almost as if it had somehow *shifted*. Again the assailants drew back, and a few low moans escaped them. Lucinda had summoned something. Darkness sculpted its form. And it began to flow downwards and around the slender form of the girl.

Drusilla must have realised something dreadful was coming, as she rose to her feet and gripped my arm.

'Quickly! We must get away at once.'

A deep, primeval terror within me prompted me to accede and we began anew our flight around the house. As we turned a corner, I heard a united shriek, a positive scream of agony as whatever it was that Lucinda had brought into this world, from whatever horrendous nether region, rolled forward and engulfed the hybrids. Fortunately I did not see what transpired as Drusilla and I staggered across the gravel to where my car was parked. I bundled her in.

I spared a last look at the house. Fires had broken out. Any chance of going back and attempting a rescue of Nigel or the other worthies who fought alongside him would simply not have been practical. As I took my place in the driving seat, I looked up and there, at a high window, I saw the face of that vile lord of the vampires, Vladimir Kazar.

I switched on the engine. I knew, though, that no matter how fast I drove away, that fanged horror would catch me easily enough.

Something behind him must have drawn his attention and he was gone.

'Drive!' urged Drusilla.

I did so.

Well, as for the rest, there is not a great deal to tell. That wonderful old house burned with a ferocity that turned it into a smoking pile of rubble long before the Fire Brigade could prevent it. Our worthy defenders escaped with their lives, though all were badly mauled and would carry scars of one kind or another for the rest of their days. Nigel, to our deep sorrow, was lost, his charred remains eventually recovered. It is my belief that he knew his own exposure to the defences he had erected against evil also worked against him and would inevitably destroy him, so he had made the ultimate sacrifice to secure victory. Of the vampire lord and his servants there were no signs that they had ever been there. And I have learned since that none of them have ever returned to the Monster Club.

I like to think that whatever Lucinda had raised had either disposed of them or carried them back to its lair in a hitherto uncharted region of the underworld. As for her, she, too vanished. Her mother insists that she is alive and although Drusilla's health is fading, there is a happy glow to her, fuelled by that secret knowledge. A kind of mental bond unites mother and daughter. Rather a human thing. Probably Lucinda has chosen to move far away, to a remote country region, where she can begin life anew, unmolested and free of the night's grim predators.

There is a footnote to this macabre tale. Word has reached me recently (several years after the events I have described) that the Monster Club, in steady decline for a while, has closed and in all probability moved back to the continent, far to the east.

A DAY WITH THE PROFESSOR

By

Marion Pitman

MERITT HAD DRAWN up his plan of campaign carefully. The rumours about Professor Stavanger were so far just rumours; any publication would clearly be libellous. Once he had evidence, however, Meritt was confident he could get a long price for the story – unless, of course, the Professor persuaded him to keep quiet. Which would cost the Professor an even longer price.

In his preliminary emails and phone calls, Meritt had used another name, and in fact another man's identity – his own name, though not well known, might have come to the Professor's attention nonetheless. He didn't want to arouse any breath of suspicion. It had taken a long correspondence and a lot of patience to persuade the Professor to invite him for this visit, but now at last he was about to set out. He made one last check of his equipment – the recorder in his jacket, to tape the Professor's conversation, the unobtrusive camera disguised as a tie pin, the phone that would film all the time he was holding it; the briefcase with sterile containers in case he could lay hands on any physical evidence.

He put his case on the passenger seat, closed the driver's door, which made an ugly clunk, and thought that if this went well, he could afford a new – albeit second hand – car. He was seriously worried this one wouldn't make it through the next MOT. He felt resentful that the world did not more lavishly reward his efforts to expose truth and reveal wickedness. Most of the time gratitude was sadly lacking, let alone remuneration. He sighed, let in the clutch and started out.

Professor Stavanger was a geneticist, in his sixties, widowed, childless, and reasonably well-off; he had had a satisfactory if unremarkable career in a government laboratory, working on no-one was quite sure what. Such unexciting facts were common knowledge and reasonably certain; the rumours, however, were vastly more lurid. People said that he had done illegal work in genetic modification, that he had been threatened with dismissal and unspecified charges, including assault, and that since his retirement he had devoted himself full time – to creating monsters. Why he should want to create monsters no-one knew, and Meritt was well prepared to find the truth less dramatic than the stories, but on the "no smoke without fire" principle, he reckoned there must be something pretty juicy to uncover. He looked forward to having the papers outbidding each other for the story – and not only papers, but TV companies, internet firms – the number of people providing for humanity's insatiable curiosity about itself was expanding every day. It was a great time for an investigative reporter to be alive.

Not that investigative reporter was what most people called Meritt – muckraker, blackmailer, tripehound, prying insidious toad, and other less printable descriptions were more usual. But Meritt was secure in his conviction of his own virtue, because he always made sure, firstly, that his facts were rock-solid, and secondly, that the object of his interest could not, for one reason or another, afford to sue.

The professor's address in Kent was off the beaten track, on the outskirts of a small village that had not yet acquired encrustations of new housing. It was a large building set well back from the road, and well out of sight from everywhere, his closest neighbour a good quarter of a mile away. Meritt drove through the tall gates and round the circular drive, and parked by what seemed to be the front door, at one end of the frontage. He had a look at the outside of the house, mentally compiling descriptive adjectives – wondering whether he could get away with "sinister" and "crumbling", or would have to settle for "ancient" and "rambling". In fact the house seemed to date from the late nineteenth century, imposing in red brick, with three stories, a turret, and complicated porches and verandahs. Various outcrops and projections, to be glimpsed behind the main edifice, suggested a good deal had been added on before local planning departments had a say in the matter. Architecturally it was a mess, but in the mild mid-morning sunshine, brooding evil was not, he regretfully concluded, its obvious quality.

He rang the bell, and the Professor answered it himself, opening the door with a smile. 'Mr. Bagshaw,' he said, that being the name Meritt had borrowed for the occasion, 'do come in. You find me alone – my secretary has her day off – but I hope I can entertain you. Come into the kitchen.' He put out a hand, which Meritt shook, once more disappointed – the Professor was no more sinister than his house, being of medium height, slightly plump, with thinning grey hair and metal-rimmed glasses. He wore a loose grey suit and white shirt, but no tie. He led the way into a large, airy kitchen, and waved Meritt to a stool at a breakfast bar, saying,

'I generally have coffee now, would you like some?'

Meritt accepted, and watched the Professor make the coffee, very efficiently, and not at all like a man who doesn't know his way around a kitchen. The coffee was good. The Professor sat down and said,

'Now, Mr. Bagshaw, I gather you are a scientific journalist, with quite impressive credentials, though I admit I have not come across your work. You have no doubt heard the absurd rumours about my own work – tell me now, do you think I am a crank? A traditional "mad scientist"? Have you come here with the idea of exposing me?'

Meritt gave a very good performance of astonished denial: 'Professor, I assure you absolutely that that thought never crossed my mind. Your work – though not an area with which I am over-familiar – is of great interest to me. The enormous possibilities of genetic science in the treatment and prevention of some devastating medical conditions...' He broke off and looked away – 'You might say I have a personal interest, I suppose...' He had prepared a touching story of a severely disabled offspring, but discarded it when the Professor said harshly,

'Mr. Bagshaw, I am not interested in your personal problems. I am not working to cure your congenital conditions, or those of your nearest and dearest. A scientist pursues a line of research because he can – do you understand? I am seeking to push forward the bounds of knowledge, to establish scientific facts, to impose order upon chaos. No doubt the facts established may be used for the good or ill of humanity, but that is not my job. If the facts turn out to be of no use whatever, that makes no difference. My job is to establish the facts, and I regard that as its entire justification. Do you understand? We must be clear on that. I am not trying to improve the lot of mankind.'

'I see. Yes, I understand.' Meritt was doubtful about the man's sincerity. Everyone had a personal interest, whatever they were doing, even if it was only making money. 'May I ask, though – what about your funding?'

'Funding! God, that dreadful word. Yes, you're right – to do anything one must persuade some idiot that it is in his interest to support the work. However, you may have heard that I inherited a sum of money from a relative, which augments my rather meagre pension. That sum of money was a great deal larger than anyone knows, and so far I have mercifully avoided the need to go cap in hand to the guardians of wealth. You may reveal that secret – I realise that to keep it now would make people suspect far more fantastic things.'

'Professor – may I record our conversation? It will be easier than trying to take notes. And may I have some photographs of you and of the house?'

Stavanger started and knocked over his cup, which fortunately was empty – 'Photographs! Why on earth should anyone want to know what I look like, or my house?'

'If I write a feature piece—'

'Feature! I'm not a feature! I thought we were discussing a serious report.'

'Of course! Of course, I'm sorry. But a feature would introduce your work to more people—'

'I thought you understood that I don't care how many people know about me. I just think it is better if those who do know understand what I am really doing. The great mass of people don't interest me at all.'

'Of course, I apologize. No photographs then.' That was no problem, since he had the hidden camera. He had brought an ordinary camera, too, in case Stavanger expected him to have one, and got suspicious, but it was no trouble to leave it in his case.

The Professor poured more coffee, and offered Meritt a biscuit. 'I'm sorry,' he said, 'I am perhaps a little too emphatic sometimes. I understand your desire to inform and educate. I'm afraid years of working under restrictive conditions and cumbersome bureaucracy have left me somewhat intolerant.'

'It must have been very frustrating for you.'

'Indeed. But now, I hope, I have the opportunity to follow my own line, which I think will lead to some pretty remarkable discoveries. I am making considerable progress, though of course it takes time. Come into my study, and I will show you some of my work.'

The study was large, with several computers on the desks that ran round three sides of it. There were other devices which Meritt did not recognize, and a great many files and folders.

He said tentatively, 'Somehow I was expecting a laboratory, rather than a study.'

The Professor laughed; 'Don't worry, I have a lab. But this is where I correlate and analyse my results, and I wanted you to see the approach I'm working on.'

The next half hour or so was taken up with the Professor's discoursing on his methods, in language which was largely incomprehensible to his visitor. Meritt kept recording, hoping perhaps he could get something out of it on a second or third hearing. What he did grasp was that Professor Stavanger, rather than manipulating DNA in a seed, egg, or foetus, was attempting to alter it in the adult plant or animal, to fuse life forms – to turn one thing into another.

Meritt's initial thought was that the man was in fact potty, deluded; in which case his own work had been wasted – Mad Professor Is In Fact Just Mad wasn't a very lucrative headline. Still, there might be more to it. Having come this far he wanted to see everything.

He made appreciative noises, and eventually the Professor said, 'You see what I'm aiming at? Now I shall show you the labs, and you will see how it's working out.'

This is more like it, thought Meritt. He envisaged monstrous hybrids, animals with parts of other animals grafted on – minotaurs, centaurs, griffins. He remembered a newspaper picture of a mouse with a human ear growing on its back. He was aware that actual griffins or centaurs were unlikely, but he was always an optimist. He could never have continued in his line of work if he hadn't hoped every story would turn out to be a sensation. He followed the Professor down a corridor, and into a large room that had been reconstructed as a laboratory. There were no fantastical creatures, just more machinery, and Stavanger's lecture became more enthusiastic and even less comprehensible. Meritt wondered if in fact the experiments had yet led to any concrete results, or whether the Professor were still working on the theory. Surely not.

The coffee began to make itself felt; he asked the Professor the way to the bathroom.

'Oh of course – I'm sorry. I'll just lock up here, then show you the way. This is rather a rambling house, I'm afraid.'

They came eventually to a small cloakroom under the stairs. When Meritt came out, the Professor said,

'I have just looked at the time – would you care for some lunch?'

They returned to the kitchen, where the Professor set about preparing lunch – a very good pasta salad, with garlic bread, and a bottle of quite decent red wine, of which Meritt had two large glasses – he thought he might as well get something out of a day he was now convinced was going to be a complete frost.

He said, 'Professor – tell me honestly – you are clearly doing entirely legitimate and respectable research, so where did the rumours come from? What gave people these bizarre ideas?'

'My dear fellow, it doesn't take much to give people ideas. A public that cannot tell the difference between a paedophile and a paediatrician will hardly distinguish a geneticist from Dr Moreau.' Meritt must have let his incomprehension show: the Professor went on, 'Or Frankenstein, if you prefer. I left government service with something of a reputation for being difficult, and when I came to live here and built on my laboratories, naturally the local peasants Feared the Worst. It's irritating, but so far they have refrained from marching on the house with pitchforks.

'Will you have some more coffee? I don't myself after lunch, but it's no trouble.'

Meritt accepted, and wondered if he had misheard, or had Stavanger said "laboratories" in the plural? He said, 'An excellent lunch, thank you. So have you more to show me, or have I seen it all?'

'All? Heavens no, by no means. I have simply been giving you the background. When you have finished your coffee, I will show you the main laboratories.'

The main laboratories required an even longer walk, and Meritt realised as they went through a steel door and down a short passage that this was the large, rather ugly addition to the house he had glimpsed from the front. So the Professor had built this himself – with or without planning permission. Perhaps, at last, he was going to see something.

"Something" was putting it mildly.

It was a vast room, with a gallery around two sides, and the walls were lined with cages. Almost all the cages were occupied. The first thing that struck Meritt was the quiet. Nothing was hooting, or barking, or howling; nothing was scuffling or pacing or rattling. The occupants of the cages sat, staring into vacancy. They seemed to take no notice of the visitors.

The second thing was the smell, of which there was as much as might be expected and more, although all the creatures looked quite clean.

The creature in the first cage reminded Meritt of the mouse with the human ear growing on its back: only this wasn't human, and it wasn't an ear. There were mammals with scales, and reptiles with fur. There was a monkey with hooves, and a goat with hands, there were creatures with extra limbs, sometimes in unlikely places. There were things whose origins he didn't recognize. The Professor continued talking, explaining, theorising, but Meritt was no longer listening. This was far more than he had even hoped for. More bizarre, more extraordinary, more fascinating, more horrible. It sent a thrill of fear down even his cynical spine. What a story this would make! But why had Stavanger kept it secret? Fear of animal rights campaigners, perhaps? No doubt he had been bending some laws on animal welfare. But in that case he would hardly invite Meritt to write an article, however scholarly. So maybe fear of rivals, and now he had reached a point where he felt safe from the competition...

Meritt was now staring at what was more or less a pig. The differences were hard to pinpoint, but they were there. The Professor was saying, 'Of course, the pig is one of the more intelligent mammals. I have unfortunately had to confine myself to land-dwelling life forms; the possibilities with the octopus and squid are fascinating, but I have had difficulties with the habitat. I had an octopus, but it escaped before I could begin.'

Meritt fleetingly wondered where the octopus was now. He stared again at the pig, the pig stared back, and the man realised what was most unnerving about all these creatures. They all had expressions of deep sadness, which was perhaps not surprising, except that most of them had faces he had never thought of as having expressions at all. But now they had. And all of them were unbearably sad. He shook himself. The Professor looked at him, and said,

'I suppose this is rather much to take in all at once.' He looked at his watch; 'It's nearly tea-time, let's take a short break.'

He led the way back into the house, and along more corridors, into a room Meritt had not seen before: a curious mixture of laboratory and Victorian drawing-room, with clinical looking equipment at one end, and at the other heavy mahogany armchairs and velvet curtains.

'Have a seat, my dear chap. I shan't be long. You look tired.'

Meritt was tired, he realised, enormously tired. He lowered his heavy limbs into one of the chairs, and looked at the opposite wall. Beside a long dark red curtain hung a painting, of a cat with a human face. The expression, however was entirely feline – immense superiority, and vague dissatisfaction with the incompetence of the help. Meritt checked his recording equipment. All seemed to be in order. He had managed to take some photos, but had not dared to attempt any filming. Pity. He had hoped to be left alone at some point with the experiments. Perhaps he would manage it later. He felt slightly sick; some of the things he had seen were a bit too strong even for his stomach. Still, it was an amazing scoop. The cat gazed at him superciliously. He closed his eyes.

Meritt started awake with the visceral terror that follows a serious nightmare. He tried to open his eyes, and to move his arms, but could do neither; nor could he speak or cry out. He told himself to calm down – this was just sleep paralysis, a well known phenomenon. It would pass in a moment. He tried to relax and breath slowly. Breathing seemed to be more of an effort than usual, as if something were constricting his chest. He thought back. He had fallen asleep while the Professor was making tea. Why had the Professor not woken him? He managed at last to open his eyes. He saw the picture of the cat on the wall, and beside it the curtain had been drawn aside, giving a view into the next room. What he saw there made him catch his breath.

This was surely the pinnacle of the Professor's work. It was huge, to begin with. The basis seemed to be a mountain gorilla. The hind legs more resembled those of a gazelle, and there were small horns on the forehead. The forelimbs were smoothly scaled like a snake, and ended in long, elegant hands. The face – the face gazed back at him, as the creatures in the lab had done, with something close to despair. The creature made no sound. It was seated in some kind of chair, to which it was bound with metal bands. Meritt stared for a long time; then he tried to move his head, but found he could not. He heard Professor Stavanger's voice from somewhere to his right:

'Ah, you are awake, Mr. Meritt.'

For a moment he couldn't think what was wrong with this sentence, then he realised – Stavanger had used his real name, he had rumbled him. His uneasiness turned to panic. What was the Professor likely to do? He tried to speak, but his tongue felt thick and heavy. The Professor continued,

'Did you really think you had fooled me? I'm not a fool; I contacted Bagshaw. I worked out your real identity before I agreed to see you. It amused me to act as if I believed you – the would-be fooler fooled, the biter bit. I do not think, Mr. Meritt, you will be missed. I do not think you have told anyone where you were going. Your car is already somewhere else. And you will certainly not be a great loss to the human race, despicable though most of it is.'

Oh God, thought Meritt, *he's going to kill me. He's going to vivisect me, use me for his experiments. He really is mad.* The voice went on,

'The drug I put in your coffee after lunch was timed to act precisely when it did. It will wear off gradually, but it will take some time. You have been unconscious for a considerable while, of course.'

Drugged! thought Meritt, *I should have guessed,* though he could not have said why. *He's taking revenge for my lying to him. What can I do? He said the drug will wear off; if I pretend it's lasting longer, if I make out I'm still unable to move when I feel it wearing off, maybe I can get away. He's an old man, he doesn't look very strong; I should be able to overpower him, if I wait till I have my strength back. Don't try to move, that's the thing. Let him think I'm still completely paralysed.*

Which was really the triumph of irrational optimism, since so far he could move nothing but his eyelids.

The Professor spoke again from the right: 'In a way, of course, I'm grateful to you. I've been longing to see how my methods work on humans, but it's really quite difficult to get hold of one. I need to investigate the subjective effects, but of course most of my creatures can't tell me about them. And to be honest, despite what I said earlier, I am getting short of money. You really are a godsend, Mr. Meritt, in a strange way. I'm sure you never thought of yourself as that.'

Meritt concentrated on breathing. It would be OK. People didn't get away with things like this. He would bide his time. And then it would be an even better story – "Mad Professor Held Me Hostage, intended to use me for experiments". He would even be famous.

Suddenly, the Professor's face appeared, behind the gorilla creature in the next room. This was disorienting; the voice had seemed to come from quite a different direction. Ventriloquism? The Professor said, 'I look forward to some very interesting interviews, once you regain the power of speech. You realise, of course – ' a hand fell on Meritt's shoulder – 'that you are looking into a mirror?'

MADAME ORLOFF'S LAST STAND

By

John Llewellyn Probert

'MR WINKIE-POO IS MISSING!'

Those words, uttered by a voice so strangled-sounding it suggested their speaker might benefit from releasing the tight grip they had on their necklace of imitation pearls, fell on uncaring ears. They had all heard it too many times before. Indeed, they had already heard it too many times this morning.

'It's all right, Gertrude.' Mr Walbert Cummings spoke from the safety and comfort of his armchair. 'I'm sure he's around here somewhere.' He had only retreated behind his copy of *The Observer* for a moment before Gertrude hit him over the head with a rolled up copy of *The Mail on Sunday*. Under other circumstances he might have quipped that it was the only decent use for such a scandalous rag, but this morning he just released the kind of low growling sound he usually reserved for especially difficult bowel movements.

Gertrude Watkins, still in distress, raised the newspaper for a second blow, only to be divested of her weapon by the imposing form of Nurse Balstock. The meaty woman wrenched the newspaper away from her considerably slighter charge with perhaps just a little more force than was strictly necessary.

'Now we don't hit the other residents, do we?' Her stentorian tones echoed off the magnolia-painted walls. 'Especially when they are trying to help.'

Gertrude's face creased into a scowl. 'He's not trying to help. He's revelling in the fact that Mr Winkie-Poo is gone.' She glared at the defenceless old man. 'Aren't you? In fact I bet it's you who's hiding him.' Now she was down on her hands and knees. She would likely need helping back up. 'Have you got him under the chair?'

Two of the three other residents of the Happylands Home for Sociable Seniors currently occupying the day room ignored the drama completely. Agnes and Dingle Payne, the building's only brother and sister residents, were engrossed in a daytime repeat showing of their favourite soap opera, *It Was Much Better Back Then*. At that moment a beleaguered miner was telling his family how they would likely starve to death now the strike was on.

Only one other person was paying attention to the fracas. Only one person was considering chiming in. And that was because only one person could actually see Mr Winkie-Poo, a self-satisfied-looking ball of overfed Persian Blue disdain. As Gertrude was lifted from the ground in one of Nurse Balstock's beefy arms, Madame Orloff decided it was time to intervene.

'He's over by the radiator, dear.'

All eyes turned to the corner of the room, to where the individual who had uttered the words was sitting. She was so festooned with bangles, baubles and gaily coloured draperies that if she hadn't spoken she could have been mistaken for last year's Christmas tree someone had decided to prop up in a chair.

Now it was Nurse Balstock's turn to glare. 'I beg your pardon?'

Madame Orloff ignored her. 'Actually he's *under* the radiator. He doesn't like the cold, you see. But he's very happy. He's watching you right now.'

She neglected to mention that Mr Winkie-Poo seemed to be finding the entire situation utterly beneath him, but that was only because she didn't think it would help.

Gertrude's eyes darted to the far wall and her expression transformed into one of almost beatific relief. 'Oh he is! Thank you! You naughty puss puss. What are you doing over there? Mummy was worried. Didn't you hear her calling you?'

From Mr Winkie-Poo's expression it was likely that he had, but that the piece of fluff on the floor he was currently studying was more important than his mistress' distress.

The situation defused, Nurse Balstock released her grip on Gertrude, who scuttled over to where the spectral presence of Mr Winkie-Poo was not sitting at all. Madame Orloff didn't correct her because that wouldn't have helped either. Besides, the nurse was now marching over to her.

'You mustn't encourage her.'

'I merely did it to calm things down.' She looked over Nurse Balstock's shoulder to see Gertrude petting her imaginary cat. Two feet away from Gertrude the ghost of Mr Winkie-Poo regarded her with vague disinterest. 'And it seems to have done the job.'

Nurse Balstock was having none of it. 'Even so, most of the residents know of your previous "profession".' That last word was invested with all the sneering disbelief Nurse Balstock could muster. 'And I just want you to know I won't stand for any of that ghost nonsense here.'

'Not nonsense my dear, but then I hardly expect you to understand that.'

'I beg your pardon?'

'Oh nothing, nothing.' She made a mental note to whisper more quietly. 'I promise I shall keep my thoughts to myself in the future.'

'You do that.'

Madame Orloff was tempted to whisper something else as the nurse strode away. Instead she gave Gertrude a warm and sympathetic smile as the old lady stroked something that wasn't there, in any realm or dimension. Sometimes it was important just to make people happy.

And later, when Gertrude was discovered dead, Madame Orloff was at least able to take solace in the knowledge that she had helped make the old lady's final hours happy ones.

It is, of course, a common occurrence for the residents of an elderly care home to one day take that final step of passing on to meet their maker. Even so, at Happylands every attempt was always made to keep such matters as quiet as possible. Unfortunately the ambulance was late and so poor old Gertude Watkins ended up being carried out of the building through the dining room. At breakfast time.

The pale blue blanket that covered most of her body did little to disguise who it was. Some residents stared, while others pretended the event wasn't taking place at all. Only one had a quizzical look on her face.

Madame Orloff put down her plastic fork (no metal utensils were allowed in case residents fell on them, she had been told) and immediately forgot about the dreary taste of her milky grey scrambled egg. Something far more pressing was on her mind.

Where was Mr Winkie-Poo?

The ancient Egyptians had almost got it right. It was customary for the ghost of a pet, especially a cat, to accompany its owner's body until the difficult transition to spectral form could be made and the two reunited friends could journey to the afterlife together. Madame Orloff frowned. Surely Gertrude had not ascended already? Despite the claims of cheap literature and even cheaper television, spectral transfiguration was a lengthy process that could take days and, in some cases, weeks. This time yesterday Gertrude had been alive and kicking. Well, alive and shuffling. Which meant right now her spectral form should still be within her corpus. Which again begged that nagging question.

Where was Mr Winkie-Poo?

She was almost at the point of intercepting the stretcher bearers and their charge when Nurse Balstock loomed up to block her.

'Nothing to see here, Mrs Orloff.'

The psychic drew herself up to her full five feet three inches. Despite the fact the nurse still towered over her, the woman took a step back as Madame Orloff used tones she had employed in the past to dispel elementals, banish hadel-monsters, and give a fly-by-night a terrible case of the runs (or rather, the flies).

'It is *Madame* Orloff, and I wish to say goodbye to Miss Watkins.' It was probably best to embellish that. 'She was my friend.'

They were nearly at the door. Nurse Balstock didn't move.

'You've only been here three days Mrs Orloff, and I don't remember you having anything to do with Gertrude other than that nonsense with the cat yesterday.'

They were having trouble opening the door because it was on a very heavy steel spring to stop elderly residents escaping from breakfast before they were allowed. They'd be through in a minute, though.

She had to do something.

When all else has failed, sometimes one has to resort to the kind of desperate measure that, fortunately, Madame Orloff had had some practice in.

To the surprise of Nurse Balstock, the assembled diners (all of whose attention she grabbed effortlessly) and even the ambulance men, Madame Orloff let loose the most almighty wail, ducked past her oppressor, and threw herself to her knees beside Gertrude's prostrate form. This action also included a gentle but deliberate nudge of the stretcher, thus encouraging a pallid left arm to flop forth from beneath its coverings.

'Oh why, Gertrude? Why?' Madame Orloff bellowed in the hope it would distract everyone from how she was clutching the dead old lady's hand and concentrating.

Gertrude's spirit was indeed still resident within her body, and it had quite a tale to tell, one that was revealed to Madame Orloff in the blink of an eye, the flutter of a bird's wing or, in this particular case, the time it took for Nurse Balstock to make it over, wrench Madame Orloff's hand away and escort the ambulance men out while simultaneously giving the psychic an "I'll deal with you later" kind of glare.

But Madame Orloff wasn't paying attention. She was far too busy wondering why, and indeed exactly how, in the early hours of the morning the by definition insubstantial spectral form of Mr Winkie-Poo had smothered Gertrude Watkins until she was good and dead.

It was three days later when the next incident occurred. Jimmy Bickerstaff, eighty five and fighting fit until the day he fell down a flight of stairs in a part of the building where he shouldn't even had been venturing, was taken away with a broken neck. The pathologist who ended up having to perform the post mortem had to resist describing the poor man's cervical spine as "like a violently shaken box of Lego".

Madame Orloff knew, though. The general pall of gloom cast over breakfast proceedings one horrible Wednesday morning, plus the absence of Mr Bickerstaff, meant it was easy to put two and two together. Once again there was a delay in the removal of the body, giving her plenty of time to disappear into the toilets and then come out just in time to coincide with Mr Bickerstaff's exit.

'You were in there a long time, Mrs Orloff.' Nurse Balstock's eyes were once again narrowed at her nemesis.

'Madame.' She wasn't going to back down about that. 'I'm afraid something had got a little bit stuck, dear. I'm sure you've encountered such things before but you don't really want me to go into the details in front of all these people, do you?'

As Madame Orloff threatened to describe just what exactly might have got stuck and where, she brushed a palm over the dead man's head.

Jimmy Bickerstaff's pre-ghost also had a very interesting story to tell.

'Did Mr Bickerstaff own a dog?'

'Jimmy?' Walbert Cummings looked up from his newspaper. It appeared to be the same copy of *The Observer* he'd been reading for over a week now. In fact, Madame Orloff wondered, had he even ever left that armchair? She dismissed the thought as she waited for his reply. 'I'm not sure. Why? Did he say anything to you about one before he left us?'

Not exactly. But according to his ghost his beloved Alsatian "Chancy" had tripped him up after chasing him into the utilities area. 'He just struck me as the kind of man who loved dogs.'

'We never liked dogs,' said Agnes Payne as the end credits rolled on yet another episode of *Buy My Rubbish*, or whatever the awful auction programme currently showing was actually called.

'And we've never been cat people, either,' interjected Dingle, thumbing the remote control repeatedly until *Let's Redecorate Your House In Appalling Taste* came on.

'Of course there were the rabbits,' said Agnes. Her brother shushed her as viewers were shown a very nice if rather scruffy

Victorian interior doubtless soon to be transformed into something fit only for decadent degenerates. 'Flopsy and Fluffy and Tallywacker and Biggles.' Mr Cummings' snigger was muffled a few seconds too late. It earned him an admonishing glance. 'Our twelve year old nephew came up with those last two so I would ask you not to make fun of the innocent imagination of a child.' Agnes went back to counting on her fingers. 'Then Tallywacker died and we replaced him with Montague who turned out to be a lady rabbit and she gave birth to Pippin, Wacksy and Bodrun.'

'Who looks after them now?' Madame Orloff asked.

'Oh that must have been twenty years ago!' Agnes sniffed. 'They're all gone, now. Rabbits don't live for very long, do they? At least ours didn't. Did you have any pets?'

'No.' The psychic got to her feet. The cracking of her knee joints could probably be heard in the next town.

'Really, Madame Orloff?' That was Walbert. 'You strike me as someone who would have enjoyed animal companionship.'

'I'm afraid not.' She'd certainly had pets, but Madame Orloff was in no mood to go into detail about what a Grundlechaser or a Slow Larkin was, and since the former was always a vicious little fellow and the latter tended to turn invisible and empty its bowels whenever it was upset she didn't think anyone in the day room would want to hear about them anyway. 'What about you, Mr Cummings?'

The old man in the fraying armchair was silent for a moment as a wistful, faraway look came over him. 'Barney,' he said eventually. 'Barney the Brindle Bull Terrier. He was such a good boy. There's a lot of rubbish spoken about them but you could never have met a more affectionate animal.' He rustled his paper and turned a page. 'Mind you, if he didn't like you, you could watch out.'

That night all was quiet.

The next night, however, there were screams.

So loud and so terrifying were they that they roused Madame Orloff from her slumber in an instant. She sat bolt upright in bed and waited, just in case they had been a component of an especially disturbing dream.

Then there was another one – a long, drawn-out howl. It was difficult to tell if it was a man or a woman and it didn't matter – Madame Orloff was out of bed and into the corridor with all the speed her elderly frame could muster.

The corridor was in darkness.

It was also empty.

Where was everyone? Surely she couldn't have been the only one to have been woken?

Another scream.

And then Madame Orloff realised.

The screams were spectral. Only she could hear them. Which meant whoever was uttering them was either already dead, or very nearly.

The sounds had come from the left, and so she made her way in that direction cautiously and quietly to avoid tripping over anything, but mainly so as not to wake Nurse Balstock.

She came to a halt outside Room eleven, where Alice and Dingle had their twin beds. She was about to knock gently when another scream wracked the inside of her skull.

The door opened at her touch.

Madame Orloff slipped inside. The room was in darkness, the two occupants mere outlines in the shadow of night. First she made sure the door was closed. Then she switched on the light.

To behold a scene of horror.

Alice was in the bed on the left, Dingle on the right. Both had kicked off their bedclothes. Both were convulsing as if being stabbed repeatedly.

Or rather, as if they were being bitten.

For as Madame Orloff watched, she saw tiny puncture marks appearing, marks that added to the multitude of minute bleeding wounds that had already been visited upon their persons. And though their mouths remained shut, with each bite they cried out in their sleep.

Her first thought was to get help, but this was quickly superseded by the realisation that physical intervention was not what would save Alice and Dingle's lives.

Madame Orloff took a deep breath, put her fingers to her temples, and concentrated.

It wasn't long before the perpetrators of the atrocities began to take shadowy form. Madame Orloff had expected something vampiric, perhaps something looking to suck what little life essence the Paynes still possessed.

What she did not expect was rabbits.

To be fair, they were bloody horrible-looking rabbits. The four large, semi-rotted shapes nestling on the bodies in the beds seemed to know they had been seen, and they turned as one to regard their observer with milk white eyes. Bloodstained teeth were bared and, though Madame Orloff expected them to snarl, the insidious hiss that escaped their bone-exposed jaws was far more terrifying.

It had been so long, and her reflexes were so rusty, that it took Madame Orloff a moment to collect her thoughts. Then she raised her arms and uttered the first spell of expulsion that came to her:

Rotting things from down below
Back to hell I command you go!

Nothing happened. Except that one of the rabbit-ghoul things pulled what remained of its mouth into the semblance of a grin. The other three went back to biting.

She had better try something else.

Eaters of flesh, be ye gone!
Your presence here is entirely wrong!
Return now to your astral plain,
And do not bother us again!

Was that a laugh? From somewhere behind her? Perhaps coming from whoever, or whatever had brought these accursed things into being in the first place?

Right, time to bring out the big guns. She was going to need a large brandy after this. Hopefully Mr Cummings would have a stock, and if he misinterpreted her intentions visiting him at this late hour, she'd soon put him right.

Oh ye ministers of the eternal realm
I call on thee to use blade and helm
To vanquish these damned eternals four
And prevent them coming back for more!

The four hell-bunnies didn't seem to like that one little bit. Rotting ears pricked up (or tried to) as an ethereal wind passed through the room. The creatures tried to hold onto their victims but the harder they dug their claws into flesh the more fierce the wind became. Eventually, making sounds like four cats being put through a mangle backwards, they flew across the room, passed straight through the wall, and disappeared – hopefully back to wherever they had come from.

The wind was just dying down as the door burst open.

'What on earth is going on in here?'

Madame Orloff was too busy checking the pulses of the Payne siblings to worry about Nurse Balstock. It was only when she realised they were dead that her mind turned to the problem of how she was going to explain herself.

'The Paynes are dead,' she said in as calm a voice as she could muster.

'I can see that.' Nurse Balstock sounded nonplussed. 'What did you do to them?'

'Not me.' Madame Orloff pointed to the wall. 'I sent them through there.'

'Sent what?'

'The...' Oh why were these things so difficult to explain? 'The things that killed them.'

Nurse Balstock's expression turned from shocked to sad. 'Oh

Madame Orloff, you just don't know what you've been doing, do you? You're not in control.'

This change of approach was, if anything, much worse than the angry Nurse Balstock Madame Orloff was used to dealing with.

'You don't understand!' She protested.

'Oh yes I do.' The nurse was holding out a placatory hand now, one that no doubt possessed a very powerful grip. 'You've been feeling tired, haven't you? Been suffering blackouts, perhaps? Not sure of how you've ended up where you've found yourself? I've seen it all before. You come with me and we can have a nice chat about it, perhaps over a cup of tea?'

Nurse Balstock took a step forward. She would have taken another were it not for the fact that at that very moment something small and brown shot out from beneath the late Agnes Payne's bed, passed between the nurse's feet and squeezed through the barely open bedroom door.

'What on earth was that?'

'I must have missed one.' Madame Orloff's fear of the nurse had vanished now that there was spectral business to deal with.

'Was it a rat?' The colour drained from Nurse Balstock's face. She glanced at Agnes' bed, presumably with the intention of climbing onto it.

'Worse than that, I'm afraid.' Madame Orloff pushed the distraught woman aside, gently opened the door, and called outside. 'Now where have you got to?'

She placed her fingers to her temples and concentrated, looking first to the left down the corridor.

Nothing.

She swung her gaze to the right.

Something.

Just the bare remnant of something, a trace of a stink of corruption, of graves reopened and coffin lids lifted.

'Come on.' she said to Nurse Balstock. The other woman exhibited no inclination to follow her. 'If we don't go now we may lose him!'

She wasn't surprised to find herself alone on the corridor, nostrils aflare as she followed the unholy odour of the supernatural creature that had created it.

She didn't have to go far.

The trail ended at the door next to hers, at the room she knew was occupied by Walbert Cummings. The moment Madame Orloff pushed the door open she knew something was wrong.

To begin with, the lights were on. Mr Cummings wasn't in bed but was sitting up in his chair, pipe alight, newspaper open in front of him. He looked understandably startled by the intrusion into his privacy.

'Madame Orloff! Is everything all right?'

'I should ask you the same thing.' Her eyes darted around the room. The smell was stronger in here than it had been outside. Perhaps the creature was hiding somewhere, waiting to strike.

'In that case, would you mind leaving? I'm very tired and I really should be getting to bed.'

'Please give me a moment if you would, Mr Cummings. I hate to play the melodramatist but I fear your life may be at stake.'

Mr Cummings did not seem to appreciate her concern for his safety. In fact his usually benign expression had now become a distinct glower. 'Madame Orloff, I am afraid I must ask you to leave. I have had a very trying day and...'

Madame Orloff was so busy scanning the room for supernatural phenomena that she didn't immediately register that Mr Cummings' words had tailed off. By the time she had turned to look at him his eyes were closed.

Something moved. Underneath his newspaper. It was only the briefest of twitches but Madame Orloff was sure something was there. She took a step towards the seemingly sleeping man.

The newspaper twitched again, more violently this time.

Then it began to move, rhythmically, in and out, like a paper bag being used to quell a panic attack.

Madame Orloff didn't really want to see what was beneath the crumpled copy of *The Observer*, but she knew she had no choice.

With one deft movement she plucked the newspaper from Mr Cummings.

There was something in Mr Cummings' lap.

Actually, it looked more as if there was something that was part of Mr Cummings. Something attached to the sagging flesh of his belly where his shirt had been torn open. Something small and furry and brown, with disproportionately tiny arms and legs that appeared to be embedded in the hapless pensioner.

Aware that it had been discovered, it turned its wrinkled, wizened, gargoyle-like head, opened a mouth that, despite its minuscule size seemed to contain about a hundred minute, pointed teeth, and hissed at her.

'Dear God.' Nurse Balstock had made it down the corridor and was now staring, aghast, from the presumed safety of just behind the door. 'What is that?'

Madame Orloff was regarding the tiny creature with all the fascination of an entomologist who has spotted a butterfly rare to these shores. When she remembered she had a voice, she spoke with all the awe of an expert who knows all too well how uncommon the thing is that she has happened upon.

'That, Nurse Balstock, is an elemental.'

'A what?'

'They're usually invisible, so you'll have to forgive my excitement. I have only very rarely come across these things in the flesh.' She took a step back and then bent over to get a better look.

The creature glared at her.

'My, my yes you're just a baby, aren't you? Now what's a nasty thing like you doing running around in a place like this, eh?'

'What are you talking about?' hissed the nurse.

'Well you see, usually once an elemental gets hold of you it's almost impossible to get rid of it. They become embedded in the flesh like a tick or a parasitic worm.' There was another angry hiss from over in the corner. 'Yes that's right my lad, I'm talking about you.' She turned back to Nurse Balstock. 'What I don't understand is how this one is quite obviously mobile, or what it was doing in the

Payne's bedroom. Unless...' Madame Orloff suddenly felt herself gripped by the kind of terror and panic she had not experienced for many years. She regarded the creature again. '...unless you're not the one responsible for all this at all. Because actually...'

But it was too late and Madame Orloff wasn't close enough to the door as it was slammed shut by another of the creatures. Two more emerged from the lampshade overhead while a further three crawled from beneath the bed. All hissing, all smelling appalling, all the offspring of the thing in the armchair.

She could hear Nurse Balstock hammering on the door, demanding to be let in. 'It's best you stay out there, my dear. Otherwise one of them will be into you while the others scatter in search of further hosts.' She gave Walbert a gentle tap on the cheek, then progressively harder ones until he came round. She knew he was dying. But she had to know.

With rapidly dimming eyes he regarded her, his breathing weak, his face growing pale.

'It was Barney, wasn't it?' Madame Orloff spoke slowly and clearly in the hope her words might get through. 'He wasn't a dog at all, was he?'

What was left of Walbert Cummings shook his head.

'But he had been with you most of your life, hadn't he?'

A nod.

'And you brought him here with you here, didn't you?' Even the strict no pets policy wouldn't have stopped him.

Another nod.

'And when Barney discovered he had happened upon a treasure trove of victims near death, and the means by which to do away with them, Barney decided it was time to reproduce, didn't he?' Or rather she. Or possibly it. The sex of elementals was a subject very little had ever been written about. Any observer of a brood tended to end up on the menu pretty smartly.

One more nod. A very weak one this time. But it confirmed all Madame Orloff's suspicions.

'Bugger.'

She had dealt with elementals before, of course. But they had been single, invisible, and far weaker than what she now found herself surrounded by. It had been damned clever of "Barney" to think of using the ghosts of the residents' pets against them, bending them to his/its will, forcing them to do its bidding.

And then a thought struck her.

Those ghosts wouldn't be under the elemental's spell now. The creature didn't need them any more. And besides, it was unlikely it could control more than one at a time. The baby elementals (elementalings?) were too weak to do anything other than hiss and smell terrible right now. But if they drained her they'd soon be strong enough to start causing mischief of their own.

The ghosts...

It was likely they were still around, and it was also *extremely* likely that they were keen to avenge the deaths of their owners.

There was only one way to find out.

Madame Orloff took a step back and raised her arms. The elementalings crouched, preparing to pounce, as she bellowed as loudly as she could.

You were their great comfort, their best friend,
I know you weren't responsible for their end
I beg you now to join with me
And cause these monsters to flee, flee, FLEE!

Mr Cummings' body began to twitch as "Barney", his host now exhausted and of no further use to him, decided to put in an appearance.

If its babies were scary, Barney the Elemental was positively terrifying. To Madame Orloff it looked as if a gargoyle the size of a two year old was tearing its way from Mr Cummings' stomach, all the while glaring at her with tiny red eyes filled with hatred.

'Come on, come on,' she muttered to herself. As the elemental tore itself free from Walbert's corpse and reached for her she raised her arms and repeated the incantation once more. The creature was almost upon her, its taloned claws reeking of mould about to touch her cheek.

A wind passed through the room.

And with the wind came a mighty sound.

It was difficult to describe but Madame Orloff imagined it likely consisted of a number of furious dogs, cats, rabbits and other creatures Barney had seen fit to make its slaves.

Suddenly the room was filled with spectres.

They swooped down upon the elementalings and scooped them up, crushing them between jaws, tearing them between claws. They attached themselves to the parent and tried to tear it apart.

But it was no good. "Barney" was too strong for them. Even more furious now that its brood had been destroyed it leapt at Madame Orloff.

But it didn't reach her.

Because something was in the way.

Something huge and ferocious and invisible.

Something with bigger claws than an elemental, something with sharper teeth, and something with a tremendous sense of propriety regarding its threatened owner.

'Bartholomew!' Even though she couldn't see her former pet Hadel-monster, Madame Orloff knew it was he, come to her in her hour of need.

The elemental didn't stand a chance.

When it was all over, Madame Orloff opened the door to be faced with an almost catatonic Nurse Balstock.

'I wouldn't go in there for a bit if I were you my dear,' the psychic said. 'It's all a bit whiffy, if you get my meaning. Best let the authorities deal with it.'

Madame Orloff turned to leave.

'Where are you going?' Nurse Balstock croaked after her.

Madame Orloff beamed the biggest smile she had in years, and certainly since coming to this place. 'Just to get some sleep my dear. I thought staying somewhere like this would be dull, but now I've a very big job ahead of me. Next year's annual meeting of the British

Psychical & Paranormal Research Society (Middlesex Branch) is going to be audience to a presentation that will shock their socks off!' She paused, as if considering something. 'In fact I wonder if they'd be prepared to hold the meeting here?'

For once, Nurse Balstock had no words.

FAMILY PLOT

By

Fred Adams, Jr

CHESTER ARRIVED AT Saint Mark's Cemetery late in the day. He had again been held up at work by his boss. Mr Canty was the sort of employer who delighted in tugging at the strings attaching a man to a paycheck and yanking him back like a trout from a brook, just as the poor fellow was about to punch the clock and liberate himself from servitude.

Elias Canty would have been stoned to death in Biblical times as a usurer, but in London's enlightened climate, he was regarded a legitimate businessman, a money lender who rubbed his hands and rolled his eyes like Uriah Heep at the prospect of foreclosure. He was a hulking brute in a tailored coat who bragged, 'I don't need a magistrate; I settle my accounts with my fist,' accounts that Chester tallied as his bookkeeper.

'Oh, Hastings,' he'd say just before the stroke of five, 'before you leave, I wonder if you could take care of one little thing for me.' And Chester would find himself elbows deep in some tedious chore as Canty donned his hat and coat and went whistling down the hall toward the lift.

Someday, thought Chester, I'm going to tell that rotter to stuff it. But today hadn't been that day. The sun was setting through the dark boles of the elms and about to dip below the hedges that bounded Saint Mark's Cemetery. Chester had to walk briskly to make it to the graveyard before dark when the grumpy old sexton with his rheumy eyes and gnarled fingers locked the iron gates and left until morning.

He carried a small bouquet of pink roses, his aunt Tillie's favorite, to lay on her grave. It was her birthday, and he tried to honor all of his late relatives in the family plot on their special days. They always remembered his birthday as he grew up, and even as an adult, so he felt an obligation to remember theirs, especially Aunt Tillie, who raised him from childhood after his parents were killed in a rail crash at Chesney in 1919.

The Hastings family plot rested on a gentle grassy slope under a canopy of branches that kept it in a sort of perpetual twilight and brought the night earlier there than the rest of the cemetery. The plot was enclosed by a wrought iron fence with spear point balusters and pineapple finials on the gate posts. The cemetery grass had been mowed the day before, and the green scent tickled Chester's nostrils.

Not a headstone teetered one degree. They were all as severely upright as were the people whose graves they designated. Blue-nosed Puritans all, the Hastings family descended from Cromwell on Chester's maternal side. Chester strode among the phalanx of granite to the far corner of the plot where the stone read: Mathilda Hastings Tolliver, September 23, 1868 - June 13, 1942. He doffed his Homburg and gently laid the roses on the grave.

'Hello, Aunt Tillie,' Chester said. He turned the brim of his hat in his fingers. 'Happy birthday.' He stood silent for a moment then returned his hat to his head and began to walk away. He hadn't quite reached the little iron gate before he heard a voice say, 'It's about time you got here. A few more minutes, and the gate would've closed, and you'd've missed my birthday.'

Chester turned and stared at Aunt Tillie's tombstone as the lines of its incised inscription began to twitch and to crawl like earthworms until they formed a nose, mouth, and eyes that decidedly belonged to Tillie Tolliver. He might have been shocked had he not seen it happen so many times before.

'Well,' the face said, 'Don't stand there gawping at me, boy. Explain yourself.'

'It was Mr Canty. He made me stay late.'

'Again?' said another voice, this one deep and phlegmy. 'That man is an unholy pain in the arse,' The headstone formed the features of his great uncle Clive. 'Why do you put up with him, Chester?'

'I need the job, Uncle.' He looked down at his frayed shirt cuffs. 'You all died and left me next to nothing.'

'There you go again, whining and poor mouthing,' Aunt Tillie snapped. 'Ask that pinchpenny for a raise if you're so destitute.'

'I did, Auntie. He laughed at me and told me to be grateful he let me work for him at all.'

'He's a right bastard, that one,' said a nasal voice belonging to Uncle Arthur, Aunt Tillie's husband who preceded her in death by twenty years. 'He needs a good thrashing, he does.'

'That's right, as does all bullies.' It was Uncle George, who was a boxer in life and his broken nose had a sideways semicolon for nostrils. 'If I were alive, I'd teach you a few tricks that'd lay the bugger low, or maybe even go after him myself. I'd teach him to bully a Hastings.'

Chester sighed. 'I wish you could. I wish I could, but it's no use. I'd be no match for him. He's twice my size.' The sky was turning indigo in the west and black in the east. 'I have to go now, or I'll be locked in for the night. Happy birthday, Auntie, and a good night to you all.'

A voice he hadn't heard for a long time caught his ear. 'Come back tomorrow, lad. Mayhap we can be of some help.' A stern old man's face stared from the granite, Abijah Hastings, Chester's grandfather.

'All, right Grandfather. I will.'

'And don't be so late,' Aunt Tillie chided.

Chester had to run to reach the gate before the grizzled old sexton padlocked it for the night. 'Out jawin' with the dead again, eh, boy?' The old man could hear only Chester's voice in the graveyard. The family council was for Chester's eyes and ears only. The Sexton let out a mean laugh that turned halfway into a wet cough. 'Makin' me wait. Get out before I lock you in for spite.'

The gate clanged shut, and as Chester walked away, head down, he thought again of his grandfather's offer of help. What could his family do in the ground? Nothing, he thought, the dead can do nothing.

The next day passed as did so many for Chester, working through lunch, but this evening, at quitting time, Canty was occupied in his office, "consulting" with a widow who was behind on her mortgage.

Chester wasn't one for peering through keyholes, but had no doubt that the widow was paying her arrears with her flesh. He quietly pulled the roll top closed on his desk and as quietly slipped out the office door.

Saint Mark's was peaceful in the early evening, a few visitors here and there on the grounds, but no one hovered near the Hastings family plot. Chester passed through the gate and stood a full ten minutes contemplating the stones. He had the hope that his relatives' counsel might actually be of some help, but when no word came from the monuments, he finally lost his patience and said, 'All right. You said come back and you'd help me. I'm here. Well?' he said his voice rising. 'Well?'

'Isn't he the impertinent one?' said his Great Aunt Beatrice. 'Chester, you know we can't speak before the sun sets.'

'Hush, Bea,' Grandfather said, his face appearing on his stone. 'Time is short. Come here, lad.'

Chester stood at the foot of Grandfather's grave and watched as the face on the stone wrinkled its brow and squeezed its eyes as if great in concentration or perhaps effort. 'Unngh,' Grandfather grunted. Again. Again. Then the face pursed its lips and spat. Something flashed in the grass in front of the stone. 'Pick it up, boy.'

Chester knelt and picked up a coin between his thumb and forefinger. It was gold and shone dully in the fading light. The face on the obverse was Victoria, and the date was 1855. Chester turned it over and saw the words SYDNEY MINT on the reverse. 'I don't understand,' he said.

'Do you remember me telling you that I once adventured in Australia? I didn't come back wealthy, but I had a cache of those. By the time I died, only two remained, and when I was buried, they were put in my waistcoat pocket – to pay the Ferryman, you know.'

'Oh. Bosh,' said Aunt Tillie. 'Superstitious claptrap.'

'Be that as it may, Tillie,' Grandfather continued, 'I think my superstition may yet be of some benefit to young Chester here. It will soon be dark, lad, so listen closely...'

The next day, Chester rapped his knuckles on Canty's doorframe.

His head snapped up and he grumbled, 'What is it Hastings?' When Chester didn't speak at first, Canty said, 'Well, out with it, man. What is it?'

'I'd like to speak with you sir.'

'You are speaking with me, damn it.'

'Something has happened, and I'm not quite sure what to do about it. I thought perhaps you could advise me, perhaps give me some help with the matter.'

Canty's irritation was ill concealed. 'Help? What kind of help?'

'Last night at Saint Mark's I was visiting the graves of my family. It was almost dark when—'

'Yes, yes. Stop wasting my time. Get to the point, Hastings.'

'I saw something shiny in the grass in front of Grandfather Hastings' headstone. It was this.' Chester held out the Sovereign in his palm.

Canty plucked the coin from his hand and held it between his thumb and forefinger. 'It's old. Australian.' He put it between his teeth and bit down. 'And it's no counterfeit.' His eyes narrowed. 'You say you found this at your grandfather's grave?'

'Yes, sir. It was half out of the ground as if someone had pushed it into the soil – or pushed it out.'

'What are you suggesting, Hastings?' But Canty's greedy mind was already two jumps ahead of the conversation.

'That there might be more in his grave. I heard more than once his stories about his adventures in Australia and the rumors that he brought back a bag of gold with him, but after he died, no one found it. He was a miserly old bugger, and I think he might have had it buried with him. The coffin rots in the ground, and what with frost and such, this coin was pushed up to the surface.'

'And how do you think I can help you?'

'You know much more about the law where money's concerned, sir. Is there a way I could legally open Grandfather's grave to retrieve the gold?'

'Hmm.' Canty rubbed his lantern jaw and pretended to ponder Hastings' question, when in fact, he was pondering one of his own:

how to turn the situation to his advantage. 'I'm having dinner with Copstone, the attorney tonight. I'll ask him about the legalities of the matter – without naming names, of course – and we can discuss it in the morning.'

'Thank you, sir.' Chester hesitated. 'Uh, may I have the Sovereign, sir?'

'What? Oh, yes.' Canty reluctantly returned the coin as if he were handing over one of his own ears. 'When you come in tomorrow, we'll have a talk about it. I should know what can be done then.'

'Thank you, sir.' Chester gave a nodding bow and left Canty to his scheming thoughts.

At the end of the day, Canty didn't hold Chester back, in fact he sent him off a half hour early then left the office himself to buy a shovel.

When he left Canty's office, Chester did something he hadn't done since his school days: he went to a pub, the Flute and Fiddle, to name names. Then he did something else he'd never done before, he got roaring drunk. He got so drunk, in fact, that he stood on a table and sang bawdy songs until two Bobbies wrestled him out the door and into a waiting Mariah to take him to the Nick for the night.

About the time the constables were turning the key on Chester, Canty was standing in the shadows across the road watching the old sexton lock the Saint Mark's gate. Once the old fellow had shuffled off into the gloom, Canty looked one way then the other for prying eyes, crossed the road and studied the eight-foot wall for a moment. He Spotted a few protruding stones that looked to be likely hand and foot holds and threw his spade over the wall. Then with an agility that belied his size, he quickly scaled the wall and dropped to the grass on the other side.

A few bob to the right informant had secured the location of the Hastings family plot and in particular, the location of Abijah Hastings' grave. The cemetery was nearly pitch dark by this time, and Canty had to be careful as he followed the interconnecting pathways, using the handle of his shovel as a blind man uses a staff.

In a few moments, he stood at the low fence and the wrought iron gate that separated the Hastings family from the rest of Saint Mark's tenants. Canty struck a match on one of the stones and cupped it in his hands, leaning in to read the inscriptions. Roger Hastings, Clive Hastings, Tillie Hastings Tolliver, Oliver Cromwell Hastings, and finally, Abijah L. Hastings. 'The Golden Goose,' said Canty under his breath. And sure enough, when he looked down at the grass before Abijah Hastings' marker, he saw the glint of gold.

Canty scooped up the coin and studied it until the match burnt low enough to singe his fingers. He felt the tightness of excitement constrict his breath. There was more, There had to be.

Canty set a lantern behind a nearby stone so it couldn't be easily seen then began to dig, but carefully, skimming the sod from the grave and setting it aside in the hope of replacing it so that no one would know the grave was disturbed. Then, for each shovelful of earth he dug, he crumbled the clods and rubbed the dirt between his fingers so as to not leave one precious Sovereign behind. Two feet. Three feet. Four feet. No more coins. They must be in the old goat's bloody coffin, Canty thought, and dug some more.

He was chest deep in the grave when a voice startled him. 'Looking for something? You won't find it here.' Canty's head snapped up and he found himself staring into the granite face of a stern old man. 'Being of sound mind and body, I spent it all before I died. And by the way, thank you kindly for digging your own grave.'

Canty's mouth worked, but no words came out. He put his hands on the edge of the hole and tried to lever himself out. That was when he heard a grating, shuffling sound and saw the stones of the Hastings family plot closing in around him. Canty clawed his way out of the hole and tried to run, but his foot caught on the stone platform of Clive's tombstone and he sprawled headlong at the feet of Tillie's stone. 'Thief! Thief!' Tillie shrieked, and when Canty tried to put his hand over her mouth to silence her, she closed it on his fingers, biting off three at the second knuckle, then spat the bloody stumps in his face.

A strangled howl like that of a scalded cat flew from Canty's mouth. He heaved away from her and landed on his back to find himself staring up at the scarred brows and broken nose of Uncle George. 'Bloody git,' the stone face snarled, then tipped forward to land full weight on Canty's screaming head.

The next morning, Chester woke behind bars with a throbbing head, paid his fine and was turned loose in the grey light of dawn. Apart from losing his shoes somewhere during the night, he was none the worse for wear if one discounted the tidal slosh of his brain in his skull.

He opened the office a few minutes late, after a stop at the Chemist for headache powder, but Canty didn't show his face. Lunch came and went, and his clientele came with crowns or pennies to pay their debts all morning, but Elias Canty was not present to collect them. By day's end, Chester had a goodly heap of money and nowhere to put it, since Canty carried the only key to the office safe in his pocket.

Chester rolled up the money in his handkerchief, stuffed it in his pocket, and locked up the office. After a stop at a cobbler's, where he bought a pair of used shoes, Chester made his way to Saint Mark's, where he sat on the grass until the sun sank through the elms. Grandfather's grave had been so cleverly filled in and the sod replaced, that no casual observer would ever know it had been disturbed.

Aunt Tillie was the first to speak. 'Look what the cat dragged in.'

'Oh, hush, Tillie,' Uncle Arthur said. 'The lad's been through a lot.'

'Quiet, all of you.' Abijah's voice cut through the chatter like a fog horn. 'Chester,' he said, 'I see you did as you were told.' Chester nodded. 'We also did as I promised. Canty won't trouble you again, nor anyone else. He and I are sharing quarters now, in a manner of speaking. And if the coppers come looking, they know damned well where you were the night he disappeared.'

'That's all well and good, Grandfather,' Chester said, 'but now I have no job, no income.'

'We thought about that,' Abijah said. His face folded into his look of strain and concentration. Unngh. Unngh.' The granite face pursed its lips and Grandfather Hastings spat something that landed at

Chester's feet. He picked it up. It was a key.

'That's the key to Canty's safe, lad. We've helped you as much as we can.' The old man's face folded into a smile. 'Now it's time you help yourself.'

'And you be back here tomorrow,' chided Aunt Tillie,'and don't be late. 'No excuses.'

'No, Auntie.'

As the dark closed in, Chester walked through the Saint Mark's gate and thought, *No, Auntie, no excuses, not anymore.*

THE CREEPING CRAWLERS OF CLAVERING

By

Josh Reynolds

In swch a place, no man kin be sayd to walk alone.
Henry Cooper,
Ye Historie of Clavering, 1532

'THERE IT IS. Clavering Grange.' Charles St. Cyprian leaned against the side of the Crossley, his hands in his pockets. He studied the edifice in question with a wary eye. 'Proof of the old adage that there are certain houses that are not.'

Ebe Gallowglass took their bags out of the boot and peered at him in confusion. She rustled the bags from one hand to the other, trying to keep a grip on all of them. St. Cyprian gave a moment's consideration to lending a helping hand, but decided against it. She was the assistant, after all. He'd carried his fair share of bags when he'd played batman for Carnacki; now it was her turn. 'Not what?' she asked.

'Not houses.' St. Cyprian was lean and dark, dressed in the best Gieves and Hawkes had to offer, and wearing it well. Some said he resembled Valentino, but privately, he fancied it was the other way around.

She glanced up at the looming pile, and sniffed. 'Looks like a house.' In contrast to her employer, Gallowglass was shorter, darker and dressed like a bricklayer, in a worn duffel coat and a flat cap that hid a head of short cropped, dark hair.

'Looks can be deceiving.'

'So what is it?' She started towards the front door, a bag in either hand, and one under her arm. The edge of her coat had rumpled back, revealing the worn grip of a Webley-Fosbery resting snug in its shoulder holster. The revolver was more in the way of a faithful pet than a pistol at this point, and Gallowglass was never without it. It made a wonderful conversation starter at garden parties, if nothing else.

St. Cyprian fell into step with her. 'Theories abound.'

'Wonderful. Care to share one?'

'Dee claimed it was a menagerie.' He said the name with some reverence. Dee was his predecessor's predecessor, at some remove. The first to bear the office of Royal Occultist, back in the days of Good Queen Bess, and the first to try and hold that which bumped in the night accountable to the Crown. Here in the year of our Lord nineteen and twenty-five, those responsibilities had fallen to St. Cyprian – a fact he often had cause to regret.

Gallowglass gave him the side-eye. 'What's that when it's at home?'

'A private zoo, you might say.'

'Someone made a zoo full of ghosts?' Then, 'On purpose?'

St. Cyprian shrugged. 'We have borne witness to stranger compulsions.'

Gallowglass frowned, but didn't argue the point. 'So why are we here? Someone forget to feed the animals?'

'In a manner of speaking.' The door was an innocuous square of green, with gold fittings. St. Cyprian gave the knocker a try. The echoes of his knock reverberated audibly through the open windows on the ground floor.

'Must be airing out the old pile, what?' he said.

'Place like this probably needs it,' Gallowglass murmured. Abruptly, she dropped a bag, nearly catching his foot. He twitched aside as she spun, free hand on her pistol. He turned with her, but saw nothing save the desolate drive and their motor-car, sitting all by its lonesome. She vibrated, tense as a cat.

A few dead leaves skittered across the rocky path. Beyond that, he saw nothing to explain her sudden alarm. 'Did you see something?' he asked, softly. While Gallowglass seemingly had all the psychical sensitivity of a rock, her other senses were almost preternaturally keen.

'Something was creeping around the Crossley.'

'Something, or someone?'

'I said what I said.' She relaxed. 'Whatever it was scarpered.'

'A rat, maybe. This drafty old heap is supposed to be full of them.' He paused. 'Keep an eye out, though. Never know what might be lurking in a place like this.'

'What I'm here for, innit?'

Before he could reply the door was yanked open with such force that the hinges squealed in protest. 'Charles! Is that you?'

'Who else would it be, Philip?' St. Cyprian studied the portly, red-faced apparition before him. Philip Wendy-Smythe looked as if he'd run a half marathon in his sleep, and then collapsed in a hedge. His hair was askew, and his dressing gown was unbelted, exposing silken pyjamas. 'You look more flustered than usual, old thing. Catch you in the middle of your morning ablutions?'

'Oh ha-bloody-ha, Charles. Get in here – quickly! It's back!'

'What's back?'

'The crawling horror,' Wendy-Smythe intoned. 'This way, quick. Quick! Before it gets out of the billiards room!' He bustled them inside and slammed the door, but not before taking a quick glance at the drive.

'You never mentioned nothing about a horror,' Gallowglass said, dropping the bags in a heap. St. Cyprian winced as his socks spilled onto the floor.

He cleared his throat. The air was thick with dust, mould and something else – a peculiar odour he could not immediately name. 'I wasn't aware that there was one to mention. Philip, what's going on? Your telegram was rather sparse on detail.'

'Just come on, and bring your whatsit!' Wendy-Smythe sped across the entry hall with nary a look back, dressing gown flaring about him like wings. St. Cyprian glanced at Gallowglass, who shrugged and gave her pistol a fond pat.

'Got my whatsit right here.'

He gestured. 'By all means then, after you.' They followed Wendy-Smythe through the foyer. St. Cyprian saw that it was larger than he'd first thought, and in the process of renovation. Clavering, like many organisms, outgrew its skin every so often. Scaffolding had been erected to either side of the room, and the portraits that had once hung on the walls had been haphazardly stacked on the floor.

Wendy-Smythe wasn't built for speed. They caught him at the first turn. At the other end of the hallway, a man was hunched up before a door. He was a long stretch of Kentish aristocracy, all but chinless and with hair the colour of curdled milk. Like Wendy-Smythe, he was clad only in a silk dressing gown and pyjamas.

He had both hands on the knob of the door, holding it closed. As they arrived, he braced one foot against the door frame, losing his bedroom slipper in the process. The door bucked like a restless stallion, nearly flinging him to the floor.

'Philip – you're back! Help me,' he bawled.

'Coming, Oscar,' Wendy-Smythe panted. 'Charles, this is Oscar Sinclair...Oscar, this is Charles St. Cyprian...' The man shook his head as the door flumped in its frame.

'Now's not really the time, Philip! I can't hold this door shut for much longer.'

'Why are you holding it shut at all?' Gallowglass asked. The door bowed and squeaked alarmingly in its frame. The bolts were even beginning to work loose from the hinges. Whatever was on the other side seemed to be growing more determined.

'I told you, we've got it trapped in the billiards room,' Wendy-Smythe said.

'It?' she said.

'The crawling horror, I assume,' St. Cyprian said. He leaned forward. 'I say, is that the Sign of Koth marked on the door?' He tapped the symbol and sniffed his finger. 'And in jam?'

'Needs must when the devil drives,' Wendy-Smythe said, determinedly. 'We were in the middle of breakfast, and that was all I had to hand.'

'It's not even strawberry, Philip.'

'What does it matter?' Sinclair nearly shrieked. 'Help me!'

St. Cyprian glanced at the panicked man. 'Help you do what?'

'Kill it! Banish it! Do something,' Sinclair howled.

'Well, for a start, perhaps you should let it out of the billiards room.'

'Philip?' Sinclair squeaked, eyes wide.

Wendy-Smythe stared at St. Cyprian. 'Are you – are you sure, Charles?'

'If I'm not, we'll find out soon enough I expect.' St. Cyprian gestured. 'Step aside.' He cracked his knuckles. 'Let's see what we're dealing with here.'

Sinclair's reluctance was evident, but with some cajoling Wendy-Smythe managed to pry him loose from his post. The door flew open almost immediately, as what was within came out in a rush, spilling about them, knocking them from their feet. The roiling presence crashed outwards and filled the hallway with a thunderous teakettle hiss.

St. Cyprian had only a moment to take in the immense, shapeless mass before it sprang upwards in torrential geyser. A great brownish patch of damp spread across the ceiling plaster as the thing vanished with a gurgling howl.

'What the hell was that?' Gallowglass demanded, snatching up her cap from where it had fallen. She ineffectually tried to wring it out.

'An elemental,' St. Cyprian breathed. 'How wonderful.'

'Wonderful?' Sinclair yelped. 'It's tried to eat me!'

'And how did you come to that conclusion?' St. Cyprian asked. 'It requires no sustenance that you could provide.' He peered up at the dripping patch on the ceiling. 'In fact, I'd say it looked rather more scared of you, than you are of it.'

'Where'd it come from?' Gallowglass asked. She'd given up on her cap, and was peering into the billiards room.

'It just appeared. But I believe it's been rushing about through the walls for days now,' Wendy-Smythe said. 'The whole house sounds like the bloody overnight to Penzance around sundown – moanings, groanings, clumpings and crashings.'

'No doubt,' St. Cyprian said. Clavering Grange was home to over forty-five recorded abnatural manifestations, including, supposedly, a giant that was said to climb out of a washbasin. He paused, noting the lack of comment from his assistant. She could rarely resist needling Wendy-Smythe. But she was paying them little attention.

Instead, Gallowglass was still studying the billiards room, her fingers tapping the butt of her pistol. 'What is it?' he murmured.

She grunted and turned away. 'Thought I heard something.' She waggled her fingers. 'Like rats. Or stoats. Only not.' She looked at Sinclair. 'Rodent problem, innit?'

'Rodents?' Sinclair looked horrified, and for reasons unrelated to the elemental. 'Good God, no. That's the one problem this pile *doesn't* have. Rot in the foundations, rising damp, creaky joists and a leaky roof – but no vermin.'

'Maybe something ate them,' Gallowglass said.

'Like an elemental, maybe?' Wendy-Smythe said, hopefully.

'Possibly,' St. Cyprian said.

'I've never seen one before,' Wendy-Smythe said, excitedly. 'Read about them, though. Even got one of Vance's monographs on the subject – and signed, to boot!' He grabbed Sinclair's arm. 'I told you, Oscar. We'll get it sorted, now.'

St. Cyprian sighed at this display of exuberance. Wendy-Smythe wanted so very badly to be a member of the secret set, but he had too much enthusiasm and too little common sense to manage it. He'd been expelled from more than a dozen eldritch societies and psychical circles, and been banned from joining at least as many others.

Worse, he'd frittered away a good deal of his family fortune on occult tat like powdered werewolf teeth and dragon eggs. And on the rare occasions when he did manage to acquire something with a bit of actual mojo, it inevitably bit him square in the sensitives. It didn't stop him trying, though. He was as persistent as a terrier.

'I told Sinclair you were the chap to see when it came to the spooky business, Charles,' Wendy-Smythe went on. 'He has a bit of a problem, as you can see, and it's quite outside my bailiwick. I'm strictly a curses and conjurings man, me.'

'Or is it because you don't actually know anything about

anything?' Gallowglass asked, without looking at him. Wendy-Smythe sniffed.

'I'll have you know I'm coming along quite smashingly with my studies into the abnatural, thank you very much I'm sure. In fact, I've just completed the first English translation of the Book of Minor Grotesques.'

Gallowglass laughed but St. Cyprian silenced her with a glare. 'You've done quite well, Philip old thing. But best leave it to the professionals from here on, eh?' He patted Wendy-Smythe on the shoulder. 'We'll have it sorted in two shakes of Shadmock's tail.'

'Do they have tails?' Gallowglass asked.

'Don't know, never had the misfortune to meet one. My point stands. We're here and the little blue devils shall get hence momentarily.' St. Cyprian looked at his hosts. 'Maybe you two would like to get dressed before we go any further. Panoply of war, and all that. Wear something you don't mind getting dusty.'

While Philip and their host were getting dressed, St. Cyprian made a careful study of the billiards room, with Gallowglass' help. There were damp patches everywhere, marking the elemental's rampage. It had overturned the billiards tables and loose balls rolled across the hardwood floor. The curtains had been mangled, the window frames gnawed, and the chandelier all but pulled from the ceiling.

St. Cyprian stood in the centre of the room. 'What do you see, apprentice-mine?'

'Assistant,' Gallowglass corrected. 'Looks like something wasn't happy about being here.' She crouched and retrieved a billiard ball. It had been all but bitten in half. 'This the usual sort of thing you'd expect?'

'Fairly. Elementals are unpleasant things, by and large. Rather like ectoplasmic Tasmanian devils, what?' He looked around. 'Rather reminds me of when that dog got into the Drones that time. Quite the mess.'

'Can't blame it. Half a dozen booze-jockeys were chasing me around a club, I might wreck stuff as well...' She trailed off. Her gaze sharpened. 'Oh. I see. Something was chasing it.'

St. Cyprian nodded, pleased that she'd reached the same conclusion. 'I suspect so. The question is... what? And why?'

'That's two questions.'

'Pedant,' St. Cyprian said. He could feel a dampness on the air – a sort of gelid chill quite unlike the traditional Kentish damp. 'Do you feel that?'

'Like somebody left an icebox open.'

'Ectoplasmic residue. And quite a bit of it. Our recently departed friend must have stirred it up.' St. Cyprian stripped off his jacket and slung it over a nearby chair. 'Right. Best it were done quick, as the Bard had it.' He rolled up his sleeves. 'Be ready.'

'For what?'

'Anything that might occur.' He bent his fingers into the appropriate – if somewhat painful – shapes and traced the signs of Hlooh and Hloh upon the chilly air. As protections from the unearthly went, they were uncertain at best. But they would serve, for the moment.

Thus reinforced, he closed his eyes and allowed the gates of his mind to swing wide. It was a sort of talent – one he'd honed into a skill at the feet of the acknowledged masters of psychical projection. To see, not with his two mortal eyes, but with the third immortal one that all men possessed, but only a few could open.

Which was, in itself, a good thing. Mankind, as a whole, was ill-prepared to see what walked beside them, separated by the thinnest of membranes.

The process was so routine by now as to be dull. The world turned soft at the edges, frayed and faded. Colours lost their vibrancy, and he felt his *ka* – his spirit-self – disassociate itself from his physical form. He felt himself as an echo of a thought, watching at a remove, as the membrane between realities wrinkled, split and peeled back.

At first, things looked little different. But gradually, he became aware of a curious undulation, just out of the corner of his eye. As if something were intent on keeping itself out of sight. He was reminded of the movements of a stoat, as it stalks an unwary rabbit.

There were sounds as well – soft chitters and dull thumps; the scrabble of sharp nails across hardwood floors; moans and groans and the clanking of ethereal irons.

When he saw the ghost, he was careful to give no sign. Such entities homed in on the psychically gifted the way a shark might follow a blood-trail. They battened on the emanations of a sensitive mind, feeding on the fear and uncertainty. The ritual gestures he'd made would mask his presence from such spirits – at least in theory.

In any event, this particular spirit did not seem in fit state to haunt anyone. It...limped. It lagged, trailing tatters of its essence behind it. It had been a man, once, clad in the ragged finery of another age, its ruff askew and doublet torn. Now it was a wizened, hopping thing, with palsied claws and a face like a Peruvian mummy.

It staggered through the billiards room, slapping at itself in curious fashion. It made for the door, brushing past him and leaving behind the stink of the unearthly. He followed it into the hall, and saw more spectres racing to and fro along the stairs in a panicked tide – no, a stampede. Like frightened beasts.

They were of all shapes and configurations – headless matrons, bifurcated aristocrats, towering executioners, bearing the tools of their ghastly trade. Grunting dawn-men shambled down the steps, eyes wide beneath beetling brows. Creeping, gaunt shapes leapt from one end of the hall to the other and back again, like agitated grasshoppers. There was even a horse, or something that resembled one. And things with no definable shape fluttered through the air, seeking succour in the rafters and cornices of the hall.

They moaned and wailed, speaking in dialects older even than England itself – but faintly, as if from an impossible distance. He could make out nothing of what they said. The tide broke around him, and swept along towards the foyer or back up the stairs. They raced in all directions, through walls and doorways, up to the ceiling or through the floor. Again, he perceived that strange furrow of motion among them, as if something were leaping and gambolling among the procession of the dead. Harrying them – savaging them.

He caught sight of the spectre he'd glimpsed in the billiards room. The shrivelled thing stumbled, and the air around it seemed to crinkle. There was a presence there – many presences – small, weasel-like. They crept and crawled about the ghost, gnawing and biting, reducing their prey to pitiful rags of ectoplasm. The phantasmal courtier came apart before his eyes, and the writhing weasel-shapes seized on another spirit.

Nauseated, St. Cyprian turned away...only to find himself face-to-face with one of the creeping crawlers. His first impression was that he had been correct – it resembled a stoat, or mink. A long, hairy tube, topped by a blunt muzzle full of sharp teeth. Eyes like twin embers bored into his own. It perched atop a bust of one of Clavering's previous owners, balancing on too many legs, its broad lash of a tail wrapped about the bust's plinth. Its nostrils flared wetly, and he felt, rather than heard, the intake of aether. A chill ran through him, as an expression of malign glee passed across the thing's brute features.

'Bugger,' he said.

As if in reply, it gave out a shrill chitter. The unearthly noise was echoed by several of its fellows and all at once they began to converge on him, creeping through the spectral tide. St. Cyprian backed away. He was vulnerable here, outside the safety of his physical frame. They circled him warily as he backed towards the door to the billiards room. The one perched on the bust leapt to the wall and scampered along it, quick as a spider.

They were trying to cut him off. St. Cyprian turned and lunged for the door. A disturbingly solid weight struck his legs and he went to his knees in the doorway. They were on him in an instant, crawling across him, biting, clawing...he fell forward, and they went with him, knotted about him like serpents.

His physical form blazed like a beacon of light, and he crawled towards it. Fangs sank into his shoulder and his thigh, and he screamed in pain. He rolled onto his back, kicking at them, hoping to throw them off, even if just for a moment. But they were stronger now. Somehow larger.

More real, a part of him added. As if they were leeching away at his strength. They bit at his hands, and scraped claws across his face. Bits of him wafted through the air. He was losing himself, even as the ghost had.

They were going to eat him alive. Panic surged through him as they began to back away, dragging him back out into the hall. He clawed at the edges of the doorframe with insubstantial fingers. Somehow, he managed to grab hold. They continued to pull.

He could feel himself stretching thin – like a bit of rubber pulled past the point of snapping. Soon, his essence might give way entirely, and there'd be nothing to return to his body. His fingers began to slip as his strength waned. He cried out.

A billiard cue shot down, nearly splitting one of the creatures. 'Got you,' Gallowglass crowed. The creatures reacted like light-struck roaches, scattering in all directions. She pursued them, cursing and jabbing at the floor. St. Cyprian clambered to his feet and heaved himself towards his body. The ectoplasmic tethers snapped back, and he jolted upright, sucking in a lungful of air. He found himself sprawled on the billiards table.

Wendy-Smythe was at his side a moment later. 'Charles – is that you?' he asked, holding up a grotesque sigil of gilt and brass. It resembled a squid, albeit one designed by an opium addict. 'Touch the Solemn Effigy of Escalup to be sure.'

'Please don't wave that thing in my face, Philip. My stomach's loose enough as it is.'

Wendy-Smythe wilted in relief. 'Gads, I was worried there for a few hot moments. Thought something nasty might have taken up residence, what?'

'What were you planning to do if it had? Hit me with a bit of costume jewellery?'

Wendy-Smythe frowned. 'Now see here, I have it on good authority that this symbol is anathema to free-floating entities of all sorts...'

'If it were real, it might. That thing is made of paste and a bit of paint.' St. Cyprian swung his legs off the table with a groan.

Everything ached, though he'd suffered no physical wounds. His soul would need time to recover, however. 'What happened?'

'We were hoping you could tell us,' Sinclair said, looking perturbed. 'We came in and you were flopping about on the floor like an epileptic. Then your assistant started whacking at the floor with my favourite cue stick.'

'Something attacked me,' St. Cyprian said. He felt about himself, wincing at the memory of spiritual hurts. 'My *ka,* rather.'

'Your what?' Sinclair asked.

'My spirit-self. Miss Gallowglass?'

Gallowglass poked her head back into the room. 'Yeah?'

'What did you see?'

'Creepy, crawling things. Like rats or – or...'

'Stoats,' St. Cyprian supplied. 'Vermin, regardless.'

'And lots of them,' Gallowglass added. She tossed the broken cue onto the table. 'They scarpered quick enough, though.' She frowned. 'Same things I saw outside. Only bigger, I think.'

'More real,' St. Cyprian said. He looked at Sinclair. 'I'm afraid you have an infestation, of sorts.'

'We know all about the ghosts, Charles,' Wendy-Smythe said. 'Clavering is infamously lousy with them, even if Tipsy here doesn't believe in them.'

'Tipsy,' Gallowglass said. Sinclair flushed.

'A nickname from my school days, and I'll thank you to keep it to yourself.'

'On my honour as a lady, Tipsy,' Gallowglass said, grinning wickedly.

'Enough, assistant mine. Go get our bags, please. And keep an eye out for more of the wee beasties.' St. Cyprian turned to Sinclair. 'When did you begin the renovations?'

'I didn't,' Sinclair said. 'The owner before last started them, I believe. Back before my father took possession of the place.' He looked around, his expression one of distaste. 'And now I'm lumbered with it, scaffolding and all.'

St. Cyprian went into the hall, and found the bust his attacker had perched on. He ran his fingers along the marble scalp. Searching for what, he couldn't say. He was certain he would know it when he found it. 'You're not a direct inheritor, then?'

'Lord no. We're a bit of a hop, a skip and a jump to the left of the family line. Same name, bit of money, but little else. Until recently, at least. Why?'

'It might have some bearing. Or perhaps not. Clavering is a curious beast.' St. Cyprian turned towards the stairs. He wondered if the ghosts were still running. The thought wasn't a pleasant one. 'According to certain noteworthy sources, it sits on tainted ground.'

'Meaning?'

'Meaning from such sour earth only evil fruit doth grow, to mangle a saying.' He turned his attentions to the floorboards, and he began to tap them with his foot, one at a time. 'Is it any wonder, then, that such a place might draw in malign spirits? Like moths to a flame.'

'Wasps to gin,' Gallowglass said, as she returned, a heavy Gladstone bag in hand.

St. Cyprian glanced at her. 'Do wasps like gin?' He paused. 'No. Never mind. Sounds like something I'd rather not know. In any event, Clavering is a well-documented draw to ghosts, spirits and various other ghastlies and ghoulies. Including elementals. Some are born here, but others are transients – or were.'

'And you know this because...?' Sinclair asked.

'Clavering is one of the most infamous haunted houses in Britain. Though not so well-known as Borley Rectory and Berkley Square, it surpasses both in sheer nastiness.' St. Cyprian pressed his ear to the wall. Beyond the plaster, he could hear a faint *thrum,* akin to an electrical generator. Or perhaps it was the reverberations of an unseen stampede. He gestured to Gallowglass. 'Come here and tell me what you make of this.'

She took off her cap and listened. 'Sounds like a ruddy great heartbeat.'

'It rather does, doesn't it?' St. Cyprian frowned, considering. 'Or like many feet, moving all at once. The undead inhabitants are on the move, stampeding to and fro.'

'Maybe we should burn this place down,' Gallowglass suggested.

Sinclair blanched. 'What?'

'It has burned down,' St. Cyprian said. 'Twice. An acquaintance of Carnacki's had a theory that what stands here now is not a house at all, but a sustained ectoplasmic construct.'

'It's the ghost of a haunted house,' Gallowglass said. She knocked on the wall. 'Feels solid enough.'

'That or an abnatural manifestation of some sort.' St. Cyprian looked up at the ceiling, and the brown patches there. The elemental was likely still loose in the house, unless the verminous entities had caught up with it. 'Regardless, it functions as a sort of spirit-trap. Things come in, but don't go out. And not all of those things are best pleased by their new circumstances.'

'Is that why the elemental was so...aggressive?' Wendy-Smythe asked.

'Oh, it wasn't being aggressive. As I said earlier, it was afraid.' St. Cyprian turned, scanning the walls and cornices. 'Though as to what an elemental might fear – well. That is a conundrum.' He rubbed his arm, as an echo of pain twinged through it. 'Though having endured their savagery first-hand, I don't blame the poor blighter one bit.'

'These...things that attacked you, Charles...they weren't ghosts, then?' Philip asked. 'Perhaps a form of minor elemental or something of that nature?'

'No. They were quite unlike anything I've ever encountered.' St. Cyprian retrieved his coat and slipped it on. 'Reminded me of foxes in a henhouse, honestly. They're ravening among the local wildlife with abandon.'

'What?' Sinclair asked.

'They're eating your ghosts.'

Sinclair looked about, visibly alarmed. 'Surely that's a good thing?'

'Depends entirely on why they're doing so. Having been face to face with them, I can safely say that they are not doing so out of any sense of civic-mindedness.' St. Cyprian straightened his neck tie.

'No. The little beggars are decidedly malign.'

Wendy-Smythe frowned. 'So what do we do about them? We can't bally well see them, Charles. Or the ghosts for that matter.'

'I can,' Gallowglass said, as she peered about the corridor. 'Only out of the corner of my eye, like.'

'Not all of us are possessed of your perspicacity, assistant-mine. But I might have a solution.' He took the Gladstone bag from her and popped the clasp. It contained an assortment of esoteric necessities, most of them hand-me-downs from his predecessors. Clumps of amulets and blessed sigils, moleskins stuffed with incantations for all seasons, tiny, stoppered vials of various unguents, concoctions and waters taken from various blessed springs. He rummaged through it for a moment, until he found what he sought – a small, wooden box, decorated in early Hyperborean iconography.

'Ah, here we are – everyone gather round.' He opened the box, revealing a small, crude clay amulet bearing a curious symbol. Wendy-Smythe gasped appreciatively.

'Is that...?'

'Yes, Philip. The Voorish Sign. One of the few remaining originals.' St. Cyprian preened slightly as he hung the amulet about his neck. 'In conjunction with certain ritual gestures, it can reveal that which is hidden.'

Wendy-Smythe made a reaching motion. 'May I...?'

'No, Philip. You may not.' St. Cyprian lifted the amulet and gave it a gentle tap, causing it to spin. As it did so, he gestured sharply. For a moment, nothing happened. Then, there was a chime like that of a bell, and the hairs on the back of his neck stiffened. Slowly, imperceptibly, the ghastly tide from earlier became visible.

Sinclair gave a strangled curse, and Wendy-Smythe paled. 'So many,' he murmured, turning as a phantasmal horse galloped past. Upon its back was a nude hag, her withered frame marked by primitive tattoos and a hempen noose about her throat. She cackled wildly as she and her steed vanished through a wall.

'They do accumulate in these old places,' St. Cyprian said. There were not so many of them as there had been, and he could see the faint traces of savaged ectoplasmic residue on the floor and walls. There seemed to be more of the creeping crawlers than he'd noticed previously, as well. As if their numbers had increased as those of their prey decreased. They weaselled about, clinging to everything, beady eyes watching the remaining ghosts hungrily. Their chitters were audible now – and even more disturbing than before. In fact, they sounded eerily, oddly human, as if one person were speaking through multiple mouths.

'What – what are they saying?' Wendy-Smythe asked.

'I don't think we want to know,' St. Cyprian said. 'In fact I – hsst!' He held up a hand, silencing the others. The verminous apparitions had fallen silent and were studying them. All at once, those closest to the group began to edge forwards. St. Cyprian glanced at Gallowglass. 'Get the arbutus blossoms – quickly!'

She rifled through the Gladstone and came up with a small paper bag of whitish, bell-shaped blossoms, which she tossed to him. St. Cyprian whipped out his lighter and burnt one, releasing a fragrant, herbal odour. The creeping crawlers hesitated, their black nostrils flaring. Then, as one, they turned and scampered away – a flood of narrow, squirming forms, heading past the stairs, and for the rear of the house.

'What the devil...?' Sinclair croaked. 'They're fleeing!'

'*Arbutus unedo,* to give it its scientific classification,' St. Cyprian said. 'Blossoms from a Killarney strawberry tree. Various ancient peoples supposedly used the bally stuff to drive away noisome spirits.' He dropped the burning blossoms to the floor and carefully trod on them, ignoring Sinclair's wince of displeasure. 'Any idea where the little beasts are headed?'

Sinclair shook his head. 'The only thing back that way is the kitchens – oh, and the ah, the cellars.' He looked doubtfully at Wendy-Smythe. 'We're not going to have to go into the cellars are we, Philip?'

'Why? Something wrong with them?' Gallowglass asked.

Sinclair frowned. 'No! No. Just...' He hesitated. 'I just don't care for the place, is all.'

'They give me the creeps and no two ways about it, Charles,' Wendy-Smythe supplied. 'You know I'm no bantam weight when it comes to unseen terrors, but I couldn't bring myself to stay down there longer than it took to find a bottle of wine to go with dinner. Even then, I was in quite a rush. Found I'd gotten the wrong dashed bottle, too – white, donchaknow? And us having beef stew!'

'Oh Philip, no,' St. Cyprian said, in sympathy.

'Tragic, innit?' Gallowglass said. 'So, we going down there or what?'

St. Cyprian hefted his Gladstone. 'Indeed we are – Philip, lead the way.'

'Are – are you certain?' Wendy-Smythe asked. 'Perhaps we could just board it up?'

'Boarding up cellars rarely solves the underlying problem,' St. Cyprian chided. 'You know that better than most, Philip... remember Shaftsbury Avenue? The slug-ghost?'

Wendy-Smythe flinched. 'Don't remind me.' He took a deep breath. 'Fine. Tipsy – your house, you lead the way.'

Sinclair looked as if he wanted to protest, but refrained. He led them through the winding corridors to the kitchens, past towering stacks of paint cans and plaster tubs that formed makeshift bulwarks. The kitchens were in a better state than the rest of the house, but only just. Here too, there was evidence of half-completed renovations, as well as the ravages of the creeping crawlers – the remains of a wraith hung from the ceiling beams, its ghostly limbs gnawed to the ethereal bones by leaping stoat-shapes.

The creatures scattered as St. Cyprian and the others came into the kitchens, fleeing the fragrance of the burning blossoms. They squeezed themselves beneath the doors to the cellars, or through chinks in the walls. St. Cyprian marched to the heavy wooden door and snatched it open. A set of slabbed stone steps led down into the dark. A rush of damp air rushed up to envelop him, and he stepped back. 'Well. Who's up for an expedition?'

'I'll stay here,' Sinclair said, hurriedly. 'Hold the line, and such.'

Wendy-Smythe patted him on the shoulder. 'Good show, Tipsy.' He produced a heavy pistol from somewhere about his person and brandished it wildly. 'We'll go down and sort the blighters out.'

St. Cyprian snatched the pistol from Wendy-Smythe's grip and shoved the Gladstone into his arms. '*We'll* sort things out. You will observe.' He checked the pistol cylinder and snapped it shut, before tossing it to Gallowglass. 'If there's any shooting to be done, Miss Gallowglass will be more than happy to do it.'

She grinned and twirled the pistol. 'Ecstatic,' she said. 'Want me to go first?'

'If you wouldn't mind.' St. Cyprian retrieved an electric torch from the cellar head and clicked it on. A wash of pallid light illuminated the steps, and the cobwebs drifting in the draft. There was a rank smell mingled with the usual cellar-odours. A sort of musky, animal-stink. As they descended, he could hear the soft susurrus of vermin pattering through the baseboards, just out of sight.

'Reminds me of Exham Priory,' Gallowglass said. Her words echoed back at them.

St. Cyprian frowned. That had been a bad one all around. 'Let's hope it's nothing like that, eh? Fingers crossed.'

They reached the bottom of the steps fairly quickly. The cellars were wide, but not deep. That didn't make them any less unpleasant, however. They seemed to stretch for vast distances, back into lightless gulfs. Toadstools and other fungi covered the flagstones and bunched on the walls in disturbing patterns. Here and there, they could see evidence of more building work – dislodged bricks, uprooted flagstones and new supports built to replace older, rotting ones.

'Tipsy didn't mention it, but I get the impression that the fellow who started all of this was a bit doolally,' Wendy-Smythe murmured. 'Lived here since he was a boy, and all that.'

'Yes, such surroundings might well have an adverse effect on a developing psyche,' St. Cyprian replied. His breath pooled about his face as he spoke. The cellars were cool – cold, in fact. The shadows seemed deeper, like great abysses gouged into the substance of the cellar. St. Cyprian felt a prickle of something creep along his spine, and had the sudden urge to flee back up the steps and away from Clavering Grange entirely. A glance at Gallowglass told him that she felt something similar.

'Do you feel that?' Wendy-Smythe murmured, teeth chattering. 'What is it?'

'Fear,' St. Cyprian said. His breath puffed out in white clouds that stretched into unsettling shapes before his eyes. 'That is what it is. Raw and unbound. The fear of the dying and the forgotten. Seeded in this ground and left to grow wild.'

He turned, raising the torch. The light washed away the shadows, but only for a moment. And when they returned, something – some*things* – came with them. 'What are you feeling, Philip?' he breathed.

'It's like a – a lump of ice in my chest,' Wendy-Smythe said, his voice almost a squeak. 'I can hear a voice in my head – telling me to run.' He took a deep breath and leaned against a wine-rack, causing the bottles to rattle. 'Tipsy – Tipsy said that the workmen just – just never came back one day. That was the rumour, anyway.'

'What happened to the previous owner, the one who started all of this?' St. Cyprian could hear something scrabbling in the dark. It reminded him of a hedgehog, snuffling for worms. A rather oversized hedgehog.

Wendy-Smythe shook his head. 'No one knows. Vanished one day. Majorca, I heard. Or maybe the Riviera.'

'Or maybe he joined the menagerie,' Gallowglass said. 'We should definitely try burning this place down. And then salting the ashes. Third time lucky, innit?'

St. Cyprian swung the torch about like a machine gun, chasing the shadows from one side of the cellar to the other. He saw no sign of the creatures, but that didn't mean that they weren't close to hand. 'Maybe,' he said, doubtfully. The fear gnawed at his certainty. 'Perhaps we should retreat for the moment – wait for the beasts to reappear...'

In the darkness, something hissed. St. Cyprian heard a shout from the kitchens, echoing as if from a great distance, followed by the booming crash of the cellar door slamming shut. 'Tipsy? *Tipsy!*' Wendy-Smythe bawled.

'Stand still, Philip,' St. Cyprian barked. All at once, the darkness seemed to surge forward, stopping at the edges of the torch light. The three of them drew closer together, huddling in the light.

'Listen,' Gallowglass said. St. Cyprian did, and heard the tell-tale chittering of the strange creatures. They seemed to be climbing through the piping, and skittering across the stones. Drawing closer and fading away all at once.

'They're all around us,' Wendy-Smythe murmured. 'May I have my pistol back?'

'No,' St. Cyprian and Gallowglass said as one. Gallowglass handed St. Cyprian the weapon and drew her own. While he doubted it would do much good, its weight was reassuring. A new sound intruded on the scuffling shuffle of the beasts – the sound of something heavy being shifted.

'It sounds like they're digging beneath the flagstones,' Wendy-Smythe whispered. 'Rooting around like badgers. Why would they be doing that?'

'Obviously to get at something beneath the stones,' St. Cyprian said, more harshly than he intended. He hefted the pistol and started towards the sound, torch beam playing across the ground, seeking any sign of their quarry.

They pressed on, past the edge of the house as it currently stood. Brick archways gave way to oaken beams gone black with age, and cobwebs shrouded everything. The refuse of generations of storage had been broken and scattered, and the irregular flagstones gave way to an older set of foundation stones, worn smooth by time.

'I've seen enough stone floors to know those are older than they should be,' Wendy-Smythe said. 'Then, Clavering is supposed to have ancient foundations...'

'Not this ancient – and if they were, why this close to the surface?' St. Cyprian played the light across the flagstones. He stopped, as the light was reflected in dozens of pairs of beady eyes. Gallowglass nudged St. Cyprian, and he saw a low, lean shape scuttle along the edge of the torch's glow. Then another, and another. They were surrounded.

'How much arbutus do we have left?' Wendy-Smythe asked tremulously.

'Enough.' St. Cyprian lit another clump and waved it about. The hissing faded, and the shapes retreated. They seemed less solid than before, as if they'd become a part of the cellar's darkness.

'There,' Gallowglass said, pointing. 'Something in the corner. Shine the torch that way.' He swung the torch around and illuminated several twitching, thrashing masses in a far corner of the cellar, where the floor dropped steeply away.

'God above,' he murmured. The mass was not one thing, but many – the creatures, roiling about one another in tempestuous frenzy. They tangled themselves up and it was all but impossible to tell where one of the beasts ended and another began. More and more of them raced to join the throng, slithering and slinking from all directions. Hundreds of them, of varying sizes and solidity.

'What's happening?' Wendy-Smythe whispered.

St. Cyprian shook his head. 'I don't know.'

The things were beginning to merge into each other in some fashion that he could not understand. Becoming something else... something solid.

Something real.

There was a thick sound, like water sloshing in a bucket. The torch beam flickered, and St. Cyprian felt a tug deep within him, as if in memory of the bites and scratches his *ka* had endured. 'They're all part of the same entity...' he said, in realisation.

As he spoke, there came a deep, animal sound – an intake of breath, as if from something that had not breathed air in time out of mind.

Gallowglass cocked her pistol. 'Wait,' St. Cyprian said.

'Until I see the whites of its eyes,' she said. 'If it has eyes.'

'What is it?' Wendy-Smythe said.

'We'll know in a moment.' St. Cyprian raised his pistol.

Something reached out of the darkness – a flat, wedge-shaped paw, like that of an otter or a rat. Hairy finger-claws scraping against the stonework as a wide, flat skull emerged into the light, black eyes shining.

It resembled the smaller creatures, but was a titan, in comparison. Massive. Like a giant stoat, plucked from prehistory. Maybe that was what it had been, once upon a time. Now it was something much worse. Teeth like spear-blades shone wet in the light. A square nose wrinkled as it scented the air. It loosed an echoing hiss.

'Is it me, or does it look hungry?' Gallowglass said.

'It's not you,' St. Cyprian said, as the thing began to squeeze its bulk towards them. Glistening slaver pattered from its jaws. It lunged, more swiftly than he expected. He shoved Gallowglass aside and threw himself against the wall, losing his pistol and the torch in the process. Wendy-Smythe scrambled away as the beast clawed at him.

'Philip – get back!' At his cry, the beast spun, knocking crates and paint cans clattering. Its tail sent the torch spinning across the floor. Wicked jaws snapped shut just shy of his face as he shoved himself back. It clawed at him, tearing flinders from the nearby shelves as he ducked. A wash of hot, rancid breath enveloped him.

He could feel its heat, hear the bellows-creak of its lungs, smell the stink of its fur. It was alive – or, if not alive, then the next best thing. He rolled back through a section of broken shelving, dropping into the gap between it and the wall. It tore at the wood, trying to reach him. It seemed to recognise him – maybe it still had the taste of his *ka* in his mouth. As it raged at the shelving, he saw splinters jab its hairy limbs and muzzle – and the rivulets of blood that resulted. That gave him an idea. 'Somebody distract the bally beast,' he shouted.

He heard glass shatter, and saw Wendy-Smythe stumble into view with an armful of wine bottles. The little occultist sent another sailing towards the beast, causing it to turn. 'Over here, you great brute! Have a taste of Christmas port.'

'Good show, Philip – keep it up,' St. Cyprian said as he snatched up the last of the arbutus. Carefully, hand shaking, he lit the entire bag. When it was properly smoking, he scrambled into the open. 'Now, back to me, beastie,' he called out. 'I've got something for you.' He readied himself. He was only going to get one shot.

The beast whirled, jaws agape, and undulated towards him. As it did so, he flung the burning sack into its open jaws. The effect was immediate. The beast squalled and reared, thumping into the roof of the cellars. It pawed at its muzzle, squealing in apparent agony, though whether from the fire or the blossoms he couldn't say. 'Any time, Miss Gallowglass,' he called out, hoping she'd understand.

The beast bent towards him, scorched muzzle wrinkling back from blackened teeth. Before it could do much more than glare, however, Gallowglass appeared beside it. 'Oi, over here,' she called out. As it twisted around, her pistol boomed six times.

For a moment, he thought he'd gotten it wrong. Then, slowly, the beast toppled onto its side, thrashed once, and expired. Again.

St. Cyprian picked up the torch and played it across the thing's body. Already, it was beginning to lose cohesion. Stolen ectoplasm drained away into the stones of Clavering. Gallowglass grinned at him. 'I was wondering how you were going to get it to stand still,' she said. 'Couldn't just let me pot it in the first place?'

'I wasn't sure bullets would work, until I saw that it was bleeding.'

'You – you shot it?' Wendy-Smythe said in disbelief.

'It thought it was alive,' St. Cyprian said. 'And if it was alive, it could die.' He picked up a fallen bottle of wine, blew dust from the label, and stuffed it under his arm. 'A celebratory drink is in order, I think.' He gestured with the torch. 'Up we go.'

A shamefaced Sinclair was waiting for them at the top of the stairs. 'I'm sorry about the door. Something blew it shut...'

'Never mind, Tipsy,' Wendy-Smythe said, consolingly. 'All's well that ends well.'

'Indeed.' St. Cyprian popped the cork on the wine and poured out four glasses. 'I can only imagine the trouble if that thing had gotten loose. Even Clavering might have proved a flimsy cage for such a beast.'

'But what was it?' Wendy-Smythe asked. 'Not a ghost, surely?'

'Of a sort. An old ghost, something older than Clavering itself. A prehistoric monster, from the dawn of time. Who knows how long it had been sleeping down here, before the renovations woke it. And like any beast, after a long hibernation, it woke up hungry.'

'And what do ghosts eat?' Gallowglass said. 'Other ghosts, of course!' She laughed.

St. Cyprian nodded. 'And once it had eaten enough it became a sustained ectoplasmic construct of some sort. That's my theory, at any rate.'

'And now?' Sinclair asked.

'Now its dead twice-over. With luck, it'll stay that way this time.'

'What about the ah – the others?' Sinclair looked around nervously.

St. Cyprian lit a cigarette and leaned back. Above him, an ectoplasmic something with too many limbs and the face of a wizened pensioner crawled across the ceiling. Carefully, he took off the Voorish Sign and banished the thing from sight.

'Never fear, old thing. Still plenty of them hanging about the old pile, I suspect.'

He smiled. 'This is Clavering Grange, after all.'

MR BEGOT'S BESPOKE MANTLES

By

I. A. Watson

'THIS IS IT!' Diamante cried excitedly. 'Just like Quaggy said! Look. Only that little brass sign there on the door. That's the place!'

Diamante's current beau and lifestyle financier did not like her mentioning her previous boyfriends. 'Never mind about that *dweeb*,' he growled – except he didn't say "dweeb". 'All that matters is if this is the shop we heard 'bout. But it don't look like no shop to me.'

The exclusive stores along Oxford Street had brightly-lit picture windows under designer awnings, with tasteful well-lit displays of expensive merchandise. Many of them also had discreet little boasts in gold lettering somewhere below their bold modern logos, saying things like "Est.d 1823" or "By Appointment". This lone mahogany door was squeezed between a well-known chain store's senior branch and a gentleman's tailor shop where even the combs started out at fifty guineas.

The overweight celebrity in the baseball cap and sneakers on whose arm Diamante hung looked doubtfully at the small sign. 'So is this it or not?' he demanded.

Eli Rothwell, a mid-twenties man in a shiny business suit and a Bluetooth earpiece answered his employer. 'Many of the most elite of establishments in London have only a brief nameplate to establish them. It is assumed that if you are a suitable client then you are already in the know. Other visitors are not encouraged.'

'Keep the plebs out. Right.' Grunge-hop rapper Stabby D, owner of the arm that Diamante occupied, nodded his jowly head. 'Makes sense. No point letting in the *dweebing* riff-raff.' Again, he used a different adjective.

The discreet nameplate simply said: *Begot's.*

Diamante tried the door. After a moment's pressure it swung open, allowing admittance up two disabled-unfriendly steps into a long half-panelled hallway. An antique open-cage lift waited at the other end of the passage.

'Boys,' Stabby D prompted his entourage, nodding them to go ahead and investigate. Bulky, tattooed Jagged thudded down the hallway to summon the elevator car. Kagel stayed on the street, covering Stabby's behind, alert for paparazzi or autograph-hounds.

Jagged pushed the pearl lift button. Pre-war winding mechanisms shuddered to life with a strained groaning. The car slowly descended and arrived at corridor level.

'You'd think a place this posh could afford a decent lift,' Stabby D objected.

'I guess it's all part of the image, Stabby,' Diamante persuaded. 'Come on!'

Jagged thumbed the 'up' button and the art deco compartment rose to the first floor. The elevator-cable strained a little under the combined weights of Stabby, Jagged, and Kagel. The slighter forms of Diamante and Rothwell made negligible difference.

The lift disgorged into a well-lit waiting room with ornamented plasterwork, fancy coving, and ceiling roses. Two thin leaded windows looked out over the muted bustle of Oxford Street. Three leather couches and two armchairs stood on plush shag carpet. The walls were decorated with framed clothing designs, hand-drawn designer originals.

A catalogue on a low coffee table was inscribed with italics that read *Mr Begot's Bespoke Mantles*.

'See,' Diamante insisted triumphantly. 'Quaggy wasn't fooling. There really is such a place.'

Stabby D pursed his lips. Diamante sometimes liked to provoke him. She could be annoying like that and she was certainly high maintenance but she offered other compensations and she looked good on the publicity.

As the bulky young man was again calculating the Diamante downsides/compensations ratio, an interior door opened. A slim young woman in a superior black and white shop uniform stood aside to allow a short broad man with a great shock of red hair and beard to precede her into the lounge. 'I'm sure you'll find it more comfortable now, sir,' she was promising. 'Are you sure you wouldn't like a tentacle to go with that?'

'Perhaps another time,' the customer said in a strange multiple voice that sounded like it had been spoken by half a dozen serpents. 'Thank you for your assistance but I must run or I'll miss my taxi and be late for the assizes.' He gave her a polite head-nod and hurried past Stabby's entourage, into the lift.

The mechanism clanked its way down to ground level. The shop assistant looked at the new visitors with well-concealed dismay. 'May I assist you?'

Jagged and Kagel had spread out to take opposite corners of the room. They planted their feet apart and folded their arms, doing their best impressions of the bodyguards in action movies, right down to the designer shades. Rothwell, Stabby's fixer, moved forward to engage the hired help. 'This is Begot's Mantles? We're here to buy.'

'This is *Mr* Begot's *Bespoke* Mantles,' the shop-girl clarified, in old-school BBC tones of received pronunciation. It was an accent perfectly designed for speaking emphasis italics. 'Visits are usually by appointment.'

'I don't do no appointments,' Stabby insisted. 'I do what I want.'

'What Stabby D means,' Rothwell interpreted, 'is that he is a man whose time is valuable. He would appreciate immediate attention.'

The assistant eyed the running-to-blubber would-be customer, measuring up his New York baseball cap, pre-stressed designer jeans, edgy t-shirt with a sexist caption that could not be repeated in polite company, approximately six pounds of jewellery in the form of neck-chains, rings, and wrist-chains, and his truculent expression. 'I will inform Mr Begot of your arrival,' the shop-girl conceded.

'Inform him to shift his ass out here now,' Stabby commanded.

The assistant vanished back into the depths of the shop. Diamante called her companion's attention to the catalogue on the table. 'Look at this, Stab! Look what's in here!'

The document was a ring-binder containing handsome six inch by nine inch head shots of more-handsome male models. Each of the images portrayed the subject with some different set of horns protruding from his forehead. Some of the tines were mere stylish stumps, while others curled, bifurcated, twisted, or in one case became a full antler rack.

'That's easy to do these days with CGI,' Eli Rothwell sniffed. 'Or if they're real, it can be done with prosthetics. You see that stuff in cinema all the time now.'

'I don't want no horns,' Stabby D insisted firmly. 'Though I might get matching sets for Jagged and Kagel. Hey boys, you want horns?'

Diamante shook her head. 'Quaggy said they don't do prosthetics. It's all natural. And not just horns. Fangs, claws, hooves, wings – you name it. Quaggy got his feelers done here. They were much better after that, didn't leave lots of little sucker marks on my...'

'I don't want to hear 'bout *dweebing* Quaggy,' snarled Stabby. "You want to talk 'bout him, how about you crawl back to that loser, eh?'

Diamante used her hurt expression. 'Don't be like that, Stab. I only told you about this place because I care so much about you. Mr Begot's Bespoke Mantles, where you can become the monster of your choice!'

'That is not quite correct, I am afraid.'

Even Jagged and Kagel jumped at the unexpected voice from the unnoticed newcomer in the room. The ascetic tones were a perfect blend of Christopher Lee and Peter Cushing, while the speaker's appearance was nearer to Vincent Price. His three-piece suit was as well tailored and tasteful as any shop on Oxford Street could offer, a rebuke to the rack-bought outfit that Eli Rothwell wore.

Around the tailor's neck was a tape measure, the sole concession to his business.

'What'chu mean?' Stabby D demanded.

'The young lady's assertion was slightly erroneous. One cannot become a monster here. One can only customise the kind of monster one is.'

Rothwell moved forward. 'Mr Begot, is it? Well I've got to tell you that it's my job to protect my employer from all kinds of scams and hustles. If you've really got some kind of extreme surgery shop or some kind of genetic manipulation process then I'm going to need firm proof and some binding indemnities before we do business.'

'I am Mr Begot,' the proprietor of the establishment acknowledged. 'It is customary to seek an appointment before attending a consultation. Nor are all requests for a fitting granted. We are an old-established firm with an exclusive client list.'

'I am right here!' Stabby D shouted. 'Don't you know who I am?'

'I am afraid I have no idea,' Mr Begot admitted. 'I presume that you know?'

'This is Stabby D!' Diamante intervened. '*Stabby D!* Britain's top white rapper. He's number one in the clubs. Two Grammies. Nine million followers on Twitter.'

'Ah.' Mr Begot's faint answer might well have masked a lack of information on any of rappers, Grammies, or Twitter.

'And he is not accustomed to having to wait,' Eli Rothwell added.

'I don't like it,' Stabby cautioned. 'And when I don't like it, my boys don't like it.' He nodded to Jagged and Kagel. 'And when they don't like it, things get broken.'

'I see.' Mr Begot glanced at the hulking bodyguards, then ranged his gaze over Rothwell, Diamante, and then the white rapper himself. 'May I enquire what brings you to this establishment?'

'I heard things 'bout you. 'Bout your shop. You do body-mods and stuff.' He didn't say 'stuff'. 'Give guys add-ons, level-ups.'

'You can make people into... into vampires or werewolves,' Diamante burst in. 'You can make them immortal.'

Mr Begot winced. 'Vampires and werewolves are very... last season. As for immortality, that is a rare and precious commodity that comes only with the most superior refurbishments.'

'Give us your pitch,' Rothwell demanded sceptically. 'What do you claim to do here?'

The proprietor took a breath before gesturing around him. 'Mr

Begot's Bespoke Mantles caters for clients who wish to eschew their existing bodies and purchase new ones. We do not simply add or delete body parts. There are other establishments that undertake such crude and simplistic works. At Begot's, we craft an entire mantle, a complete transformation from one mode of monstrosity to another.'

'But what does that *mean*?' probed Diamante.

'Perhaps, for example, sir or madam is tired of lycanthropy. It is, after all, somewhat passé in contemporary society, which is hardly governed by the phase of the moon or the migration of herds. Perhaps he might care to try on a shadow aspect, lurking in the pools of darkness between the urban lights of the West End? Or else he may enjoy one of the North African forms of nosferatu, so refreshingly different from the European clichés? Perhaps with a dash of ghoul? A hint of barghest? Or if the client prefers a period in less human guise, he might consider a psychic waveform or an elemental grue? Begot's will custom-make the appropriate mantle and fit it to taste.'

'You pimp up monsters?' Stabby D translated.

The proprietor shuddered. 'We refine horror for the discerning customer. Mr Begot's caters for all tastes for creatures of the night; but it is rare that a human is allowed upon the premises.'

'It's rare that a human has an unlimited platinum card,' Rothwell pointed out.

'Quaggy said that sometimes you *will* upgrade a... a mortal,' Diamante remembered. 'If the price is right.'

'Quaggy?' Mr Begot enquired. The affectionate name was not known to him. 'From whom came your intelligence of this establishment, Miss...?'

'Diamante,' the orange-tanned blonde insisted. 'Diamante Sparkle.' Well, that was her stage name. 'I heard it from... from a gentleman I knew before. Quentin MacDocherty.'

'The Laird of Dunbeggat,' Mr Begot recognised. 'I must speak a word with him about the necessary discretion required to remain on our client list.'

'Oh, don't tell him I told you!' Diamante pleaded. 'Only, Quaggy isn't just a... a Scottish laird or whatever they call it. He's a... a jerrymoth.'

'He is a *geriamoothe*,' Mr Begot corrected her. 'That is, an entity sired by a redcap or tower-haunter upon a freshwater kelpie during a neap tide on a Friday. That, however, does not excuse him from an unconscionable breach of confidentiality regarding the services of this establishment.'

'Who cares about that *dweeb* and whatever the hell he is?' Stabby D interrupted irritably. 'Only thing matters is, he came to you, traded in his... feelers or whatever, and got a whole bunch of other parts. Like, maybe, a really huge...'

'I cannot discuss the personal requirements of our clients,' the proprietor insisted. 'Confidentiality is a watchword at Mr Begot's Bespoke Mantles.'

Rothwell grinned like a shark. 'Is it, now? So I'm guessing you *wouldn't* like a front page exposé of your business in the tabloids, then? Or a visit from a nosy news film crew? I can only guarantee that *if* you see to my client's requirements, Mr Begot.'

The gaunt shop owner looked down his nose at the irritating fixer in the shiny ill-cut suit. 'One does not speak about this establishment. It is not done.'

'*Dweebs*, it ain't!' snorted Stabby. 'One little Tweet from me an' all my followers know all about your spooky little secret, pal! So make less with the lip and more with the... whatever it is you do. Show me the goods!'

Mr Begot took a breath, then clapped his hands to summon his assistant. 'Miss Cadever? Are you free?'

The same shop girl from before appeared from a different door, pushing aside a changing room curtain and setting down a pile of garments to be re-hung. 'Yes, Mr Begot?'

'I shall be doing a measuring. Would you please assist Mr... Stabby here onto the podium so I can establish his vital statistics.'

Miss Cadever showed the rapper where to stand on a low stool, then positioned a pair of full-length wheeled mirrors to flank him.

Stabby D tried to toss her a wink but her stare somehow managed to freeze it in mid-air.

Mr Begot moved into place with his tape measure. 'You better keep yo' hands away from my junk,' the client warned him.

'I can already see that sir dresses to the obtuse,' the tailor replied. 'If sir would extend his arms and raise his chin I will attempt to measure his ego.'

'Tell me what you can really do,' Stabby demanded. 'I mean, I heard Diamante's stories about... that guy. I'm not sure I really *believe* her. I mean, it would be cool to have claws and stuff. So much cooler ways to off punks than just using a piece or a razor, you know? But monsters? Really? Vamps and Creatures of the Black Lagoon and that? Or aliens that jump out of your chest?'

Mr Begot held his tape along the length of his client's back. As he suspected, the spine was rather lacking. 'I can't speak for aliens, sir. If one wants chest-exploders I might recommend a transplant of gremlin, or one of the gastric poltergeist packages. And while there is a certain customer base for anthropomorphic amphibious predators, careful consideration must be given to the geographical preferences of the aquaform.'

'Huh?' Diamante contributed.

'Adaptations suitable for a sub-tropical black lagoon would be most inconvenient, and of course considered rather provincial in a Nordic fjord venue or in a metropolitan sewer environment, for example. Nor are all our customers willing to accept the necessary regimen of skin and gill care required to maintain a proper piscine hide consistency.' Mr Begot sighed. 'The number of patrons who are back here only months after their new purchase to have lesions or minor parasitical incursions rectified... you wouldn't believe it. We get more such repairs nowadays than gentlemen who return to have bullet holes removed from pelts or garlic stains purged from their evening wear.'

'But you do monsters,' Stabby D checked again. 'Monsters that live forever, like Draculas.'

'Many of the nosferatu have significantly extended longevity,' Mr

Begot owned. 'Similar benefits accrue to djinnforms, to elementals, and to many of the noncorporeal mantles. Of course, each has its limitations as well, and long life is not the same as immortality.'

'Well I wanna live forever,' the rapper insisted. 'I wanna be this lethal, immortal bad-ass that makes everybody *dweeb* their pants! A real heavy, tougher than anyone – and with a real big endowment, yeah? I'm'a be the baddest motha ever to be a monster!'

Mr Begot made no comment. That may have been because he was trying to parse why his unwanted customer wished to become pregnant or whether Stabby D had actually expressed a desire for a dash of lepidoptery in his modifications.

'How does this work, anyhow?' Eli Rothwell enquired. 'Does he try on monster suits till he finds one he likes? What's the fee-scale anyway? Where's the price list?'

'Ours is a bespoke shop, sir,' Mr Begot scolded the fixer. 'Every mantle is made to measure, an exclusive creation for that client alone. Even if a customer insists upon one of the rather overused "traditional" mythological identities, every one of them must be properly crafted to offer a tasteful, well-suited morphology that says that monster has gone for the best – that is, Begot's.'

'I want the best, yeah,' Stabby D declared.

'*We* want the best,' Diamante chipped in. 'I mean, you'll want to buy a little present for me, too, won't you, Stabbykins?'

'We'll see, woman. I still ain't sure 'bout whether this guy can do what he says.' The rapper glared at Mr Begot. 'And if he can't, then he's gonna have a problem wit' Jagged and Kagel.'

'Lots of t'ings can kitch fire in here,' Jagged spoke for the first time, in a thick Russian accent.

'Why don't you buy me an adaptation first, Stab?' Diamante suggested brightly. 'That way you'll *see* if it works.'

Stabby D frowned down from his stool at his girlfriend/groupie/lifestyle coach/physical therapist. 'Is this why you told me 'bout this place, girl? So *you* could get done up?'

'Come on, Stabby. You like buying me things. You know I get all... *excited* when you buy me things.'

The rapper snorted. 'What'chu got that will shut her up?' he asked Mr Begot. 'You got something that can make her boobs bigger?'

'Miss... Sparkle is not quite a suitable client for this establishment,' the proprietor regretted.

'Hey! Are you saying I'm not good enough?' Diamante objected.

'Quite the opposite, miss,' Mr Begot assured her. 'As I mentioned, we cater only to monsters, and you do not yet qualify. However, if Mr Stabby insists on being a patron of the establishment, he may seek to... accessorise. He might elect to have us modify his... accessory.'

'I'm not...' the brassy blonde began to argue, then clamped her mouth shut. 'Okay. I'm his accessory. Like a purse. Do me.'

Mr Begot circled the young woman, frowning. There was so much to improve. 'Miss Cadever, would you be so good as to step into the stock room and bring me a pair of Nahemah encapsulates, please?'

'A pair of what now?' Stabby asked.

'In Hebrew myth and middle ages scholarship, Nahemah was one of the four beautiful concubines of fallen Samael. You want to enhance your commensal's physical attributes? Consumption of materials derived from a daughter of Lilith is a proven method of achieving what you wished for. And it will perhaps provide the demonstration that your other minion required.'

'I'm not his minion...' Rothwell began to argue, but Stabby D interrupted him and said, 'Shut up, Eli. You kind of are.'

Miss Cadever returned with an oriental box of carved jade and ivory, which she set on the coffee table. 'Do you consent to this modification as your principal's commensal, under the accords of the Fourth Treaty of Malebolge?' she asked Diamante. 'If so, open the Casket of Nü Gui and swallow down the objects placed therein. Would you like a glass of water?'

Diamante glanced from Stabby to Mr Begot, then down at the box. She made a decision, opened the lid, and peered inside. Two gelatinous orbs the size of large plums lay on a red silken cushion. 'They look like raspberry jelly,' she said.

'Eat 'em, then,' Stabby D told her impatiently. 'What's this costing me, by the way?'

'If you have to ask, you can't afford it,' Mr Begot told him. 'Be assured that I am keeping a tab.'

Perhaps afraid that her sugar daddy might change his mind about the sugar, Diamante grabbed up the encapsulates and gulped them down.

'Oh...!' she gasped, 'They taste like... cigarettes and sour rum. Ohhhh!'

And then she cried, 'Owww!' – for good reasons. Diamante Sparkle's 36-C chest had suddenly expanded to 38-D and didn't seem to intend stopping there. The young woman was having trouble breathing and her bra was trying to kill her.

'Ah, perhaps you would take Miss Sparkle into the changing room and find her some more comfortable attire?' Mr Begot requested Miss Cadever.

As the newly-endowed model hastened away to be freed from her restraints, Rothwell turned a shocked, open-mouthed gaze on the dapper proprietor. 'It's true. It works!'

'How did you do that?' Stabby wondered. 'Boob pills?'

'A trifle,' Mr Begot assured him. 'That kind of cosmetic change is really only appropriate for a fashion item. When we craft a mantle for an actual client the change is entirely more profound, a culmination of art and destiny that speaks to the whole of creation.'

The rapper grinned hungrily, revealing a designer gold tooth. 'Okay then. So never mind her. What do you got for *me*? 'Cause I deserve the full treatment. The best.'

'I can provide exactly what you deserve, sir,' Mr Begot promised. He raised his tape again. Nobody had noticed him picking up what looked like an unfinished felt outline of an Inverness cape, but he held such a thing now. He draped it over Stabby's shoulders and spent a moment or two making marks on the fabric with a tailor's chalk.

'What's this thing?' Stabby interrogated the proprietor.

'A pattern guide. It will help me to ensure that your mantle fits perfectly. You'll need to answer a few questions about your preferences.'

'Girls,' the rapper insisted emphatically. 'I'm suing that *dweebing* magazine that printed...'

'Other preferences,' Mr Begot clarified. He threaded a pin at the template's collar and asked, 'When did you kill your first victim?'

'What? I mean...'

'Rumours of my principal's criminal behaviour are just that,' Eli Rothwell interjected. 'That kind of reputation is necessary marketing to his fan base. It doesn't mean...'

'What passes between a man and his tailor is strictly confidential,' Mr Begot assured the agitated fixer. 'However, as I have previously explained twice, I can only offer transformative mantles to *monsters*. I'll need to hear details about what a monster Mr Begot is. My measurements have already informed me of some of his aspects – I know how much he "likes" girls, for instance, especially very young ones. I can tell that he has "got away with murder" on several occasions, often with your assistance, Mr Rothwell. But the devil is in the details, as they say.'

There was something about the calm routine of the tailor circling, of the patient chalking and pinning, that encouraged confession. 'Alright,' Stabby conceded, still balancing on the podium stool. 'I might have done a few things...'

He had done more than a few, and many of them deeply unpleasant. Mr Begot listened without comment or reaction, labouring away at the felt garment, as his client unburdened himself of his misdeeds; even boasted of them.

'...And that was when the bitch learned to shut the *dweeb* up!' Stabby D concluded.

'Monstrous,' Mr Begot agreed, 'but does that make you a monster, Mr Stabby?'

'I can be a monster,' the rapper promised, balling his hand into a sharp-ringed fist. 'Need me to show you?'

'So you want to be a monster? And I believe you specified immortality.'

'Oh yeah. And power. I gotta be big and unstoppable.

Indestructible Stabby D! That's what I want.'

'Such a transformation is rather expensive, sir.'

'Name a figure,' Rothwell told the proprietor with a smirk. 'You won't believe how much cash my client has!'

'The fee is not only financial, Mr Rothwell.'

Stabby D frowned. 'I gotta sell you my soul?'

'Whatever makes you think you have one? No, such intangibles are a rather variable market and this establishment prefers to deal in less risky currency. For the most part a financial settlement will be sufficient.'

'How much?' Rothwell asked suspiciously.

'One half of Mr Stabby's total current net worth,' the tailor answered promptly. And then, to cut off the fixer's haggling, he added. 'Our fees are non-negotiable. If one wishes to purchase the best, one meets our costs. Otherwise, one goes elsewhere for an inferior fitting.'

'It's cool, Eli,' Shabby interrupted his assistant. 'I can make more money, easy. I got real dumb fans.'

'You said "for the most part" money would do,' Rothwell reminded Mr Begot suspiciously.

'That is correct. In addition to a sum equal to one half of your principal's worldly estate, we shall require him to trade in his present accessories as well. Mr Begot's Bespoke Mantles is a discreet and private venue; we do not permit casual visitors to leave with the knowledge of our existence. This would have been explained to Mr Stabby had he arranged an appointment in the usual manner. Clients simply do not bring their retinues along without prior provision for confidentiality.'

Rothwell frowned. 'When you say "trade in present accessories..."'

'Other and more appropriate ones can be provided as required,' Mr Begot assured Stabby D.

The rapper tried to keep up. 'You want... my posse?'

Rothwell realised that he had just been put on the bargaining table. 'Hey, hold on...!'

In his corner, Jagged began to understand the turn of the

conversation. 'Boss? What this? Are you t'ink...?'

Kagel, also not employed for his brain-power, took a step forward and went, 'Whut?'

'This guy wants to shut us up?' Jagged objected. 'Wants you to get rid of us?'

'It is a necessary and non-negotiable prerequisite of Mr Stabby's transformation,' Mr Begot warned.

'*Dweeb* that!' Rothwell shouted, his polished veneer slipping as he realised that his employer was considering the deal, whatever that deal was.

'Yeah!' Jagged agreed, stepping forward menacingly.

'Hold it there, boys,' Diamante called from the doorway. 'Don't move a muscle. None of you. That means you too, Kagel.'

The three angry men ground to immobility. They all looked surprised that they could no longer lunge at Mr Begot.

The rapper's newly-enhanced companion emerged from the changing rooms in a slinky low-cut number that accentuated her most obvious upgrades. But it was her command that held the men in Stabby D's entourage motionless. 'Hmm,' she admired herself, 'Not bad.'

'How did you do that?' Stabby asked her.

The blonde looked in the mirrors that flanked him. She ran her palms over her fascinating curves. 'Succubus implants,' she explained. 'Very effective on the weaker sex.' She winked at the bodyguards. 'That's you, boys.'

Mr Begot nodded approvingly at Miss Cadever and returned to his negotiation with the client. 'Miss Sparkle's minor modification is irrelevant now, Mr Stabby. We were discussing the matter of remuneration. You wish to receive an indestructible, eternal, powerful and... endowed body that properly houses your inner monster. I have outlined the required fee, which includes trading in your "posse" in part-exchange. I always find use for spare components. So the question is, how much do you wish to be a client of Mr Begot's Bespoke Mantles?'

'Stabby, no...!' Rothwell managed a choked plea before a glance from Diamante silenced him.

The rapper eyed his improved girlfriend. 'Including her?' he checked, reluctantly.

'That is acceptable to me,' the buxom blonde told him coolly.

'What? You don't mind me trading you to this weird freaky dude? That's...'

'Oh...' She comprehended now. '*You* think that little Diamante is speaking. But you might recall that in addition to wishing her to be physically enhanced you also wanted her to be shut up. That's why we are in control now.'

'We? We who?'

Diamante leaned forward, allowing an even better view of her cleavage. 'The implants,' she whispered. 'Flesh of Nehemah, one of the Four Sacred Prostitutes of Hell.'

'The what?'

The blonde made a delighted moue. 'You agreed to the contract and so did little Diamante. So thanks for the new ride, "Stabby". And sure, speaking as Diamante's new management we'd be much happier if we weren't tied in to you.'

Stabby D turned an accusing gaze on Mr Begot. 'You never said that would happen.'

The proprietor stepped back. 'Well, never let it be said that my customers don't come first. If sir is dissatisfied, we can restore Miss Sparkle to her former characteristics, sans her new intellectual capacities; of course she may prefer not to associate with you further thereafter. Your companions can enjoy freedom of movement and speech again, though they may harbour ill-will at being used as bartering chips. And you may hand back that template garment and leave as you came – without the mantle that you sought.' Mr Begot spread his hands. 'It is *entirely* your choice, sir.'

The proprietor, Miss Cadever, and Diamante's chest waited to see what Stabby D would decide.

'I gets to be immortal, invulnerable, everything you said?' the rapper checked. 'But you get half my dough and these four guys?'

'That is the required sum, yes,' Mr Begot agreed. 'If you accept the arrangement, I can fit your mantle while you wait. Or you can depart.'

'I am a monster,' Stabby D decided. 'I should have the power of one. Mister, you got yourself a deal!'

Rothwell, Jagged, and Kagel might have objected had they not too been smitten by the enthralling new version of their employer's mistress. Instead they watched and listened helplessly as Stabby bargained them away.

'Consent. Splendid,' approved the proprietor. 'Miss Cadever, the order book, please. Sir will need to sign here and here, and initial at the bottom. One moment while I issue you a receipt, and then we'll see about the final fitting.'

Jagged actually managed an independent step forward then, but another smile from Diamante halted him in his tracks.

Mr Begot regarded the entourage with a faint distaste, as if he was handling a soiled rag with the tips of his fingers. 'Take these spare parts to the box room, please,' he requested Diamante. 'Miss Cadever will accompany you and show you how to dismantle and store them.'

Diamante gestured with one finger. Rothwell, Jagged, and Kagel followed her out, eagerly yet unwillingly, past the changing rooms, into the darkened space beyond. That was the last of them.

'Now for you, sir,' Mr Begot told Stabby D. 'Just slip off that template so I can fashion a full mantle from it. No, don't worry if you don't understand what you are seeing, sir. It is rather beyond mortal senses. Transformations of this kind are necessarily difficult to explain.'

'I'm feeling bigger,' Stabby reported. 'Stronger too.'

'As promised, sir. Now kindly raise your hands above your head, palms upwards – as if you were supporting a table, perhaps. Steadily, please.'

'My skin's goin' grey and hard.'

'Calcifying, in fact,' clarified Mr Begot.

'So what's happening to me?' Stabby D suffered a flash of panic. 'What am I becoming?'

'You are familiar with the nature of telamons, no? They are the male equivalent of a caryatid.'

'I dunno what that is either. 'S getting hard to talk.'

'That would be the transmutation setting in, sir. Telamons and caryatids are respectively categories of statuary, specifically male and female figures that support columns or archways. They are a subsection of decorative chimerae that includes gargoyles, cherubs, atlantes and so on. When mystically imbued with a resident spirit to gain sentience they are quite unbreakable. Powerful, indestructible, immortal entities, just as required. And carved with the physical attributes you ordered.'

'But ah cnn't m've!'

'Sir never specified mobility as one of his requirements.'

The rapper was larger, more muscular, with sharp ridges on his arms, legs, and spine to make him dangerous. His skin was now impenetrable stone. A prodigious granite member dangled below his paunch, between his squatted legs. Only his single gold tooth remained unchanged, a style accent to set off his feral carved expression.

''M stk...!'

'But stuck in impeccable style, Mr Stabby. Your mantle is quite the fashion statement. I assure you that it will occasion significant remark. True, you will live out the rest of eternity conscious but petrified to immobility, unable to irritate the world any more with your obnoxious personality, but our mantles are guaranteed to be exactly what you deserve.' Mr Begot circled the Telamon. 'Suits you, sir.'

'Mmm...'

The last remnants of flexibility left Stabby's new form. Now he was entirely composed of silicone. He stood nine feet tall, with arms upstretched to usefully support a lintel. He was quite deadly – if he happened to be toppled onto someone. His face had a somewhat shocked expression, as if outraged blubber had been solidified mid-protest and immortalised forever.

'It really is best to call ahead for an appointment,' Mr Begot mentioned to him. After all, Stabby D could still see and hear what was going on around him. 'I'll see you delivered to your house, shall I? Oh, and your new entourage, as promised. I'm thinking pigeons.'

He regarded the statue, admiring its artistic features, brushing a flake of dust away here and there. He produced a pocket handkerchief and polished the gold tooth. Mr Begot's Bespoke Mantles was nothing if not fastidious.

He closed the order book.

'Begot's thanks you for your custom, sir. Good day.'

TEMPTATIONS UNLIMITED

By

William Meikle

G EORGE JENKINS HAD peculiar enthusiasms, ones that led him to spend much of his time in the back rooms of second hand bookshops and dilapidated video stores where expensive deals were done under the counter for brown-paper packages tied up with string. His hobby, for want of a better word, took up many of his spare hours, and invariably led to him scouring the four quarters of London for shops frequented by others who shared his furtive interests.

He knew he could very easily save a great deal of time in this modern age by utilising the Internet to indulge his particular cravings, to join what he knew was a burgeoning community online. But for George this had always been a solitary activity, even from as far back as his schooldays, one to be kept hidden from parents, friends, and eventually Mrs Jenkins. Besides, the thrill of the chase in the shelves and corridors of those grey establishments was ingrained in him by many years of questing for the really good stuff. There was also the not insignificant fact to consider that Mrs Jenkins was a great deal more technologically savvy than he, having got a diploma at night school and all, so George had of necessity to be circumspect. And by doing things the old fashioned way, he didn't need levels of computer security or encryption to keep his secrets from his wife, just his old shed out in the garden and a stout lock both outside and in.

On this particular Saturday morning, it was the hopes of finding a new addition to his back door collection that led him to take the train to Lewisham, and to find a store, new to him, tucked away in a shadowed alleyway off the high street. He'd heard whispers from a like minded chap in his local that a friend of a friend told him this place could be relied upon to deliver "the real deal", all the way from

Denmark. George's blood was up as he approached the premises.

There was no display window, just a simple red doorway. The only indication that it wasn't a private dwelling was a hand-painted sign above the door. "Temptations Limited" it said, a good start, but George's spirits fell when he ventured inside. This place was too bright, too clean and appeared to be an antique and curios shop rather than the book and video store he'd been led to expect. There were old musical instruments lining the walls, walnut covered art-deco radios and gramophones all along one side, fine scrimshaw chess pieces on ancient mahogany tables, gilded mirrors of all shapes and sizes and tall glass cabinets brimming with watches, fob chains, porcelain and jewellery. Mrs Jenkins would have been in her element, but for George it was a major disappointment. There were no books, no videotapes... none of the good stuff. He was on the verge of turning to leave when a voice spoke from a darkened doorway behind the counter.

'Can I help you, sir?'

The shopkeeper came forward out of the shadows. He was an elderly chap, balding on top with a grey goatee beard, wearing pince-nez glasses, a tweed suit long past its best and a cheerful smile. He looked so eager to please that George decided to brazen it out.

'I'm here on the recommendation of a friend, and I'm after something exotic. Something Scandinavian if you catch my drift?'

The elderly shopkeeper smiled showing twin rows of brilliant white teeth that looked to belong to a much younger man.

'I believe I know exactly what you have in mind, sir,' he replied, and, coming out from behind the counter led George to a tall wooden cabinet in the darkest corner of the store away from the main door. The old man walked with the use of a stick, a piece of polished, crooked wood that looked as old as anything for sale in the shop, and he used the length of wood to rap, twice on the cabinet door with the silver wolf's head at the handle end. The case fell open with a loud creak of ancient hinges to reveal four shelves of videotapes stacked upright with only the spines showing.

'I'll leave you to make your choice,' the shopkeeper said and walked slowly back toward the counter, his walking stick clattering out a marching beat on the hardwood floor as George turned eagerly to peruse the titles of the tapes.

It was immediately obvious that he was not going to find the usual range he might have expected. All of the titles were hand-written on the spine by the same neat, slightly crabbed, hand that he suspected was the work of the old man himself. George did not recognise any of the titles, and indeed they seemed slightly outlandish, even rather tame; *The Mock Honeymoon*, *Weredigo's Big Night Out* and *Kiss of the Faevamp* being the first three to catch his eye. But he had butterflies in his stomach, the old gut instinct that always told him he was on the right track to the good stuff, the stuff that got his juices flowing. He knew already that he would not be leaving this shop empty handed.

Each tape had a small, round price sticker at the bottom of the spine. George was dismayed to see that the average asking price was three, nearly four times as much as he might have expected to pay in his normal establishments, and certainly more than he carried with him in cash. Using any of his cards was fraught with the danger of having to explain himself to Mrs Jenkins and the possible uncovering of all his secrets. He checked over his shoulder, saw that the old man's attention was elsewhere, and took one of the tapes from the rack, slipping it with ease into the deep pocket inside his jacket before closing the cabinet door and turning back to speak.

'You have a fine stock and several I have not seen, so I will definitely be making a purchase. You're a bit pricey, so I shall need to go to the bank first, though,' he said, attempting a smile as he returned to the counter.

The elderly gent smiled, sky blue eyes twinkling behind the pince -nez.

'As you wish, sir,' he replied then, speaking slowly and clearly, as if it was somehow of import. 'I shall be seeing you again soon. I am quite sure of it.'

As George turned to leave the shop he heard the ring and clatter of the old style till, as if the elderly chap was ringing up a sale.

The tape felt heavy in his pocket, and every glance he received from people in the street, on the train, then on the Tube on the way home felt like a judgement. But this was the good stuff. He knew it in his heart, and by the time he got within half a mile of their suburban home in North Finchley he was almost running.

George had resisted the urge to check on the results of his shoplifting. He didn't take it out of his jacket pocket until he had locked himself safely inside his shed with the blind pulled down over the window, safe from prying eyes.

The tape was in a plain black plastic box. Only the title on the spine and repeated on the tape itself gave any clue as to its contents; *Snow White and the Seven Weregoblins*. His hopes sank at that. He assumed this was going to one of those cheap Seventies knock-offs that had been so prevalent at one time, a hastily produced European soft porn version of a more famous movie, and one that would be far too tame for George's more esoteric tastes. With no great sense of anticipation he slid the tape into the old trusty TV/VHS combo player and waited for the credits to roll.

It became immediately obvious that this was something out of the normal. He was used to creaky sets, atrocious acting and minimal plots; he did not after all, get this stuff to appreciate the film-maker's skills. This tape, however, although naturalistic in style, had a level of special effects far beyond anything George was used to. The puppets – they had to be puppets, what else could they be? – looked more real than any of the CGI creatures he'd seen in the recent Hollywood blockbuster movies that Mrs Jenkins watched avidly. There were seven of them, short, pot-bellied, barrel-chested, warty and green all over, all naked above the waist. All were clean-shaven and pale eyed with wide-mouthed, wet-lipped lascivious grins as they sang and danced and capered around a young, lithe red-headed girl who lay spread-eagled, tied by ankles and wrists, naked on a huge white feather four-poster bed. George felt the first stirrings of interest.

Heigh-Ho, Heigh Ho, it's off to work we go.

Then the effects got particularly impressive. The shortest, fattest of the green warty things raised its head and howled. At the same time it changed, its face lengthening at the front into a long toothy snout, its ears elongating and pointing at the tips, the green skin exploding in a sea of coarse black hair covering its whole body. The pitch of the howl rose, and rose again. The thing tore off the leather kilt it wore around its waist, and howled again, a piercing wail that set George's old shed vibrating in sympathy. It shook itself, like a dog shedding water after a swim, then leapt up onto the bed where it began lustily and enthusiastically ravishing the bound girl whose smile grew big as the camera zoomed in for a close up.

When Mrs Jenkins called George in for his supper he was red and flushed.

'What have you been up to?'

He knew she wasn't really interested, she never was, but he realised that he was also smiling broadly, and that had made her suspicious.

'Nothing much. Just moving some old boxes of magazines around that have were getting in my way.'

'We should turn that shed over to something useful like a craft room for me,' she said, but she was already drifting away, the conversation over. She was, as usual, too busy with her soaps, cooking shows and streamed big budget, low intelligence movies to show any particular interest that evening. But he knew she had her eye partly on him after noticing his unusually good mood, so he fought down the almost overwhelming temptation to return to the shed and watch the rest of his new movie.

The opening scene around the bound girl ran in glorious Technicolor in his dreams that first night, as if the tape was playing in a loop inside his head. He woke with a start as the howls rang around him, unsure if they had followed him out of the dream and into the bedroom, but Mrs Jenkins snored on her side of the bed and did not stir. All he had to do was close his eyes and the scene was there again. He could not return to sleep for fear that his urges might betray him in the night, so lay there staring up into the dark until dawn, wondering with growing excitement what waited for him in the rest of the movie.

The next morning he waited with almost unbearable anticipation through breakfast, Mrs Jenkins' reading of her newspaper, and a long promised and oft put off trip to the tip to dispose of an old carpet. Finally his wife left for her Woman's Institute craft class and he was able, after checking twice to make sure that all was clear, to once again lock himself inside the shed with Snow White and her excitable furry friends.

Initially he had thought the whole tape was going to be just one long single scene of the Weregoblins taking turns to ravish the bound redhead, but it seemed there actually might be a plot unfolding. Snow White, now freed of her bonds, was put to work cleaning and cooking for the seven who lived in a rustic old cottage in the middle of thick woodland. And just as in the old story, somewhere out beyond the forest a Wicked Witch searched for the princess, the fairest of them all. George was quickly losing interest again at this lull in the action – then the Witch showed up on screen, an old woman in a tweed coat, wearing pince-nez glasses and carrying a very recognisable crooked walking stick. She had the shopkeeper's sky blue eyes, and they twinkled as she walked straight towards the camera and rapped twice with the head of the stick on the inside of the TV screen, speaking directly to him.

'Thieves never prosper,' she said in a voice more suited to uttering warnings about the full moon and misty moors. She cackled like a cartoon crone even as George ejected the tape from the machine and sat there for the longest time, breathing heavily and wondering whether he might not be going mad.

It was almost an hour before he could bring himself to run the tape again, and when he did he took care to fast forward through any scenes involving the Witch, which were, thankfully few. His day improved when he realised that the Weregoblins proved to a lusty bunch indeed, especially when the moon was right. George soon forgot his earlier funk as, with the willing participation of the eager redhead, all seven of the goblins took on the change again. Snow White serviced each of them in turn on the white feather bed while George got his jollies the only way he knew how.

By the time he had to stop on hearing Mrs Jenkins' car arrive in the driveway he was quite exhausted and wrung out with the exertion. He hadn't enjoyed himself so much in many years.

'Heavy boxes again?' she said with a sneer when he entered via the back door, but he did not rise to the bait. He discovered that he no longer cared whether she guessed at his secret; he still had half an hour of the movie to watch, and that was all that mattered now.

He awoke on that second night with the howls of the changed ringing in his ears again. And this time, the dream had come awake with him, for the shortest, most stout of the green warty figures was standing right there, at the end of the bed, a lascivious leer on its face. George tried to wipe the sight away from his eyes, twice before he realised this was no dream, but might well be another sign of his sanity unravelling. The thing – he realised that it smelled, damp and musty like wet dog – held out a stout length of rope towards George, and pointed at the snoring figure of his wife, running a too-long red tongue over wet, fleshy lips. Its intention was obvious, but Mrs Jenkins was no lithe young redhead. She had never figured in any way in any of George's fantasies, not even the most lurid ones, and George found himself faintly repulsed even at the thought of it.

'No,' he mouthed. 'Take me to the girl and the feather bed.'

The Weregoblin shrugged, shook his head and, between one blink and another, was gone as quickly as it had come, leaving George with only the lingering smell and worry, yet again, about the state of his sanity.

His sense of reality was to take another knock in the morning. He took himself off to the shed immediately after breakfast despite Mrs Jenkins protestations that the hoovering had not been done for several days and that there was a load of laundry in the hamper that somebody better have done before she got back from the shops. George ignored the implicit order.

When he got to the shed he slid the videotape back into the machine. He'd left it just as Snow White had lain down on the bed, and he was anticipating more bawdy action. But he'd dropped his guard in his eagerness, and the first thing to appear on the screen when the tube warmed up was the smiling face of the Wicked Witch. She, still looking unnervingly similar to the old shopkeeper, looked straight out of the screen at George. She held a large shiny red apple in one hand, and the crooked stick in the other.

'What's it going to be? Pain...' she wiggled the stick. 'Or pleasure?' she offered him the apple.

'Pain,' he whispered. 'Always pain.'

The Wicked Witch cackled and rapped twice on the inside of the screen with the stick.

'Pain it is then.'

The scene returned to where Snow White lay on the pure-white feather bed. The seven Weregoblins danced and capered around her as before, but this time there was a harder, colder, edge to their singing, and the girl was no longer quite so willing as the change came over the green warty beasts. Long snouts snarled, drool dripped, and as a full moon showed in a high window above the bed all seven howled their joy before they leapt as a pack. The feasting began on a bed that quickly turned red.

George was florid and flushed again when he met Mrs Jenkins in the kitchen.

'What are you grinning about? I see the hoovering's not done. Nor the washing?' were her first words before she noticed his condition. 'There must be an awful lot of heavy boxes in that there shed of yours. Or is it bad dreams again? You were moaning and groaning most of the night last night. You can kip on the couch downstairs if you're coming down with something, for I don't want it passing to me.'

It was the most she'd said to him in months, the most attention she'd paid to anything he'd done, but it was his turn for once not to listen. All George could think about as he watched her speak was the squat warty Weregoblin offering him the rope, the Wicked Witch offering pain, and the too white sheets of a feather bed, turning bloody red.

The thoughts wouldn't leave him. Images of ripping and tearing, biting and chewing occupied the inner screen of his mind even while the television showed soap opera characters bickering their way through their petty little lives and cookery shows detailed recipes that no one would ever cook. Mrs Jenkins soaked all of it up of course, for such material was the very bedrock and foundation of all of her conversations for the next day. George was relieved when she took herself off to bed.

He gave her half an hour to let the snoring start before making his own ablutions and joining her, creeping carefully into his side of the bed so as not to waken her.

The dream came almost as soon as he closed his eyes. In it he is not a voyeur, but one of the participants, a small hairy, drooling participant, lusting and thrusting and howling at the moon in a window high above a feather bed. He awoke, dragging the howls out of the dream, in a state of priapic tumescence.

All seven of the Weregoblins stood around the bed. As before the shortest, most stout of them held a length of rope in one hand and pointed at the sleeping Mrs Jenkins with the other. This time George showed no hesitation. He nodded, expecting to be allowed to stand to one side and watch. The stout green Weregoblin wasn't having any of that. As George got out of bed the rope was thrust into his hands.

'I can't do that,' he said. 'Even after all this time, she's still my wife.'

A voice came out of the darkness in the corner, a shadow so deep he could not peer into it.

'What's it going to be? Pain or pleasure?' he heard the Witch say, followed by the distinctive sound of the wooden stick rapping against the inside of the screen. He knew in his heart that he had made his choice, had made all of his choices, almost as long ago as that fateful marriage day.

He tied Mrs Jenkins down. She snored the whole time.

Even then he hoped that he might get to play the voyeur in this last act, but two raps, the sound of the crooked stick tapping on glass, reminded him that his choices had already been made. He winced when the stout Weregoblin bit him, hard, in the web of skin between his right thumb and forefinger, then howled as the change rushed through him in an orgasmic wave of glory. When the full moon rose in the window outside he howled along with the rest of the pack, then joined in the feasting.

When they were done the bed was as red as the one in his dreams, and Mrs Jenkins had long since stopped snoring. The change left him as quickly as it had come, leaving him gasping for breath and feeling completely unfulfilled.

'Pain. You promised pain,' he whispered.

He heard a chuckle in the darkest shadow, and as a cloud moved outside he saw moonbeams glint on both the pince-nez glasses and the one-eyed gaze of a camcorder mounted on a tripod in the corner.

'Pain it is then,' the Witch cackled.

The howling pack pounced.

The shopkeeper rang up 'No Sale' in the till, and carefully removed a black plastic box from an envelope that had a bloody stain along one edge. With his crooked stick tapping on the floor in time he took it over to the tall case and shelved it with the others, its spine out showing the title that was the last thing he read before the door swung shut on his collection.

'To Catch a Thief.'

SINGLE AND SPARKLY DOT COM

By

Theresa Derwin

Looking for Mr or Mrs Right?

Or even Mr Right Now?

Well, look no further –

Here at singleandsparkly.com, we do our very best to match you with a partner for all eternity.

So, if you want a date with a girl who likes to come out at night, a guy who loves to change for a night out under a full moon, or you just haven't found the right ghoul yet...

Give our unique dating site a whirl.

It's bound to be the date of your dreams. Or if you're lucky; your nightmares.

To create your account go to www.singleandsparkly.com

Terms and conditions apply.

T & C: we do not guarantee ....

"*DEAR MS JONES*

I am most disappointed with your computerised page, requiring me to input copious amounts of information regarding my personal..."

'Oh bloody hell, not again!'

The letter, handwritten erratic ink on yellowed parchment, made Penny's heart sink. If she didn't deal with this aristocratic oaf soon, she'd have a permanent migraine.

Penny used to get annoyed at the silver surfers who'd probably witnessed the birth of Methuselah – okay, she was exaggerating – but after ten years managing her faux-supernatural dating site, *singleandsparkly.com*, she'd learned a few tricks. Those tricks included how to translate the "dating" profiles of middle aged or older clients, as well as dealing with the ones who insisted on writing in. With pen and paper, no less. She'd build their profile online after a brief interview, and they'd be off; Penny would deal with the next stages, or Shona, her partner in matchmaking, would.

She was loathe to give her partner any extra work at the moment, though. Shona had been stressed as of late, with missed calls on her mobile from unknown numbers, and this had been going on for a few weeks now. Penny wondered if Shona had gained herself a stalker. It wouldn't surprise her, in this business, and after all, most men nowadays didn't seem to have a clue how to treat a woman right. How to be a gentleman – not the door opening, pay for dinner kind – but was it too much to ask for a guy who wasn't a Neanderthal?

As for their latest client, whose file she was currently going through, she was beyond annoyed with him, but at least the business could charge an extra fee.

Lachlan Sebastian Manfred Suc-Cour – *Count* Suc-Cour – ugh, had got on every last nerve she had, twisting her guts into tight knots whenever another of his wordy tomes arrived.

This letter was his *eighth*, for God's sake.

And so, he rambled on—

"... He is a cousin, twice removed, through marriage. Not exactly family, more a close friend of the family, if you will. Though not especially close, we communicate infrequently via letter. And when Marvin informed me of his impending nuptials; I decided that I too, might acquire a wife."

Acquire a wife?! Really? Penny slammed her fist down on the latest letter, pushing bright, cobalt blue curls away from her face.

Shona, sitting in the chair opposite her, was the epitome of a polite, stylish bespectacled 1950s housewife, complete with vintage dress – and the antithesis of Penny, who was more casual goth than business manager.

'Did you *read* this bit about "acquiring" a wife?' Penny squeaked.

'I did. I mean, *seriously*, what's he gonna do? Pop to Costco to get one?' Shona asked, then laughed at her own joke.

'I doubt it. Probably too expensive.'

Shona snorted again, her standard reaction to their problematic client.

Penny glared; she knew Shona enjoyed the way he riled her up. Some friend!

Sighing heavily, she glanced at the Count's file on-screen. All she seemed to do lately was work, and dealing with the "Count" added to her load – but at least she could cope with him.

Absorbed in his letters again, Penny didn't notice the other woman had popped out of the office until Shona returned with two coffees, dumping one mug on Penny's desk.

She took a tentative sip of coffee. Just right, she thought, thinking of Goldilocks' porridge dilemma.

'So, what you gonna do?' Shona finally asked.

Penny grinned, 'Charge him premium service,' she said, and Shona laughed.

God help the freaky old wannabe-vampire. She'd put twinkly gifs all over his profile page.

'Nice one. I'm off back to reception,' Shona said, grabbing the hefty file labelled 'Old Vampire Dude' and heading out for the front desk, mug in hand.

The next morning, Penny arrived at the office, bypassing the bland, grey and white reception area which Shona looked after, and groaned as she remembered the "Count What's-His-Name's" file waiting on her desk.

Replying to his many letters had not paid dividends so far, and she returned to the office this morning determined to finish his profile. Though he still hadn't provided a photo. Maybe he was butt ugly?

She was actually losing sleep over the guy. Last night she dreamt of a vampire – a tall, sexy, dark-haired, brooding vampire but still a bloody vampire. She'd woken up, tired and grumpy, mouth dry, breath gasping and more than a little excited, just as her imaginary

Drac had been nibbling on her neck.

Holy Twi-shite, she was loosing her grip.

He'd nuzzled his face against her shoulder and as he'd been about to bite, her eyes snapped open and she groaned, squirming as she realised she'd had an erotic dream about the guy who was driving her insane, and not in an "Oh, I'm crazy about you gorgeous," kind of way.

She needed to deal with the nutter.

It seemed she was going batty, pun intended. And more importantly, it was taking time away from valuable clients who were *actually* looking for something real; not some kinky, sparkly, fang-play.

To be fair to the idiot though, it was partly her fault.

After all, she'd used the "sparkly" schtick on their adverts in the newspapers and media, to appeal to the lonely goths and weirdos out there.

Everyone knew it was a marketing gimmick, meant to rake in business.

No one could be that deluded.

Penny sighed, opening up the folder to re-read the latest of his letters.

She took a swig of coffee, glanced at her phone and groaned as she realised it was after six in the evening and she still hadn't dealt with those letters.

Sighing, she opened up a Word file, and typed "Dear Count Suc-Cour"...

She tapped her fingers on her desk, trying to come up with a way to politely invite the guy for a discussion about his technical issues.

She didn't get very far, before a familiar curly red-head peeked around her door, looking as tired as Penny felt, but unlike her, in remarkably good humour for a change.

'I've got news,' Shona mumbled, almost gleefully, 'you have, er, a *visitor* in reception.'

'It's late. Who?' Penny asked, closing the document with another yawn.

That semi-erotic dream of last night had worn her out.

She gestured at Shona to continue. 'Go on then—'

'Count Suc-Cour'

'What?!?'

He'd turned up at their office? And, without an invite, she thought, snorting at that one.

'Count—' Shona began.

'I heard! Aargh!' Penny groaned, then, dropped her head on her keyboard. 'Bitey *McBite*-Face is *here*?'

''Fraid so,' Shona answered, 'what do you want me to do with him?'

'Kill him?' Penny replied.

'I would but—'

'Ugh! What's the old guy like, then?' she asked, sitting back up and accepting the inevitable. Another late night. She'd be lucky to be home by nine.

Shona answered only with a curious smile, and went to fetch the bane of Penny's life. On her return she held open the door to admit the figure behind her, 'May I present in *one* (said in a bad imitation of a Transylvanian accent) two, three – *Count* – Suc-Cour.'

Shona grinned, obviously pleased at her own bad joke.

Penny stood up, to gain a better vantage point – it was all about perception and power – and held her hand out ready to shake that of their visitor, and play *nice*, despite her feelings towards him. He was a customer, after all.

Her hand froze, mid-air, mouth open as if catching flies, as she took in the sight of the grumpy old "Silver Surfer" who was *not* remotely old, as his letters had suggested. He was, in fact, tall, dark and as delectable as a strawberry sundae – adding insult to injury, he looked to be only in his thirties.

Her first thought was – Oh. God.

Her second was – wait, why doesn't he know how to use the internet?

Quickly, she collected herself, cleared her throat and accepted the hand he offered as he sauntered into the room.

As her hand touched his smooth polished skin, a jolt of *something* zinged through her. He was manicured, damn him. And sexy to boot.

'Ah, thank you,' she croaked, clearing her throat again, 'for coming in. I was in the middle of replying to you.'

'My pleasure,' he said, a soft smile playing on his lips.

Reluctantly she withdrew her hand from his, her senses assailed with the decadent aroma of cinnamon, verbena and a hint of copper.

'Um, chair, chair,' she whispered, flustered, then said, 'please, sit down.'

The count was certainly easy on the eye.

She watched him pull out the chair opposite her desk and sit down, completely in command and comfortable with himself.

Why on earth did this guy need their services? she wondered briefly as she took her own seat, thankful for the desk that operated as a barrier between them. That dream had messed with her erogenous zones.

She registered Shona still standing at the door, grinning at them both, and sighed.

'Mr, Er *Count*, can I get you tea, coffee? Anything to drink?' she offered their guest.

'No thank you. I do not drink – coffee,' he intoned. Shona darted out of the room, hand clapped over her mouth in an attempt to mask her bubbling laughter as a coughing fit.

Penny tried to ignore the boisterous snorts of her friend in the other room. She wasn't going to complain about anything that cheered Shona up right now, given the weird phone calls. Shona had also mentioned thinking she'd been followed home last night. That was beginning to sound serious, and something would have to be done about it. The police, maybe?

She pulled her attention back to her client.

'Well now, I can hardly call you Count, so—'

'Lachlan,' he said, his dark chocolate, brooding eyes peering into hers.

She gulped, cleared her throat again, and asked him what in the hell he'd been thinking of, sending in numerous letters on old parchment instead of picking up the phone or using the website like any other *normal* person.

'I am afraid, Ms Jones, – may I call you Penny?'

'Yes.'

'Well, Penny, I am afraid that I am not *au fait* with modern technology. My family is an *old* one.'

'I get that, but let's cut to the chase. How can I make this simple for all of us?'

She figured it was easier to play along with this façade until she got to the bottom of this guy.

She shook her head to clear away images of his bottom in tight-fitting black trousers, the bottom she'd glimpsed as he took his seat.

His lips quirked up and she flushed bright red. For a second there she could have sworn he'd guessed her thoughts.

'Penny. Thank you, firstly, to your partner—'

'Shona.'

'Yes, Shona, the delightful young lady who invited me here.'

'Sorry?' Penny asked, suddenly confused.

'Yes,' tall, dark and munch-able replied. 'When you replied to my last letter, she popped a note in saying "You are more than welcome to visit our office and discuss your needs with Ms Jones."'

'You *WHAT*!'

Penny turned red again. But this time it wasn't embarrassment. It was annoyance. OK, she had planned on inviting him herself, but that was no reason for Shona to go behind her back... and not bother to tell her!

She was about to run out to yell at her friend, but she was halted mid-stand by Lachlan grasping her hand.

'Wait.'

She knew a command when she heard one, and paused instantly.

Heat flooded through her and she dropped back into the chair, a cloud of calm suddenly settling over her.

She had no idea where that sense of comfort had come from, but *still*, she stared at Lachlan, with suspicion.

There's no way he could – *no*. Don't be stupid. You're just hormonal.

Even so, Lachlan appeared to be smirking at her.

She huffed out a loud, long breath of air to release the tension, and wiggled her hand out of his.

'Right. Back to *business*. How exactly may I help you?'

Lachlan sighed, a sudden air of yearning in his expression.

'I have been running for years,' he said, those dark, smouldering eyes peering into her blue ones, 'from – well, certain people,' he added, voice strained, 'and, the thing is—'

He took a moment to centre himself, before continuing.

'The thing is. We do not need to run any longer, I – and my family. So, I wish to find a mate.' The way he said "mate" sparked a memory inside of her. Something she'd read in a few bad romance novels that involved werewolves and stuff. The pulp that Shona loved reading. *Was he for real?*

Despite her belief that it was all a joke, or that he was insane – which would be a damned shame considering he came in such a nice package – she was hooked on his words. Like saying the word "mate" breathed power into the night.

'And?'

'And, your website says, and I quote, "If you want a date with a girl who likes to come out at night, a guy who loves to change for a night out under a full moon or you just haven't found the right ghoul yet..." I assume this also pertains to vampires? Yes?'

'Uh. Nunh—'

'Miss Jones?'

Nothing.

'Penny?'

There was genuine concern in his voice. How nice.

"Haha. I... unh... I..."

She was trying her best to hold in the mixture of amusement and alarm which threatened to erupt any moment. Vampires didn't exist. There's no way they could!

'Penny! You will calm down!'

His voice penetrated the confusion that had engulfed her.

Slowly she shook her head and recovered herself, to find the Count (Oh God, oh God, ohgod) staring at her intently.

'Better?' he asked.

'Oh yes, thank you,' she said, between breaths, 'A real vampire. Wait 'til I tell Shona!'

She made to stand up, desperate to go fetch her friend, but Lachlan stilled her again, one hand on hers.

'Shona isn't important right now.' He sounded hurt, angry even, eyebrows furrowed. 'I came here in good faith—'

Almost reluctantly, Penny took her hand back. 'You read the terms and conditions, right?'

Lachlan looked perturbed. 'Of course – *not*. No one reads those.'

'Aah.'

'What does that have to do with my finding a mate?'

Sighing, Penny explained about teenage films with sparkly vampires, and how their site was only meant to hook up fans of goth and horror films. None of it was real. It was a marketing ploy.

'An advert, really,' she finished. Flushing as though she felt his embarrassment – then his profound disappointment.

'*Crap*,' she whispered, 'you're really alone, aren't you?'

She didn't know where that thought had come from. Somewhere in her foggy brain, and in his cold, empty gaze, she felt it – an intense loneliness surging through her, a knife stabbing through her heart. She'd always been a touch empathic, which was why she'd chosen the romance business, but this was something so much more. His need was cloying, his heartache palpable.

'I'll help you,' she said, shaking her head, surprised at her own decision.

Even vampire-wannabes (or vampires her inner mind squealed) *deserved* a chance at love.

After watching Lachlan and his delightful bum leave the offices, Penny told Shona that she'd agreed to have a private consultation with him the next night.

Shona had shot her a knowing smile at that one.

'Private, huh?'

'It's not like that,' she'd protested, thinking of those dark eyes of his, the broad set of shoulders.

'I think the lady doth protest too much,' Shona answered, grabbing her coat, then rummaging around in her handbag for her bus pass.

She was still rifling through the bag by the time Penny had finished locking up the rest of the office and turning off the lights.

'Have you seen my scarf?' she asked, as Penny reached her desk in reception. 'The Dior?'

'The cream and black one?'

'Yes!'

'No, sorry. Is it at home maybe?'

Shona went suddenly pale, and dropped into her seat. She was visibly shaking.

'Shona?'

Penny crouched next to her, laying a hand on hers, and tried to think what to do.

For some odd reason she suddenly remembered Shona's ex-boyfriend, Nick, and something clicked inside. Yeah, he'd been really possessive, one of the many reasons Shona had dumped him a couple of months ago.

Maybe these problems weren't down to some unknown stalker. It might well be that git Nick, trying to unnerve her friend.

If it was him, he was succeeding.

'Do you think maybe Nick took it?'

A stray tear fell on Shona's cheek, 'I don't know! Maybe.'

'Right, we're calling the police.'

'No, it's not... not that bad.' Shona hesitated. 'Let's talk in the morning, then perhaps I'll report it.'

'Yeah,' Penny snorted, sure now that Shona's no good-ex was the one behind the weird calls and the missing scarf. 'Now I think it's you who protests too much.'

Penny's knees cracked as she stood up, went through her own

rucksack, and took out a tissue for her friend.

Once Shona had calmed down enough, they left the building, Penny locked up behind them, and walked Shona to meet her Dad who was waiting at the bus stop across the road as usual. Penny was relieved that he wasn't willing to allow his daughter to travel the streets alone these days.

'See you tomorrow,' she said, then 'Bye John,' waved at the two then turned round to get her own bus.

She didn't see the figure round the corner, watching as Shona climbed on to the bus with her dad.

The next day, for some unfathomable reason, Penny was buzzing with excitement.

She got to the office about ten, early for her. She'd always been a night owl. But there was no sign of Shona.

Maybe she'd needed a lie in after all the worry – and then having to think about Nick again.

Penny had half a mind to try and investigate the damn calls herself. She was pretty good with tech and had a knack for finding out things. She'd get the full details from Shona when she came in, and sort this mess out.

By midday, and still no Shona, Penny had moved from sending querying texts to panicked texts.

By one, she was phoning every half hour. It was dialling out.

That was it. With no replies from Shona, she would have to go to the house.

A heavy lump sat in her belly as she dealt with the minimal work queries to keep the business ticking over and logged off the computer. She grabbed a notepad, scrawling "Closing early due to emergency – back tomorrow" in marker pen, and rummaged through Shona's desk until she found the Blu-Tack.

Just as Penny was about to lock up, Lachlan entered the office.

Thank God. Relief flooded through her as soon as she saw him, knowing, despite all logic, that there was something about him which was important. She didn't know what, but she thanked the fates for their timing.

She needed his help.

Seeing the worry etched on her features, he strode over and gripped her shoulders.

'Tell me, what is it?'

'Shona,' she answered.

As she pressed against him, Lachlan inhaled the aroma of strawberries and cream that wafted from the soft strands of her vibrant blue hair. But he needed to focus on the missing girl, so he forced himself to move away from the closeness of her body, and listened to her explanation about Shona's harasser.

Creatures such as that were vile, and disgusted him.

In his day – well – men were much the same, if he were honest with himself, though they had better manners.

He sat Penny down while he fetched his car. He was grateful more than ever now that this Shona had sent him that invitation to visit the office. He'd never have otherwise progressed from sending letters.

He might never have built up the courage.

Whilst it was Penny who called to him, he thought as she exited the building and climbed into the passenger seat of his car, he liked her friend. He would see no harm befall her.

Penny gave directions and he followed them, arriving at Shona's building thirty minutes later.

He parked the car and followed Penny up to the front door.

Penny apparently had an emergency key to her friend's home – though they rarely met there, he'd been told. Something about Shona's house giving her migraines.

She unlocked the front door and walked in ahead of him.

As soon as he approached the open door, he could hear the empty stillness of the house.

Entering after Penny, Lachlan stopped instantly, a small gurgled scream escaping as he saw the most terrifying sight.

Oh, the *horror*!

Penny's equally horrified expression met his.

They were assaulted by the living room décor, swamped by a forest of lime and puce tropical leaves and ghastly flora. The room was scattered with yellow and blue furniture, and old painted, wooden bookshelves.

Worse of all, the tattered spines of the books on those shelves all had titles like *Act of Passion* or *My Bear Behind*. And they'd been read – thoroughly.

After a second's worth of shuddering, he followed Penny through the deadly living room, and into the bedroom.

To him, it appeared as if someone had projectile vomited candy floss in there. Swathes of putrid-bubblegum pink decorated walls, duvet covers, pillows, scatter cushions and even the curtains. He was no decorator, but he appeared to be in a hellish world of colour, which Penny solemnly informed him was a plethora of Cath Kidston mixed with vintage cream and – *more pink* – chintz.

And the most awful thing of all? A massive cat castle – the designer version of a cat tree apparently – minus a cat.

But that wasn't what got his attention.

There was a strange chemical scent in her bedroom. Something – *off*.

He scanned the room, looking for clues, halting when he spotted a mug on the bedside table.

He strode towards it, crouched down and inhaled the stagnant coffee – the bitter scent of caffeine mingling with the clinical and potent aroma of the sedative it had been laced with.

He was no doctor, but he knew enough about drugs from his years of surviving.

Her friend had been taken.

'What is it?' Penny asked, interrupting his thoughts.

'She was drugged.'

Penny gasped, eyes wide.

He stood, then rested one hand on her shoulder, to reassure her. 'But I promised I'd find her and I will.'

'*We* will,' she growled in response.

'Good. Do you have any idea—'

'Yes!' she answered, before he could finish. 'Hold on...'

Trying not to panic, Penny went back into the living area, plonked herself down on the sofa and started rifling around behind cushions, 'til her hand finally grasped the device she hoped Shona had, yet again, forgotten to put away properly.

'Bingo!'

She pulled out Shona's iPad, blew away dust and cat hair from the sofa and tapped in Shona's password.

'What is it you are doing?' Lachlan asked, perplexed.

'You wanted computer lessons? Well, here's your crash course. How to find your stalker 101.'

He watched mesmerised, as her fingers danced across the keyboard dragging up social media accounts, maps, search engines, then what looked to be her own website.

She stopped typing, clapped her hand to her mouth and gasped, as she scrolled through dozens of messages on Shona's account. Each message progressively more irate;

"Why are you ignoring me?" "Shona. Are you there?" "Please, just let me talk to you." "You can't treat me like this you bitch!" "No one leaves me like that, you just wait!"

And so on.

Messages Shona hadn't told her about.

Had she been embarrassed? Or thought she deserved this?

No one deserved this sort of harassment.

She cleared her thoughts and attacked the keypad once more, continued to search until she found what she needed.

'Got you you little bastard!'

'A result?'

'Oh yes!'

Penny's eyes looked half manic, with just a glimmer of tears in view.

'Tell me where we are going,' he said, and she gave him the address.

Heart thumping loudly in her chest, echoing her fear, Penny followed Lachlan to his car, her hands shaking as she tried to put her seat belt on.

'Breathe,' Lachlan said, his hand briefly touching hers and then locking the seat belt.

She did as he'd instructed, forced herself to calm down. She'd be no good to Shona otherwise.

She rifled through her handbag and pulled out her phone, opening the "maps" app.

It took less than fifteen minutes for them to get to the flat where Nick Pachinko was living, according to his Facelife account. Penny called out directions as Lachlan drove way over the speed limit.

She didn't really care at this stage. She just needed to find Shona.

If Lachlan hadn't arrived... Penny had no clue what instinct left her waiting for him, rather than calling the police. Maybe the stupid 24 or 48 hr rule.

Lachlan spun the car into a parking space and climbed out of the car, a familiar bleep sounding as he locked it after Penny jumped out.

'There,' she said, pointing to Nick's ground floor flat. 'I think.'

He hurried to the front door, surprising her with how fast he could walk and pulled what looked like a lock picking kit from his breast pocket.

'You're quick for your age,' she huffed, as she stopped just behind him. She watched over his shoulder as he worked at the lock.

'My dearest, I am only a hundred and five!' he replied, and she couldn't help but laugh.

'God, old man, just pulling your leg,' she answered. Then mumbled under her breath, '*your geriatric leg.*'

'Did I ever tell you,' he said, as he finally chivvied the lock with a resounding click and pushed the door open, 'that vampires have excellent hearing? *No?* Thought not. Wait here.'

'No.'

'Please, just a moment.'

She relented with a sigh.

He was tall, well built, and as annoying as it was, she knew he'd fare better in a fight than she would.

She heard a crash, a welp, a low growl and what sounded like furniture toppling over. Patience running low she growled herself, pushed open the door fully and walked into the darkened living room. The sight that greeted her stopped her dead in her tracks.

Lachlan was holding a six-foot-plus man, up against the wall with just one arm; the man squirmed about a foot off the floor. His meaty legs dangled like a string of chunky sausages, his face red from pain. And yes, that was Nick Pachinko – she recognised him from a photo on Shona's phone.

Boy, Lachlan is strong, she thought, admiring his physique for a fleeting moment. He was barely breaking a sweat, his one arm effortlessly bearing the weight of a nineteen stone man with blood on his t-shirt.

Blood? She gasped, barely aware she'd made the sound until Lachlan turned his face round and snarled, eyes flashing deepest black, then back to brown. 'I'll be with you in a second, Penny,' he said, flashing a row of sharp, dripping fangs.

He stared at the man for just a second or two, and the guy stopped squirming and just hung there, limply.

'What do you want me to do with him?' Lachlan asked Penny.

Lachlan looked ready to kill Pachinko, but, he wasn't worth it. Wasn't worth the trouble they might get into.

'He has to stop harassing Shona. And send him away. Please. If she sees him...'

Lachlan nodded, expression sombre. Turning back to the poor excuse for a man, he said, 'You are never to bother Shona again. Do you understand?'

The guy squeaked out 'Yes,' voice constricted by Lachlan's tight grip, and no doubt weak from blood loss.

She could now see a tear along his throat; the gash showing ripped flesh and blood splattered on his skin.

At the man's answer, Lachlan dropped him as if he were a lumpy sack of potatoes.

'Go, then, worm!'

As Pachinko crawled towards the open door, Lachlan turned to Penny. She was still standing there, staring at him, open-mouthed.

'I fear I have some explanations to give,' he said.

'Ya think?'

'But first, you need to see this,' he said, gesturing for her to follow. 'Your friend is here, and unharmed.'

Locking away her shock – though she was surprised by her lack of fear, despite what she'd seen – she followed Lachlan's broad figure as he strode into a small, dingy bedroom, which smelled of days-old pizza, rank sweat and spilled booze.

After Shona's pink nightmare, this was a nightmare on a whole new level.

She took in the rank odour of the room, and the sight of Shona sitting up, arms stretched outwards, tied to an unmade bed. She was gagged, and tears streamed down her face.

Penny took this all in instantly.

Any sympathy she'd had for the man Lachlan had – *bit?* – well, that had evaporated at the dishevelled state of the normally perfectly -turned out Shona.

Ignoring Lachlan, who was prying open a small cage by the side of the bed, she dashed to her friend, pulling at the strips of old t-shirts Nick had used to tie her up.

The second the gag was off, Shona coughed loudly, gagging like she was going to throw up, gasping 'Water.'

Before she could blink, Lachlan was gone, then back just as suddenly with a glass of cold water which he handed to Penny rather than Shona.

Penny passed it to her friend, watching her gulp greedily until she let out a relieved huff of air.

Taking the glass away and placing it on the bedside table, she engulfed Shona in her arms as she rubbed soothing circles across her back until Shona hiccuped and finally began to sob.

Penny held her and glanced at the vintage black and red 1950s dress she wore. It was dirty, and ripped, but at least she still wore it.

'Shh, you're safe,' Penny kept whispering, holding her tight. 'You're safe now.'

Lachlan finally ripped off the pet-sized cage door, dropping it on the floor with a clang. Bending down, he reached in and grabbed the yowling, ball of ginger and white fur with claws.

He put the screeching cat over his shoulder, and, watching Penny's actions, copied the same soothing circles on the furball until it stopped meowing like it was starving. There was no evidence of cat food in the small cage, only a litter tray and water bowl.

He actually found holding the annoying animal, quite comforting – until his shoulder was suddenly rather wet.

Lachlan groaned as the cat peed on him, marking its territory.

'Really?' he asked, voice laced with humour.

'Meow Meeeooow.' The tone seemed to translate as 'If you'd been stuck in that bloody cage all day...' He wasn't sure, he didn't speak feline.

'Fair enough,' he said, apparently deeming it a reasonable response.

Cats were not his animal to call, so he had no power over them, but as a rule, he quite liked them – even the ones that shifted back into irritating humans.

They were however, arrogant, possessive and occasionally playful – in between eating and sleeping.

This one though, there was something familiar about this cat.

Familiar. That was it.

He chuckled, and rubbed the cat's fur again.

'Now now, Mr Cuddlebum—'

'Yeeooow!!!'

'Ha, okay, *Finn*, if you prefer.'

'Meow.'

'No worries, *Finn* – I expect a favour though, in return.'

Finn/Mr Cuddlebum, nudged his furry head against Lachlan's chin in thanks.

Oh, this will be such fun to watch, he thought, wondering how it would pan out when young Shona discovered the true nature of her cat.

That thought was interrupted as the hefty ginger tom started meowing loudly and scrabbling up his shoulder to escape.

'Cuddlebum!'

Lachlan turned round to find Shona recovered, arms outstretched and eager to hug her feline friend. He gratefully handed her the cat.

Shona sighed in relief as Mr Cuddlebum settled into her arms. A deep rumbling purr vibrated through his body, signalling his contentment.

OMG, Penny thought, Shona's cat was adorable – if in need of a good helping of kitty lettuce. Though this was so not the right time to tell her friend that. She was just relieved they'd found them both.

That horrible man – seriously in need of a wash and a shave – was going to feel her wrath if he ever went near Shona again. Not that he was likely to. After all, Lachlan Suc-Cour had put the fear of God in him.

Speaking of which, they needed to talk.

The great lump of a cat had taken on calming duties with Shona, so Penny stood up and walked over to where the – *vampire? Really?* – stood by the bedroom window, looking out at the night time sky. He seemed to be brooding, she thought.

'Lachlan?'

He turned towards her, and she was again immediately struck by how handsome he was.

Her heart fluttered, breath caught in her throat as she tried to say what she knew she felt. What she knew was right.

It was like she was standing, exposed, on a railway track as a freight train sped towards her, demanding action. Jump, or meet the danger zooming towards her. It – whoa, that danger could just be the excitement she needed.

Before she could speak, he was on her – mouth meeting hers, his teeth nibbling at her lips, breath coming in gasps, a tidal wave of *rightness* crashing into her. Her whole body quivered in response to his tongue. The kiss lasted less than a minute, but it set everything in her on fire.

She sighed as he withdrew his mouth from hers and his hand reached up to touch her cheek.

'I'm sorry Penny, I couldn't—'

'Help yourself?' she asked, then chuckled. 'So, it's true then?'

'Yes. I am a vampire. For that, I do not apologise. For kissing you without asking, well...'

She barked out a laugh, then briefly leant up to kiss his cheek.

'Can't say I'm not surprised,' she said, 'but hey. At least I can open up the business to other vampires. If they exist.'

'Oh, they do.'

'Wow, that's – I have so many questions!'

'And I shall answer them.'

'Good. Do you *eat*? As in food – not stalkers.'

It was his turn to laugh.

'I do. Dinner then?'

'Yes, but—'

'Your friend comes first. I understand.'

Penny nodded, a smile on her lips, and pecked him on the cheek one more time, before leaving him and sat beside Shona, who was still snuggling Mr Cuddlebum on the less than hygienic bed of her psychotic ex boyfriend.

'Let's get you out of here, Shona. Yeah?'

Shona nodded, and stood up. She seemed wobbly, but happy to be standing on her own two feet again.

'Where did Nosferatu go?'

Penny glanced round the room. Yes, Lachlan had done a disappearing act. Along with Shona's Stalker, she noticed with satisfaction as they headed out through the living area.

A few nights later, after Shona had taken some time off to rest, and Penny had watched Lachlan burn his letters asking for a *wife*, he shared the sofa in her office, snuggled up next to his Penny. He stole occasional kisses from her as she introduced him to a film about teenage vampire hunters dressed in camouflage who spoke a very confusing language. He wasn't entirely sure what was happening in the film. He was too distracted by her scent, so close to him. The delicious smell was burned into his brain.

He was still inhaling her perfume as Penny yanked away from him, breathless, at a loud explosion of shattering glass from the front office.

Next thing he knew there was a scream and Shona crashed into the office, red-faced.

'Oh my God!' Shona screeched, both hands held up to her cheeks – a grim parody of the old "Scream" painting, Lachlan thought.

Penny left his embrace and pulled her partner into a hug, just as the girl started to sob.

"What is it, Shona?"

'Please, dearest, allow me.' He stood up, next to them in an instant.

Taking one of Shona's hands in his, he gently rubbed warmth back into it – ironic considering his own body held little warmth itself.

Shona was clearly in shock, so he put everything he could into nurturing her calm.

'I can see what you saw – if you let me,' he murmured.

'Just do it,' Shona said, between gritted teeth, granting him permission.

Lachlan continued to rub soothing circles on her hand, as his mind delved into hers, a shark swimming beneath the surface of her memories.

He winced, as the images flashed into his head.

Shona had been editing the website, as the man walked into their – thankfully – mostly empty office, her headphones on, as she chair-bopped to the charts.

A sallow, thin man, apparently in his early twenties – one of those goth lads, Shona had thought – stumbled into their office, two words escaping his lips before all hell had broken loose.

'Please! Help,' he'd moaned, falling to his knees.

And then he'd *whistled*.

Lachlan watched the man's lips purse, but heard no sound.

It was the shattering of the window in reception that told him what the man was.

Lachlan had heard the hounds of Hell, and the howl of a werewolf in his many years; yet he had never heard the sound that had destroyed the front room.

The poignant, anguished whistle of the Shadmock.

Lachlan saw Shona rip off her headphones and grab her keyboard, pulling it loose from its moorings. Within seconds, she had whacked the poor creature over the head, knocking it unconscious, her own scream rising as the creature fell and she saw the damage it had done.

His cold heart beat faster at the sight of the fallen Shadmock. There might still be time...

Lachlan withdrew slowly from Shona's mind, instructing her to sleep, then carried her over to the spare sofa, laying her down.

'What the actual?!' Penny asked, staring at her vampire.

'I'll explain,' Lachlan said, 'but first, put on your headphones. And oh, looks like we have our first paying customer of the... unusual kind!'

'Great! I'll get the duct tape, shall I?' Penny said, heading for the filing cabinet at the back of the room.

Lachlan laughed.

Yes, despite it all, his Penny could make him laugh, even in the midst of chaos, sex – and shadmocks.

FETCH!

By

Pauline E. Dungate

ALL CLUBS NEED some kind of security, even one like the Monster Club. I know you've heard of it even if you don't know exactly what kind of clientele party there. I don't advise ordinary humans to make it their first choice for a late night rave, not unless they are at least half out of their skulls before arriving. It's not that it's a dangerous place to visit but that the patrons are on the weird side. I mean, seriously weird.

Me, I'm Jack. I'm in security. The old fashioned kind. You have a problem like unwelcome entities casing your joint – me and Dash will sort it for you. Dash is my dog. He's a labradoodle, a hybrid of two kinds of retriever and there are times when I think he's the more intelligent one of the partnership.

I got the call from the Monster Club on a Monday in that hiatus between All Souls Eve and Guy Fawkes Day. Would I meet Theobold after dusk that night? Not a problem. Most of our work is at night. This was a little different.

The club hadn't opened when we got there – in fact most of the patrons would be barely out of their beds. Most people are unaware that they share their world with supernatural beings and would prefer to keep it that way if they had a choice. We all know the reputation vampires and ghouls have and there are other, usually peaceable, creatures out there as well. Those in London tend to gravitate to the Monster Club for company of their own kind and the freedom to be natural rather than hiding in shadows.

The entrance is inconspicuous down a gloomy flight of steps between two restaurants – an oyster bar and an Indian Take-away. Theobald opened the door for us before taking us along a dark twisting passage to a brightly lit reception area. Dash looked up at him and sniffed, pointedly running his tongue over his lips before sitting at my feet. He'd recognised that Theobald was a vampire.

'What seems to be the problem?' I asked.

'It is difficult to tell,' Theobald said. 'I close up in the morning making sure all the patrons have left but next evening things have been moved or have disappeared. I know someone has been here. I want you to find out who it is.'

'When did the first incident happen?'

'Right after All Souls Eve. There had been a party here. I initially expected I had missed a client when I closed up. I took extra care the next night, and there was greater evidence of some kind of infestation.'

I glanced at Dash. 'You want us to patrol in the daytime?'

'Yes. And dispose of whatever it is.'

'Naturally.'

Next morning Dash and I arrived as the last of the clients were leaving. Most of them needed to be sure they were in their accommodations before the first hint of sunrise. Theobald let us in and made himself scarce. We would have the place to ourselves.

The first thing we did was explore. The main room was laid out with round tables covered with what had been white cloths at the start of the evening. Spillages are inevitable and I knew that the red stains were not wine. I was sure they would be changed before the club opened in the evening. Dash was more interested in the kitchen and its walk in cold-room than I was but then he is a strict carnivore. There were facilities and refreshments for humans as clients sometimes brought enlightened guests. I found a half-decent bottle of beer and settled at a table where I could view the stage occupying the opposite side of the room to the bar. If there was an intruder, Dash would spot it first.

On the stroke of noon, Dash's ears began to twitch. I sat still, waiting. Then in a darkened corner of the room I saw her. She looked to be about twelve years old and she glowed. Dash yawned and stood up. This was not an entity to be feared. He wandered over to her and she crouched down to pet him – something he didn't often allow.

'Nice doggy,' she said. Her hands on his fur were translucent.

'What is your name?' I asked.

'Minette. Is this your dog?'

'We work together. His name is Dash. I'm Jack. Shouldn't you be at home, Minette?'

Minette sighed. 'I can't go home. She won't let me.'

'Who won't let you?'

'The other Minette.'

I studied her carefully. Dash almost seemed to be smiling. 'Tell me about the other Minette.' I said.

Minette climbed up onto one of the chairs and rested her elbows on the table. The girl started to tell her story.

Minette lived in a secluded village on the edge of the South Downs. If she climbed to the top of the hill, she could almost see the sea. She lived with her mother in a small cottage by the church. She didn't know who her father was but her mother always said he was in the churchyard whenever she was asked. Minette assumed that meant he was dead. Since she was old enough to read, she'd wandered between the headstones reciting the names and wondering which belonged to her father. It had to be one of the newer ones, she thought. It was a nice game to play, imagining what the people buried there were like.

As she grew up she discovered that she could almost become invisible. In school, if she didn't want to answer the teacher's questions she just sat very quiet and they didn't seem to notice her. It worked with bullies, too. If she stayed still and quiet, the nasty children would pass her by and pick on someone else instead. She didn't have any real friends but didn't feel the lack of them.

One day while sitting under the yew tree in the churchyard a group of boys from her class rushed under the lych gate laughing, pushing and shoving each other in a manner much too boisterous for her. She faded into the shadows as they sprawled over one of the raised tombs.

'I wouldn't want to come here at night,' one said, Thomas she thought his name was.

'Why not?' his friend Billy said. 'Scared it's haunted?'

'I've heard tales.'

'There's a ghost in the church,' a third boy, Jim, said.

'How do you know?' Billy asked.

'My sister's boyfriend's father saw it.'

'Bet he'd been to the pub.'

'Let's come back at midnight,' Alfie said. 'See it for ourselves.'

'I'd never get out at that time,' Thomas said.

Minette stopped listening. She knew about ghosts. They weren't as scary as other things that haunted the night. Her mother had told her stories about some of them – vampires, werewolves, ghouls. They were dangerous but ghosts couldn't hurt you. Minette believed her mother. She could see the churchyard from her bedroom window and had sometimes seen lights there. She didn't go there after dark. That was silly.

She watched that night to see if the boys did dare the churchyard but she didn't see anything. Most likely they had scared themselves before they got there.

Even though they lived next to the church, Minette and her mother rarely went into it. Minette was curious, though. The next time there was a service there that wasn't a Sunday, she crept down to peer in. People had been arriving wearing pretty clothes. She noticed all the flowers decorating the space and she realised she was seeing a wedding. She sat in the shadows to watch the bride walk past with the man in a smart suit that could have been her father. Minette felt wistful. One day she might want to get married and there would be no father to walk her in.

As everyone's attention was on the bride she was able to sneak in and sit in the shadows behind a pillar. The service was beautiful and she thought she might like to see more, especially the flowers and the singing. She waited until everyone had left before she came out of her hiding place – she knew weddings were only for those who had been invited – and except on Sundays, the vicar kept the church locked. There had been some vandalism, she'd heard.

Now Minette took the opportunity to look around. The windows looked so much prettier from this side and the flowers filled the space with perfume. She stood in front of the altar and stared at the life-size image of the man hanging from the cross. Was it his ghost that haunted the church, or was he a vampire that the vicar had caught? Perhaps in the darkness he came alive. Minette had no fear of him as the sun was still high outside.

She walked around the edges of the church reading the plaques on the walls. A lot of people seemed to have either been brave or given money to look after the building. The floor was made of stone slabs. Some of them looked like the headstones outside but laid flat. The one nearest the altar had a bronze drawing inlaid into it. Minette knelt down to look closer, tracing her finger in the grooves.

'Seems a shame to waste beauty on the dead,' a voice said behind her.

Startled, she swivelled round and looked up at the man standing there. He shimmered in the coloured light from the stained glass of the windows.

'I – I'm sorry. I didn't mean to intrude. It was just such a lovely wedding.'

He laughed. 'You are not intruding, little one. I don't get much company these days. Not since the vicar started locking the doors.'

'Who are you?' she asked.

'Matthew Kittery. Who are you?'

'Minette Armstrong.' She looked down at her feet and noticed where she was standing, and the name on the commemoration. 'Oh! I'm standing on one of your ancestors.'

He laughed again. 'No. The coffins are in the crypt. It would be disrespectful for parishioners to walk on the graves.'

'Is it spooky in the crypt?'

'No. Would you like to see?'

Minette wasn't sure. Teachers were always warning about strangers, but this man didn't feel like a stranger. He had a nice laugh. She thought he might be what they called good looking. The idea of going into the crypt with him was a bit scary. The boys at school wouldn't dare – they hadn't even turned up in the churchyard at midnight. If she went, she could prove that she was braver than them. 'Okay,' she said.

She took his hand. It was cool. She followed him to a doorway beside the altar. Beyond the arch were steps going down. They went down a twisting staircase which opened into a stone-flagged room.

'Is this the crypt?' she asked. No coffins were visible and it felt slightly damp rather than scary. She looked around for the lights and saw a row of bulbs along one wall. None of them were lit, but she could still see. She shrugged. She had always been good at seeing in the dark.

'This is part of the crypt,' Matthew said. 'Privileged families have rooms to themselves. The Kittery family crypt is over here.'

There was an iron grill blocking the archway he indicated. Peering through it, Minette could see shelves with coffins stacked on them. She thought she could detect an odd smell.

'Will they put you there one day?' she asked.

'They already did.' Matthew pulled a large metal key out of his pocket. 'Let me show you where I live.'

Now she was getting a bit nervous. Actually going in touching distance of the coffins didn't feel like a good idea. He must have sensed her anxiety as he said, 'They can't hurt you.'

The gate didn't make a single sound as it opened inwards. Matthew stepped through and began to walk up the aisle between the stacks. Part way along, he said, 'Are you coming?'

Minette hesitated. She was curious but she didn't want to be shut in here with dead bodies. She took a cautious step. Up ahead, Matthew had opened a door that she hadn't noticed before. Light streamed out of it making an illuminated path. She suddenly had this idea that if she stayed on that path she would be safe. She dashed along it.

The room beyond the door looked what she imagined an old-fashioned library looked like. The walls were lined with leather-bound books, their titles gleaming gold. She was too far away to read any of them but she thought she could smell the paper. There were two big armchairs and – a piano! Minette wondered how Matthew could have got that down there.

'Do you live here?' she asked.

'Do you like it?' he asked.

'It's – it's comfortable.' She looked around thinking he wanted her to like it better than she did. She noticed some pictures on the piano. She went for a closer look and frowned.

'Why have you got a picture of my mum?' she asked.

Matthew picked up the framed photograph. 'Is this your mother?'

Minette nodded.

'Is she still as beautiful?'

She took a step away from him. 'Do you know her?'

'Once, a long time ago.' He looked a little sad.

'We only live next to the church. You could come and see us,' Minette said.

Matthew shook his head. 'I cannot leave the church.'

'Why not? It's easy when the door is open.' She chewed her lip. 'We'd better go before the vicar comes back. I don't want to get locked in here.'

She took his hand and started towards the door. Reluctantly, Matthew let her lead him through the crypt and up the stairs. When they reached the door of the church, Minette stepped outside. His hand faded from her grasp. She glanced back at him and saw his body had become translucent. He was fading. When he took a step back into the shelter of the building his form solidified again.

She would have gone back in if the vicar hadn't rounded the corner at that moment.

'Run along, Minette,' he said. 'I have to lock up.'

Minette caught a glimpse of Matthew in the shadows before she turned away.

At tea that evening, Minette asked her mother. 'Do you know someone called Matthew Kittery?'

Her mother went very still before asking, 'Where did you hear that name?'

'There's a brass thing on the floor of the church with that name on it,' she said. 'And there was a man who said that was his name.'

'Where did you meet him?'

'In the church. He said he knew you.'

'The Matthew Kittery I knew is dead,' her mother said firmly. 'I don't want you talking to strangers.'

'Yes, mum.'

'And stay out of the church.'

If Minette had been a more obedient child she might have obeyed her mother but she was curious. It was two weeks before she was able to slip back inside the church. The vicar had been conducting a funeral service and when he led the mourners to the prepared grave she merged with the shadows and headed for the stairs down to the crypt. The gate when she got there was locked. She took hold of the bars and shook them. 'Matthew! Are you there?' she shouted.

There was silence except for the scratchy claws of a rodent on stone. She was about to call again when a voice said, 'Were you looking for me?'

Startled, she turned to see Matthew's form glowing in the corner. She could see the outline of the stones behind him.

'I thought you weren't here,' she said.

'Where else would I be?'

'Dunno. Are you dead?'

'In a way.'

'You're a ghost then. Is that why you got stuck in the church?'

Matthew smiled. 'I used to get a lot more visitors. I get lonely now, with the vicar locking the doors. And your mother hasn't been to see me for a long time. Will you visit me?'

'Maybe. Better go before the vicar locks the door.' Minette ran off, back to the light, not sure whether having a ghost as a friend was a good idea. Having a friend, though, was appealing.

It was two weeks before she made up her mind. It was mostly the thought of the room in the crypt that drew her. All those books. She wanted to read them all. She started to sneak in during the Sunday services, unnoticed if she kept to the shadows, treading softly so as not to make a sound on the stairs – not that anyone was likely to hear her with the organ playing. Matthew seemed to like having her there. Sometimes they talked. He wanted to know all about her and what her mother was doing. He was most curious about that. Other times she sat and read. She didn't understand all the books but she did like the poetry.

'Your mother liked poetry, too,' Matthew said. 'Does she ever mention me?'

'No. She once said she knew someone with your name but he was dead.' Minette realised what she had said. 'Oh! You're dead. Did she mean you?'

'I think she did. I was very sad when she stopped coming.'

'How long ago was that?'

'About twelve years.'

'I'm twelve. Well nearly. Why are all your books old?'

'Because I can't go out and buy more.'

'I could bring you some.' She hesitated. 'I don't have any money so I'd have to borrow them from the library. They'd have to go back after four weeks, though.'

'You could come and live here with me.'

'I don't think so. Mum would miss me. She would have policemen looking for me. Do you eat?'

'I don't need to,' Matthew said. 'I'm a ghost, remember.'

'And I'm a girl. I need food. I couldn't stay here.'

'Then give me a lock of your hair to remember you.'

'Okay.'

Matthew cut a coil from where it wouldn't be noticed. 'You will keep visiting me, won't you?' he said.

'If I can.' When she ran out at the end of the service, Minette felt a bit scared. There had been a strange look in Matthew's eyes. She waited a couple of weeks before going back, and took a couple of library books as a kind of peace gesture.

'I was afraid I'd never see you again,' Matthew said.

'I like your books,' she said.

'Do you know what tomorrow is?' he asked.

She shrugged. 'End of October.'

'All Souls Eve. The one day I can leave the church. I would like to walk through the streets with you. You can show me your school and where you play, where you live.'

'Do you want to come home with me?'

He looked sad. 'I don't think that would be a good idea. Your mother might not like you meeting me.'

'Okay.' Minette was relieved at that. She didn't think her mother would be too happy either.

The next evening, Minette escaped the house after her tea. It was the school half-term and her mother wasn't too worried about her staying out a bit later. She'd told her a little lie that she was meeting a friend. She was, but not the school-friend her mother hoped.

Darkness had fallen when she met Matthew under the lych gate.

'How did you get out?' Minette asked. 'Didn't the vicar lock the church?'

'You are forgetting that I'm a ghost,' he said. 'I can walk through walls.'

'Oh.' She didn't have an answer to that. She took him on a tour of her town, showing him the places he wanted to see. He seemed very interested though since he was an adult, she wasn't sure.

When they arrived back at the churchyard he said, 'You can come and live with me now.'

'I've told you I can't. Mum will miss me.'

'No she won't. I've made arrangements.'

'What arrangements?' She wasn't sure she liked the sound of that.

'I'm claiming you.'

'What do you mean?'

'A father can claim his daughter on All Souls Eve.'

'You are not my father.' Minette shouted at him, appalled at the thought. She turned and ran across the churchyard.

Reaching home, she opened the back door – except that it wouldn't. It was stuck. Her mother would never lock the door until she was sure Minette was home. She knocked on it. No-one came. Frustrated, Minette walked round to the front. The light was on in the sitting room and the curtains partly open. She hoped her mother was in there and she could attract her attention to let her in. She was about to tap on the window when she noticed that there was someone else in the room with her mother, someone wearing the same clothes as she was.

The other person must have sensed her presence as she turned towards the window. She was wearing Minette's face.

Dash licked her hand.

'What did you do then?' I asked when she stopped talking and seemed about to cry.

'I ran. I must've got on a train 'cos I sort of ended up here.'

'How did you get in?'

'Through the door,' Minette said.

'Like a ghost walks through walls?'

She giggled. 'Don't be silly. I followed in someone's shadow.'

'How did you know to come here?'

'I didn't. I just sort of arrived. And I'm hungry. There isn't much to eat here. Only yucky blood stuff.'

'You want to go home?' I asked.

'Yes, please. But...' She hesitated. 'There's something wearing my face.'

'I think it's a fetch. What do you think, Dash?' I looked at my labradoodle. He stood up, his tail wagging like fury, eager to be off.

'What's a fetch?' Minette asked.

'A doppelgänger. A kind of double. You said Matthew took a lock of your hair.'

She nodded.

'Then I will need some of your hair.'

'How much?'

I smiled, hearing the worry in her voice. 'One strand.' I plucked it quickly before she had time to react and tied it to Dash's collar. 'Fetch!' I said.

Dash disappeared.

'What happens now?' Minette asked.

'We wait. Dash will bring the fetch back here. We neutralise it, then you can go back home.'

'Okay.'

It took Dash less than three hours to get there and back dragging the fetch with him and less than a minute to find the lock of Minette's hair. The fetch disintegrated into a heap of earth and stones.

I took Minette back to her home on the train. She chatted most of the way as, recovered from her adventure, she regained the ebullience of a twelve-year old. It was only as we passed the church that quietness crept over her. She took my hand and held it tightly.

'He won't try to steal me again, will he?' she asked.

'I will make sure that he won't,' I said.

'How? He will still be in there.'

'Dash is quite good at fetching things other than fetches. I will talk to Matthew and if he bothers you again just let me know.'

'How?'

'A letter to the Monster Club will find me.'

'Is that where we were?'

'Yes.'

'Are you a monster?'

I laughed. 'No more than you are.'

When we got to the path leading to the back door of her house, we stopped. 'Mum will wonder where I've been,' she said.

'Just say you've been playing and forgot the time.'

'It's been three days.'

'Not for your mother. Remember, she would have thought the fetch was you.'

Reassured, she patted Dash, the turned away. I watched her run up the path into the house next to the churchyard.

Once she had gone safely inside, I looked down at Dash. I said, 'Ghoman's are rare creatures. We need to make sure this one is safe.'

He looked up at me, tongue hanging out of his mouth. 'Now we go have a word with the one who made the fetch,' I told him.

He trotted off in the direction of the church and I followed, circling the building in search of a way in. The small, vestry door at the side furthest from the graves was shadowed by the trees hanging over the cemetery wall. Dash sat in front of the door and when I tried the large, ring-shaped handle it didn't budge. I had been told that the vicar kept the place locked. Not that was an obstacle. I reached into the pocket of my coat and pulled out the key-ring I always carried when working. One of the larger keys easily opened the door. The moment the gap was wide enough, Dash slipped inside. The hinges were well oiled and it made no sound as I pushed it open enough to step inside.

I paused to allow my eyes to adjust to the lower light levels before making my way into the main body of the church. I could see why Minette had liked the patterns the stained-glass cast on the floor. Dash was sitting in the centre of the aisle before a brass set into the stone floor.

'He told the child he wasn't under there,' I said as Dash looked up at me expectantly. It seemed he was only waiting for me as the moment I stopped next to him he was off, loping towards the recess in the far corner and the steps that descended into darkness. As he disappeared, I brushed the wall, feeling for a switch. Light flooded the steps and I followed dash into the crypt. It was much as Minette had described it.

Dash peered through the bars sealing off one area containing coffins and it didn't take me long to have that unlocked as well. I couldn't see the door at the end that she had described but as I placed my hand on the wall and closed my eyes I could feel it. I pushed it open.

The man sitting in the library looked up from his book, startled. He quickly composed himself and said, 'I wasn't expecting guests.'

'Perhaps you were expecting a twelve-year old girl, Matthew,' I said.

'Hmm. I expect she's around somewhere.'

'Yes, at home with her mother.' I didn't wait for permission but sat down in the armchair the opposite side of the simulated fire from him. Dash lounged at my feet.

'Now that is unfortunate. And who might you be?'

'Most folks call me Jack. You would have done better to keep the fetch.'

'I don't like copies. I prefer the real thing. And a father has a right to have his daughter with him.'

'How were you going to feed her? Children have needs that ghosts don't.'

'She is half ghost.' He sounded a little petulant.

'She is a living creature. Why did you want to steal her?'

Matthew sighed. 'It gets lonely here. Since the vicar started locking the church almost no-one comes visiting.'

I regarded him thoughtfully. I couldn't risk him trying the same stunt again and it is very difficult to punish a ghost. 'What ties you to the church?'

'My bones.'

'So if your bones were elsewhere, you would haunt that place?'

'That is what I suspect.'

'Where are your bones?'

'In one of those decrepit coffins out there. I no longer know which one. Time has broken them.'

I stood. 'I might have a solution.'

I left him then. I would need to talk to Theobold.

I was back the next day, though, with a sack. 'Right,' I said to Dash. 'Find him.'

The labradoodle knew exactly what I meant and immediately began sniffing around the coffins stacked inside the vault. Some were in pretty poor condition and even the most recent were beginning to show the effects of damp.

'What are you doing?' Matthew was suddenly at the end of the aisle between the stacks.

'Solving your problem. I hope you have no aversion to vampires and their kin.'

Matthew shook his head. 'I do not believe I have been acquainted with any.'

'That is about to change.'

Dash gave the whuffing bark that told me he had found what he was looking for. I trusted him and didn't bother trying to find any identification on the casket which was already showing signs of collapse. There were three others stacked on top of it. I didn't try to be careful, just ripped away the deteriorating wood and reached in to gather the bones inside. Matthew had faded but I was sure he was still watching me. Once I was sure I had all of them, I tied the sack and headed back into London, and the Monster Club.

When I visited the Monster Club a few weeks later, Theobald placed a pint of real ale in front of me and a steak dripping blood on the floor for Dash. I saw at least one of the customers eyeing it.

'On the house,' Theobald said. He gestured towards the bar where Matthew stood, still in his death finery, dispensing refreshments for the clientele. 'Good idea of yours, reburying him in the cellar. Not only do I get unpaid staff but I've live in security as well.'

Matthew glanced my way. I raised my glass in salute. The ghost acknowledged it with a nod before turning to resume his conversation with the shadmock leaning on the counter. I glanced down at Dash. 'Job done,' I said.

MARJORIE LEARNS TO FLY

By

John Linwood Grant

*T*HE HOUSE IS *so quiet now, with Kenneth and the others gone. So orderly. As I gaze around the kitchen, I play my fingers across the rack of spice jars, over the slight unevenness of the plastered walls, no longer marred by the clutter of reminders and notes about the current contents of the freezer. Everything is as it should be, where it should be.*

I shall make a cup of tea.

Warm the pot; switch off the kettle just before the water boils. Don't want to drive all the oxygen out. Loose tea, never teabags. Oolong, woody but slightly sweet. Let it sit for seven or eight minutes, and then pour.

I add a dash of milk – not too much – and sip. Perfect.

This is how Marjorie likes it. She deserves this. She has plans, wonderful plans, and I am so very pleased to have her back...

It was the tea that Kenneth noticed first. He mentioned it, peering over his morning paper.

'You don't like gunpowder green, Marjorie. Too smoky, you always say.'

I stared at the jar in my hand, and then at the grey stoneware teapot.

'Getting absent-minded.' I put the tea back on the shelf, and took down the oolong. 'Going to be one of those days.'

Not that it was his place to say what I should or shouldn't drink. He paid too much attention to detail, that was the problem. If you liked something once, he made sure it was in the groceries next time. It took a whole week of Cheerios at breakfast before I broke, and told him that I'd only tried them for fun, that now I had, I thought they were dull, at best.

I downed a quick half cup of oolong, kissed him on the cheek – lipstick meeting sandpaper – and left for the office. Nothing would be different there. Typing, photocopying and too much gossip; comparisons of nail varnish and the endless talk of hair styles. It was hair. As long as it was tidy and out of the way, what did the rest matter?

I would have thought no more about the gunpowder green, except for that lunchtime, when I traipsed into the work canteen and joined the queue.

'Macaroni cheese, or goulash?' The slow, thick-browed server wasn't looking at me, just waving her ladle in my general direction. There were greasy brown smears in the vat of macaroni cheese – she obviously used the same ladle for both dishes.

'Goulash, please.'

Hungarians would have wept to see what was slopped onto my plate. More importantly, I had never enjoyed goulash, even when well prepared. I couldn't understand why I'd asked for it.

I sat alone at a small table, and as I spooned each mouthful into the inner void, I felt a soft touch behind my eyes. I looked again at the under-spiced mess in my bowl.

'No, I don't want this,' I said out loud. A couple of people looked up from their soups, then went back to desultory conversation.

I didn't want it, but my hands fed me the rest of the plateful, lump by greasy lump.

'Satisfied now?' I murmured. There was no answer, of course.

Afterwards I tried to make light of it. I told Suzie, the rather plain girl who worked at the desk next to mine, that since we moved up here, my tastes seemed to be changing.

'Though I can't imagine why,' I added. 'Our old house wasn't so different from this one; the shops are pretty much the same, and Ressington... well, it's like any other industrial town.

'You're bored.' Suzie's mud-coloured eyes met mine. 'Ressington is boring.'

'I... maybe so. Perhaps I need a hobby.'

Suzie's fingers paused over her keyboard. 'My little sister cuts herself. Says that when she's done it often enough, our Mam and Dad will let her leave this hole, go to London or something.'

That seemed somewhat extreme.

'She's more likely to end up on a hospital ward,' I said.

'Aye, there's that.'

We didn't talk the rest of that afternoon.

After work, I went for the wrong bus. I wanted a fifty-seven, but for no reason I could fathom I waited at the thirty-two stop and got on the first one which came. When the service terminated at the park – they call it a park, that sad square of bushes tangled with refuse – I got off the bus, and walked home. Two miles, in heels.

That was how it started. Tea, goulash, and a bus.

We had sex, on a cold, rainy morning in February. Kenneth lay there with the Sunday newspapers spread out over the duvet, a puzzled look on his face as I straddled him; he didn't resist, but he didn't play much of a part, either. Five inches, barely rigid enough.

Afterwards, he tried to put the sports supplement back into order.

'That was... surprising,' he said.

And it was. I'd no idea that I wanted to touch him, never mind have a bit of "the other".

Cleaning up the breakfast cups, it came to me that I really hadn't. Whoever wanted to copulate with Kenneth, it wasn't me. I'd given up that sort of thing years ago. I didn't know whether to be shocked or disgusted. I had a shower instead.

That afternoon, I watched the golf on the television.

I hated golf.

These little alterations to my routine were starting to disturb me. Was Ressington itself somehow responsible? There had been the move to accommodate Kenneth's new position at the plastics factory, and then I'd found a job in the typing pool at an adjoining firm – none of that had been planned much in advance. Nor was it what I would have chosen, myself. The town smelled of plastics and filing cabinets – an artificial miasma of made-things, overlaying what little of nature survived in the area.

We'd not liked Northampton much, but at least it had history. Someone might well have planned Ressington sixty years ago as the antithesis of the English countryside – gravel and tarmac choking the soil; grim rain-stained factories and office blocks looming over the houses, mostly post-war semis built to three standard patterns. Sometimes the construction companies seemed to have given in, and just slapped down thirty or forty copies of the same house in an estate, no longer caring to vary the facades.

If people sent postcards any more, they certainly didn't send any of Ressington.

Maybe the place was affecting me.

When I went to the doctor for a routine smear, I asked her if people's tastes could change, suddenly – drastically. She frowned.

'I wouldn't know, Mrs Eden. Not without a reason, I suppose, but there's nothing in your medical history...'

She went though the motions of checking my eyes and my reflexes, and asked if I'd banged my head or suffered any sudden shocks recently. I told her I hadn't, and in the end her opinion turned out to be much the same as Suzie's at the office.

It probably came down to boredom.

I should have walked back from the surgery, but instead, I went to the train station, and bought a ticket for the next stop up the line. A dormitory village, absorbed not long after Ressington became the pointless industrial hub that it was. King's Fletching, they called it.

It was like the bus journey, going for the wrong stop. As if another, subconscious part of me had ideas about what I should be doing.

I had absolutely no interest in King's Fletching, yet I wandered its damp streets for almost an hour, and in the end found myself staring through the window of a sad wool shop, everything half-price. I shook my head, telling whoever was in there to go away. They could spend the rest of their lives in King's Fletching if they wanted, wondering if a tangle of beige wool/synthetic mix was worth the money.

I was taking the train home.

It wasn't easy to work out what all this meant. I remembered Mother's occasional visits to psychics, and her misplaced belief in astrology, reading "the stars" in the paper every morning and trying to twist the day to fit the generalised nonsense. She would have said that I was being contacted, or even possessed. That I was "sensitive", and some poor soul was trying to get through to me.

I was sure I wasn't sensitive. I was mundane, and I knew it; never a hint of anything strange in my life. The supernatural bored me, and the only thing lurking under the bed was dust – and possibly one of Kenneth's missing socks.

The incidents didn't end there. One week I bought fresh ginger and chillies, and four or five different kinds of spices from the town's only delicatessen. I cooked meals I didn't recognise – I ate them when Kenneth was out and washed them down with pints of cold water or milk to ease the burning. I told myself that it was an experiment, that I could stop at any time. Maybe some part of Marjorie really wanted to try these things, but had never told me before.

And I saw Ressington, from the cardboard cut-out semis to the few alleys which remained of the unremarkable village it had once been. The seventies planners had all but extinguished history as well as nature by pouring concrete over it – here a last set of worn cobbles; there a set of stone gateposts which might once have announced an unimportant manor. The rest was gone.

I only worked a three day week, and so had plenty of time to indulge whoever wanted to peer at the past. These were compulsions, and yet they weren't. Once, when my back hurt, I felt a tug that wanted me to get out of the house and go wandering, and I resisted.

'Not today,' I said to the empty house. 'I'm going to take a break, read a book.'

The sensation – intrusion – receded.

It seemed like a small victory.

You might think I was going mad, but it didn't feel like that. It was... odd, maybe even disturbing, but not insane. At least, I hoped so. I didn't have much faith in the local doctors.

I went on-line, and read up on psychiatric conditions. There was plenty about multiple personality disorders. I had to check the dictionary a lot, but got through them in the end. They talked about amnesia and a lack of awareness between personality states; about trauma, and certain personalities coming to the fore under stressful conditions.

None of that fitted. Neither Ressington nor my job were stressful, they were simply dull, insignificant. They say moving house is stressful, but I'd left that to Kenneth. One day I was in Northampton, putting lightbulbs into a cardboard box; the next I was here.

And I remembered everything that happened to me when I had these sensations. Each time I could feel a slight flutter under the bone of my forehead, but I was still there – Marjorie was there – not locked away in some dusty corner of my brain. No, none of these medical sites explained what was happening to me. And who wants to go to an actual psychiatrist, even if you can get to see one? It's like admitting in public that you've cracked.

Mind you, I did find a few articles which explained a lot about my late mother. A petty personality, manipulative. That was her.

'You don't want to wear that, Marjorie. It's common.'

'Your hair doesn't suit you – you should have it long, like that nice Sally Wright down the road.'

'Your father would never have wanted you to work in an office.'

All said with a smile, camouflage spread across the mean-minded control which Mother had always sought. Mother had always thought Kenneth to be rather common, as well. Daddy, who died early – probably as a result of Mother's incessant harping on about standards – had been meant for great things on the council. That smile of hers had made me marry Kenneth, despite my own misgivings. Because Mother 'didn't think he'd amount to much'.

She'd been right about him. Lower middle management, golf on the television, and a few pints down the local every Friday. In Ressington, it was the Victoria, where the other company people drank, a mock-Tudor oasis of nothing in the middle of the estate. We went there, regular as clockwork, and I nursed a sweet sherry while he talked about golf or plastics. Kenneth was a man of minutiae, not of grand (or even large) gestures. His version of love letters was post -it notes about double-locking the kitchen window at night and remembering to order more toilet roll. Calendars marked graphically with our few social engagements, and cousins' birthdays.

I would have known if Mother was haunting me. She would have walked me to the solicitors to discuss divorce – and a sizeable settlement...

Because I wasn't the sort of person to get alarmed, I didn't let that happen. Instead, I started sorting these experiences into types. There were the food experiments and the little trips, the petty violence, and of course the sex. They all felt different, somehow, so I decided to assigned names to my visitors. That's what I chose to call them.

Visitors.

Mary was older, set in her ways. I decided she was the one who stared into wool shops, who wanted to toddle around the older parts of the area. She was also the golf watcher, and she felt like a Mary. Annoying, but not threatening.

I chose the name Sandeep for the one who was interested in cooking, in spicy and different foods. I didn't know any Asians, not personally, but I'd heard the name on the television, in one of those dramas about the Raj. I wondered if I was being racist, but it seemed to fit. The goulash was an experiment, and disappointed both of us. I could have told him it would.

Jason was more of a problem. I felt him late at night, sometimes, and his were darker whims, which I tried to hold back from when I could. He wanted me to kick random passers-by, and scrawled graffiti on walls, to do damage – to people, objects, anything that was in his way.

The one who liked sex was Anita. Perhaps the same age as I was, but adventurous, determined. I couldn't imagine being like that. She surprised Kenneth a few times – once, even, in the kitchen, before

I'd even cleared the table. Anita, I could feel, wasn't impressed by his performances in bed – or wherever else she tried to take advantage of him. He didn't know how to handle her, though he tried to rise to the occasion, as they say. I could tell Mary didn't approve, even as my bare buttocks slapped against the polished pine...

After almost two months of this, I no longer thought of the visitors as buried parts of me, as splinters of my own personality. These visitors were not Marjorie. Giving them names had allowed me to discriminate between episodes, and to realise what was happening.

These were other people. Real people.

What that meant, I didn't know, but it did push aside any suggestion that I was crazy. I almost talked to Kenneth about it, but what would have been the point? I was hardly that different when he was around – apart from the sex. Kenneth would have started leaving post-it notes so that I didn't forget to iron his trousers, and made poor jokes.

'Mary hasn't defrosted the lamb chops, I see.'

He saw nothing beyond his own needs. I let Jason smash the old wardrobe, and all Kenneth could say was that it was about time we had fitted ones – his suits were getting bunched up. And I drove my car to the reservoir, and threw a suitcase full of Mother's dreadful clothes into it, but I might have done that anyway, if I'd had the courage. She'd left me Laura Ashley dresses with little lace collars, frumpy nightgowns and horrid viscose blouses. Neither Anita nor I liked them, so it was good riddance – though Marjorie would have donated them to a charity shop.

The oddest thing was, the visitors couldn't read my thoughts. I was sure they couldn't, because I tried sending some very direct – and quite rude – responses. There was no reaction. You'd think that if you had people in your head, they'd be able to pick up that.

It was all about sensations, physical feelings, and seeing through my eyes. I didn't have to like what I ate, or be interested in where I went – following the nagging impulses didn't change what I thought about the world around me, not in itself. What I was supposed to do about the situation, I couldn't imagine. I suppose that much of the time I clung to the possibility that it would pass as quickly as it came.

But then there was that one morning, late in April.

Mary – I'm sure it was Mary – had me wandering a cramped, run-down part of town. I didn't like it much. Behind a clutter of light industries, older houses slumped together in poverty, tiles missing and the occasional boarded-up window. Battered rental signs stood at angles; bins overflowed on the edge of the pavements. The sharp sunlight made it so much worse.

I didn't know if Mary had lived around there once, or if she merely fancied a change, but I could feel wool and boiled sweets behind my eyes, urging my body to step across the road and down by a row of shops with their steel shutters down. I passed by a wrecked telephone box, crunching over shards of glass, and there was the boy.

I hadn't noticed him before. He slid around the box and put himself in my path – sallow face, mean little eyes, and a crusted cold-sore at one corner of the thin mouth. I'd have thought he was seventeen, eighteen.

He jerked his head towards my handbag.

'I'll have that,' he said, broken voice carrying over broken glass.

'I don't think so.' The shock of it left me no time to be afraid.

'Alright, then, bitch.' He pulled some sort of heavy craft knife from inside his torn anorak, letting me see him weigh it in his hand, letting me get the message.

Marjorie would have given him the bag. I didn't carry much cash, and credit cards could be cancelled. So whoever lunged forward, grabbing the knife from the kid, wasn't Marjorie...

I was the one, however, who stood over his body afterwards, watching one leg twitch, wondering how you could drive a craft knife so deep into someone's abdomen. It's not like they're meant for stabbing, after all.

'I've been... attacked,' I said into my mobile phone. I didn't need to make myself sound shaky. 'The corner of... Melton Street, by the shops.'

While I waited for the police, one of the visitors borrowed me again, and tore my jacket, ripping some of the buttons away. They bent me down, and taking hold of the boy's filthy left hand, they scratched his fingernail across my face. Painfully.

I could see why. "Evidence of a struggle", as they liked to say on the TV shows.

He wasn't dead. I leant against the telephone box, suitably pale, and let the emergency services come, let them do their thing.

The police were wonderful. Middle class white woman versus drug-using feral low-life with a history of assault.

'You had no choice, love – he could have really hurt you. And it's not as if he needs more than stitching up. Nothing vital touched.'

The way the officer explained everything, I wondered what else the boy would be stitched up for. They took me to the hospital, cleaned the scrapes on my cheek, and made me feel I'd done a good thing.

I hadn't done anything – neither had Mary or Anita. I knew that someone else had taken over and sorted the situation out, and I suspected Jason.

It was getting crowded in here.

Kenneth started to stay late at the office; I wandered Ressington doing things which spoke of too many conflicting tastes. Another trip to the delicatessen to buy things I didn't recognise; a week knitting sweaters for no one I knew. I managed to drop a stitch here and there, but the process was inexorable. I was beginning to feel a growing resentment.

When Anita had me accost one of the neighbours and fumble with them behind the azaleas one night, I didn't go willingly. Or – I should be more precise – I let things happen as far as the azaleas, wondering what was coming, but when he started to feel my breasts with one hand and work his zipper with the other, I harnessed indignation.

I resisted.

No.

It was Reggie Gault, after all – fifty, dull, and balding in that patchy way which absolutely did not make you a sex symbol.

Yes, Anita indicated by hauling out his member.

Reggie reached what heights he could all over my best tweed skirt, and I ran back into the house, ashamed.

Angry.

I stayed up that night. Kenneth was at a conference in Guildford – Extruded Plastic Mouldings: The Future – and there was no one to ask why I was still awake. I took out the twee notebook which Mother had given me for my fortieth, tore off the cover with its sickly smiling cats. I made notes.

There were at least four of them, I wrote, and I added short descriptions. Mary, Anita, Jason, Sandeep. They didn't know what I was thinking, but they knew what I was doing. They could see, feel, smell and taste through me. They...

As the pen moved across the paper, I weakened for a moment. All of this was clearly impossible, and for a moment I thought of brain tumours and strokes, of Kenneth spiking my oolong with those hallucinogens the papers talked about...

No, it was happening. I was a sensible woman, a practical one. It was up to me to handle it, or I might lose my sense of myself.

I might lose Marjorie.

After all, I was the person who had mended the broken toilet three weeks before this business started. I'd sorted out the problem with Jane Ferris's dog, and shown Suzie at work how to use a spreadsheet. Who knew what else I could manage?

I filled the next page of the notebook not with questions, but with short, bullet point sentences. What to do when strangers visit your head. I scribbled down tin foil hats, psychiatric treatment, give in, call the police, and a few other ideas, until I came to the last line.

Fight back.

Mary took me to King's Fletching, and I bought the wool she liked. Puce. Puke, I would have called it. In the evening, we knitted, but as we did so, I probed. It wasn't easy. I began to get a feeling of walnut-knuckles and frustration; she liked to knit, but it was getting harder for her. Arthritis. I knew she was interested in the old parts of town, so maybe she couldn't get around as much as she wanted. The more I sought – very carefully – the more Mary revealed herself. She was at home right now, propped in a large, high-back chair, concentrating; the wallpaper was... roses? No, carnations, pink carnations...

I left it there, not daring to push too hard. I had a feeling of her, and what she looked like now.

When Jason visited, during an argument with Kenneth, I pleaded a migraine and went upstairs. There on the bed I went through the motions of sobbing, but I was visiting Jason while I was doing it. He was in a pub, sat alone with half a bitter. I heard a jukebox, and the awful clang and shriek of pub slot machines. I could smell, through his nostrils, that he hadn't changed for a few days – and he had no idea I was there.

It became easier.

Sandeep wore a hat – no, a turban. A Sikh then, at least forty years old, working in a hardware store. Although I didn't know his thoughts any better than he knew mine, I could tell that he was very bored with his life.

Anita was a hard one. I could tell it was vital that Anita didn't sense what I was doing – she seemed to be the most powerful of them – and so I was very careful. When she had me molest the postman, I did nothing to alarm her. It alarmed him, mind you. When Reggie Gault tried it on again, I let him kiss me, and while Anita was busy with my tongue, I tested the waters. I followed her influence back, prying. I sensed a "generous" woman, which was my mother's euphemism for overweight; a pants suit or even a tracksuit, and the feeling of dyed blonde hair – and a reflection in a shop window when I was with her confirmed it. Too many highlights, and too many cheap rings on her fingers.

I left the others alone for a few days, concentrating for Anita. Which turned out to be an interesting move, because it was Anita who discovered the phone number in Kenneth's trouser pocket as she was molesting him, and Anita who smelled the cheap perfume on the piece of paper, saw the little kisses written below the number. She made my lips smile, and she took him there and then in the hallway.

Far away, deep inside me, I was thinking things over.

Now I knew the reason behind Kenneth's late nights at work, and number of "conferences" he'd been attending recently. It looked as if Anita had given my husband a taste for the carnal side.

I considered discussing the matter with him, but that would only lead to a messy argument, and to be honest, I didn't want to hear his reasons for being unfaithful. I didn't want to listen to his point by point explanations, or protestations that it would never happen again. Nor did I want to consider the unpleasant option of the inevitable divorce which would follow. It's not like anyone would fight to keep Kenneth.

In the end, I simply dealt with it.

On an overcast Sunday morning, while he was seeing to a leaky stretch of guttering, he fell off the ladder. It was very unfortunate that the foot of the ladder slipped at that particular moment, and that the guttering which had concerned me was right over the concrete patio. No prickly but survivable fall into the rose bushes which surrounded most of the house... only the satisfying crack of skull against paving stone.

'Happy now, Mother?' I whispered.

The ambulance came, and the paramedics confirmed what I already knew. I managed a suitable amount of weeping and wailing, drawing on a dreadful romantic film I'd watched for research the day before. Practice makes perfect.

Reggie Gault and the other neighbours were most sympathetic in the week which followed.

'Such a nice man, your Kenneth,' said Mrs Jones. 'It's a tragedy.'

I took her inside, where I made *masala chai* for us. I quite liked it by now; Mrs Jones struggled through half a cup, and then excused herself as too upset to stay any longer.

I finished off her *chai* as well, before it was as cold as Kenneth.

The visitors stayed out of my head until after the funeral, but they were soon back. It appeared that they couldn't resist it. And every time one of them came, I found out more. I had no distractions now, and could spend my time probing, hunting back along whatever mental or psychic link we had. I filled them out, gathering small details, noting locations, visiting them while they visited me.

I learned that I could hover in any of them, unnoticed. I didn't make them do a thing; I observed their lives and pinned them down, filling my notebooks. I was careful never to open the notebooks – or leave them lying around – when there was any sensation of another presence. At the first, the lightest, pressure or prickle at my forehead, everything was put away.

I was learning a new game.

But it was when I visited Mary one Friday lunchtime, as she went through the centre of town, that I discovered something about the game that I really hadn't expected.

She visited a few shops, poking the merchandise but hardly ever buying anything – in an hour and half, she managed to pick up one can of cat food and a loaf of white sliced bread. I was getting so bored that I was about to pull away, when she turned to hobble into a pub on the high street, which I hadn't anticipated. The place seemed familiar. Was it... yes, it was the one I'd seen through Jason, a while back. I looked around, using Mary's eyes as subtly as I could – and I saw the three other people waiting at a table in the alcove, an empty chair set to one side.

They were unmistakable – a middle-aged Sikh chap in a cheap brown suit; a pasty-faced young man with oily blond hair, and a blowsy blonde older than I was.

The shock threw me out of my travelling companion, and I was back at home, shaking.

They knew each other.

The four of them knew each other!

It took me a few days to recover from this realisation, days in which I put up no resistance at all. I let Anita make me flirt with the milkman, and Jason take me to stare into the canal – no idea why. I played along whilst I thought this out.

I suppose I'd come to believe that I was vulnerable, that I was actually "sensitive", as Mother would have said. And being so, I'd been found by whoever there was in the area who had a stronger gift, or whatever you would call it. Like the girl who is picked on at school – children can sense weakness, which is why I never wanted any kids.

But that they were a group, and that they had presumably gossiped about me, laughed at me… that made me angry. It made me feel cheap, and I didn't like that at all.

When I'd come to terms with what I'd discovered, I was more determined than ever. I took books on meditation out of the library, and I took time off work – grief over the loss of Kenneth, I told Human Resources, and they couldn't argue with that.

Human Resources. There was an appropriate phrase. I had been used by Mary, Anita, Jason and Sandeep (I was sure these were their real names, just as surely as they must know that I was a Marjorie), and not paid. A disposable resource.

I spent hours sitting cross-legged in our bedroom – my bedroom now – and I focused, finding each of the four in turn and watching, feeling, intently. They all lived on this side of town, and every four or five days they gathered in this pub to boast about their encounters. It soon became apparent that I wasn't the only one being used – there were two or three others in Ressington who had these same visitors. I must have been a delightful addition, moving here and turning up on their radar.

It took a while to grasp on what to do. My initial idea was to find out who the other victims were, and form some sort of support group, or get together and expose the perpetrators, demand they stop. But there was no proof, was there? Nothing to show anyone else – and I had no idea who the other victims were.

Even if I did find these unknown people, the thought of introducing myself and trying to explain what was happening seemed not just daunting, but rather unpleasant. Our shared experience – if it were indeed similar in each case – didn't make us friends. They might not even answer their doors to a mad woman muttering about telepathic control, or whatever I would have called it.

I drank half a bottle of sherry one evening, and decided that I should listen to Mother, just this once.

'There's nothing wrong with ambition, Marjorie.'

The following morning, despite a headache from the sherry, I sent my mind to occupy Anita. I found her in bed with a spotty young man – a garage mechanic by the stained overalls on the floor at her bedside. I slipped inside her after the act, and I made her kick the boy out of bed. I moved her hands to slap him, and her mouth to say a few unmentionable things that would have made me blush to speak. He wouldn't be returning.

And I left, before she could work out what had happened.

The day after, Sandeep was rude to a customer, and almost got the sack; Jason made a very bad job of shoplifting two bottles of cider and got barred from his local off-licence. I wasn't ready for anything grand, but it cheered me up to shift the balance of power.

Mary puzzled me. I almost felt some sympathy for her, until I thought of her uninvited jaunts with my body. Merely as an experiment, I had her knit a scarf in colours which I knew she hated.

I carried on like this for more than a fortnight, secretly hoping that they would start blaming each other. I could tell that their pub meetings were becoming more fractious, though I never heard any of them voice a direct challenge to another.

Feeling bold, I conducted more experiments – and was intrigued by the results.

Marjorie had changed.

It was time that she met her visitors face to face.

The King's Head was a scruffy public house, one which Kenneth and the neighbours would have avoided. It served very cheap, tasteless breakfasts – I knew that from visiting Jason – and from the boards outside did a Pensioners' Special on Friday lunchtimes. A stale, oily smell which greeted me as I entered the pub lounge suggested that the "special" was breakfast fried up again.

There they were, my four, toying with their food and engaged in muted conversation. They didn't look so pleased now, and I hoped that I detected a certain suspicion between them.

'Well, well,' I said, pulling up a fifth chair and sitting down at their table. 'Isn't this nice – all of us together at last.'

They stared at me, dumb.

'I'm Marjorie.' I smiled at the stout Sikh, who had been lifting a forkful of baked beans to his lips. 'So sorry to hear about your trouble at work, Sandeep.'

Fork and beans clattered to the plate.

Jason was spottier than I'd expected. He glared, squared his shoulders, and leaned forward as if he might lunge towards me at any moment.

'You – you're the one who's been messing with us and—'

'Keep it down, now,' I made his body slump, sink back into the chair.

'What the bleedin' hell do you—' Anita found herself pushing a slice of toast into her mouth, cutting off what she had been going to say.

I extended my smile to all of them.

'I don't know how you found out that you could do this, or how you came together. I have no idea how it works, and to be honest, I don't care. You see, I've found something out, thanks to you four, and it's quite exciting, really.'

Mary, who from her looks might had "grandmother" tattooed on her forehead at birth, eyed me, a watery blue gaze.

'What are you going to do, dear? I mean, I know we shouldn't ever have started this, and we shouldn't have interfered with you, but we only borrowed you. We never did any real harm...'

'That's a matter of opinion, isn't it?'

'I saved you from that thug on the street.' Jason, sitting next to Mary, was just the blend of aggression and fear which I'd expected from prying into him. 'Anyway, if you tell anyone, they'll think you're nuts.'

It's strange to find yourself in charge. I wasn't used to it, though I could see it becoming easier. Much easier.

'Saved me? I wouldn't have gone to that place if it wasn't for the four of you. And besides, some of you took more liberties than others.'

I stared hard at Anita. I wasn't going to let her speak – sex was bad enough without someone else making you have it.

'But I'm not going to tell anyone. If you want to carry on with your little games, that's fine by me. It makes no difference.' My smile returned. 'You see, you can't use me any more.'

They tried, there and then – I could feel it – and the result was on their faces. Confusion; worry. I was closed to them. And not only did they have no control over me, they were vulnerable. I don't think they'd ever felt that before.

'You... you could join us,' said Sandeep, though he didn't sound like he relished the idea. I think he was feeling cornered, which he was. 'We'll tell you who else we... know, and you can share in the—'

'We can explain how it all happened, dear,' interrupted Mary.

I laughed. 'I told you, I don't need an explanation – that doesn't really matter. And as for joining you, well, why would I bother? You can't use me – but I can use you. I can be you, if you want, and I'm beginning to think that I'm stronger than anyone here. Much stronger.'

Jason struggled in his seat, unable to reach across to me.

'There's only one of you,' he grunted.

I nodded. 'Yes, you're right. And I suppose I could thank you for that – if I felt you mattered any more.'

I spread my mental wings, and let it happen. It had been building inside me, day after day, though it had taken me a while to recognise what had happened to me...

Everyone, every single person in the pub, raised the nearest cup or glass, empty or full, and drank. Some did it without noticing; other seemed slightly puzzled at their actions.

I tasted tea; coffee; port and lemon; watered-down whisky; pale ale, and dregs from the barrel. I held up all those drinks, yet my hands were empty. If I'd wanted, I could have made the entire clientele smash those glasses into their own faces, without me moving an inch.

And only the four people at this table understood.

'Oh dear,' said Mary.

The oolong is cooling, and I have a ham sandwich prepared for dinner. It won't taste of ham, because three towns away a couple are about to cut into an enormous Porterhouse steak they decided to share, accompanied by an expensive red from somewhere in Italy.

You see, it's true that some people are more vulnerable to having visitors than others – but it turns out that a little extra effort can take you a long way. I haven't found anyone yet who can't be used – visited – at some level. No one appears to immune, if you only make a little effort. I don't bother with the four who started me off – small thinkers, small thoughts. I think Anita's already left town.

Instead, I sit at my little kitchen table, alone, and wait for the first bite of the tender beef, interested to see how it tastes on two tongues at once. When they top up their glasses, I might get to see the name on the bottle. I'll make a note. I'm quite keen on wine these days, with Kenneth's cans of supermarket lager finally out of the fridge.

These two people – friends, partners or lovers – are mine tonight. Not that I'll stay with them for any bedroom adventures. Dear me, no. I'll be off to somewhere else. To someone else. But for now, they are Marjorie.

Maybe one day, everyone will be Marjorie.

FIRE DAMAGE

By

Stephen Laws

*T*HE FIRE HAD *apparently swept through the building very quickly; caused – apparently – by an electrical fault in the wiring of an upstairs room an hour or two before dawn. The club was situated in Swallow Street, tucked unobtrusively between an oyster bar and a curry house, and reached by means of ill lit steps which ran down into a deep basement. The fire quickly engulfed the oyster bar and the curry restaurant, and when both premises collapsed, the basement club was buried and obliterated beneath burning beams, crashing masonry and rubble. Despite the best endeavors of the London Fire Service, there was no chance that the entire block of buildings could be saved. The nearest buildings were a variety of warehouses that suffered only smoke damage and since the club staff and members present that evening had left an hour or so before the incident, there was no need to evacuate any residents or night time employees.*

However, police investigation to ensure that there was no possibility that anyone could still have been present when the club was destroyed – say, anyone enjoying an early morning drink "after hours" in one of the club's private rooms – was met with a surprisingly unforthcoming response. Staff records suggested that all who should be "present and accounted for" were indeed "present and accounted for" and there were no reports of missing persons. Investigation ran its course, including the necessary insurance investigation after the police had been satisfied that there had been no "foul play". The premises were owned and managed by a Transylvanian company from afar via a number of subsidiary arrangements with ties related in some way not only to the British establishment, but also to British royalty; all professionally accounted for and registered with Companies House, its licenses, taxes and accounts all properly registered, paid for and "above board". Given the lack of injury and fatality and that all matters of finance and insurance were in order – not to mention a private word from a member of the British royal family in the ear of the Metropolitan Commissioner of Police, it was confirmed that there was no need for further investigation.

But there had, in fact, been three club members present – enjoying an after-hours drink – when the club burned and collapsed.

And they had not escaped the fire.

The remains of the site had been cleared, bulldozed, and the basement club completely filled in with fallen masonry and rubble from above, making for "level ground" across the site – and with only the odd gap and fracture to suggest that there might once have been something below and now "completely safe" to members of the public. The site was then fenced off, the funding for that operation having been paid for by sources other than the British taxpayer, which pleased those in authority – and thereafter, the site was abandoned and forgotten.

Two years before sunrise on the first year anniversary of that destructive fire, a dark figure in a wide-brimmed hat and black overcoat moved a loose plank to one side in the fence and peered across the ragged site, at that time of night only faintly cross-lit by high crane lights along the River Thames half a mile away.

A low eerie whistling sound trembled in the night.

Something that moved and looked like a small dog jumped under the dark figure's up-stretched arm and scampered quickly into the darkness of the demolition site.

The figure followed it carefully, joints aching as he shouldered past the loose plank with two canvas holdall-bags, carefully allowing the plank to slide back into place soundlessly. Following the scampering figure into the safety of darkness, he placed the bags at his feet and stretched, holding both hands on his hips to ease his aching back. Then he adjusted his wide brimmed hat, pulled up his coat collar against the night chill – and made an adjustment to the device in his ear. When that same eerie whistling noise came again, the thing that moved and looked like a dog raced out of the darkness to his side, surprisingly quiet as it scampered and whirled in tight excited circles around him. Finally, it settled at his side, eagerly waiting for its next instruction.

The man picked up the two bags again and carefully picked his way through the remaining rubble, trying to avoid the narrow beams of light that cross-hatched the area. The creature padded behind him. When he reached the area where the basement club had once existed, he carefully laid the bags down again, stooping to open one – from which he removed three small corked glass jars, placing them carefully on the ground next to each other. He stood again.

His hand went to his ear, adjusting the "device" within – and the eerie whistle came again.

The thing that looked like a dog became alert, trembling with excitement.

To any human ear, that whistle would have sounded no different from the previous sound. But there was a certain unearthly cadence, an implicit "instruction", an order – or request – that was different from the previous utterance.

The sound stopped.

The creature remained still.

But when the brief whistling came for a third time, the thing that looked like a dog sprang away from its master and disappeared into the jumbled tangle of remaining burned wooden beams and rubble that covered the "top" of what had once been the basement club.

Somewhere within that tangled mass of shadow, the thing snuffled and hunted until it had found that which it had been sent to find.

When it emerged again, it rushed back to sit obediently at its master's feet and dropped what it had found from its jaws on the ground before him.

The man stooped, uncorked one of the glass bottles and dropped that "something" into the bottle.

Standing, his hand went to his ear once more.

The whistling came again.

And the thing eagerly darted back into the darkness to perform its task a second time. Snuffling and scurrying, it emerged once more with "something" in its jaws that went into the second bottle.

The routine was performed for a third and final time.

When the third bottle was securely corked, the man placed all three into the canvas holdall while the "retriever" sat patiently waiting.

And then the man, the bags and the thing that moved and looked like a dog melted into the shadows.

The loose board in the fence slid silently back into place.

All was silent and still.

'Well, here we are,' said the man in the suit behind the desk. 'The last appointment of the day.'

He adjusted a perfectly fitted tie, smoothed back his perfectly cut brown hair, crossed his hands on the desk before him and sat forward, smiling. 'How can I help you, Mr Hayes?'

'That's Chetwynd-Hayes,' said the man sitting opposite him, adjusting his hearing aid and also smiling.

'Oh, I beg your pardon.' The other man flipped open a file on his desk and read: 'Mr Ronald Chetwynd-Hayes?'

'That's correct. You'll have to forgive me...' He finished adjusting his hearing aid. 'I'm a little hard of hearing.'

'No problem,' said the man.

'Well, it is a problem actually. A damned nuisance sometimes.'

The man's smile froze a little. 'Well – I'm Derek Pearce, Director of Pearce Insurance. I understand that you have an insurance issue that you'd like to discuss.' Pearce gestured around the office as if to indicate that every aspect of the filing cabinets, computer screen and framed certificates on the wall should bear testimony to his claim to be in charge of a very successful insurance company.

'Indeed', said Chetwynd-Hayes. 'You may or may not know that I'm a horror novelist and short story writer.'

'No,' said Pearce. 'I'm afraid I didn't know that. Horror, you say?'

'Yes.'

'Not my kind of thing, really.'

'Oh, that's a shame. Because it's pertinent to the issue I wanted to discuss with you.'

'By all means, continue.' Pearce's smile remained professionally presented. 'You've agreed to my hourly consultancy fee.'

'Indeed. One of my books, written back in 1975 was *The Monster Club*, which was subsequently turned into a horror film of the same name, starring the wonderful Vincent Price. He played the part of a vampire called Eramus...'

'Not sure what relevance...?'

'Please bear with me. All will become apparent with only the slightest of scene-setting. Eramus – Vincent Price – takes sustenance, or I should say drinks the blood of a passerby. In the book, that character is called Donald McCloud. But in the film he was renamed after me – Ronald Chetwynd-Hayes – in a part played by John Carradine, another great horror actor. The irony here, you see, is that my original horror novel was not a work of fiction. It was based on real-life events, as relayed to me by Eramus' friends, his having arranged my membership of "The Monster Club" itself – where I heard various stories from some of the vampires, werewolves, ghouls, humgoos etc who frequented the club.'

'The Monster Club...?' Pearce's smile seemed a tad faded.

'Yes, a basement club situated in Swallow Street. It burned down mysteriously a year ago.'

Mr Pearce had suddenly turned a little pale. His confident smile was now somehow not as confident as previously.

'Swallow Street? Oh yes, I seem to recall something. A club for fancy dress parties. Yes – that's right. It comes back to me now. The club had a "horror" theme. Hosting parties for those who liked to dress up as vampires and monsters, as I recall.'

Chetwynd-Hayes smiled back at him, indulgently.

After an uncomfortable silence, Pearce continued: 'Mr Chetwynd-Hayes, this is all very interesting. But I fail to see what this has to do with any insurance issue that I can help you with, or indeed...' Pearce looked at his watch. 'Or indeed what relevance...'

'Ah, the relevance.' Chetwynd-Hayes turned to the two canvas bags that he had brought with him and which lay at his feet. He hoisted one up to the edge of Pearce's desk. When he zipped the bag open, Pearce's professional affability seemed to dissolve, leaving a certain flinty aggression.

'Mr Chetwynd-Hayes. It's getting late and I really must insist that you come to the point.'

Chetwynd-Hayes reached into the holdall and placed the first of three corked bottles on the desk. It seemed to have two inches of grey dust and an indeterminate knob of matter that looked curiously like a gnarled bone.

'The patrons of The Monster Club were not, as you describe them, persons who liked to dress up as monsters and vampires. They were – are, in fact – monsters and vampires. And ghouls and humgoos and shadmocks and – well the list goes on. And The Monster Club itself on Swallow Street was burned down as the result of an arson attack.'

When he spoke again, Pearce's voice was tight: 'I recall the incident now. But I don't think that arson was proved...'

'You recall it,' continued Chetwynd-Hayes as he placed the second and third bottle on the desk – each with its portion of dust and gnarled bone, 'because your company was not only responsible for handling the insurance case, but because you personally hired the person responsible for burning the premises down.'

Pearce's face was now suddenly flushed, all affability now disappeared as his eyes bulged and sweat began to glisten on his brow.

'In a very clever insurance scam involving two other subsidiary companies – also secretly and illegally owned by yourself – you ensured that the "absent" parent company received only partial compensation and the substantive other parties – principally yourself – received the bulk of the very substantial insurance monies. You also managed to finalise this arrangement so carefully, and cleverly, that the long arm of the law can in no way investigate further and hold you to account. However, Mr Pearce – there is *another* long arm. Let me, as a writer, indulge myself in a purple prose description: The Long Arm of The Claw – the reach of which exceeds far beyond the parent company in Transylvania whose skills and talents I have the great honour of having learned and practised as a very grateful member of The Monster Club.'

'You're insane,' blurted Pearce, rising to his feet and planting both hands on the desk as if he was going to launch himself across it at Chetwynd-Hayes. 'And wasting my time. Get out!'

And then the second canvas holdall at the side of Chetwynd-Hayes chair began to move.

Pearce saw the movement, started to speak again and then halted when something made a *rippling* movement within.

'You shouldn't lose your temper, Mr Pearce,' said Chetwynd-Hayes calmly. 'My friend doesn't like displays of anger.'

With that, the zip on the bag unfurled with a slithering *rasp* and that which was inside sat up and looked directly at Pearce.

'Oh – my – *God!*' gasped Pearce, the flush of anger rapidly draining from his face, his eyes widening in horror and his breath catching in his throat. 'What – is – *THAT?*'

The thing that looked like a dog turned to give its version of a smile to Chetwynd-Hayes, and then turned its normal expression back to Pearce, who instantly flinched back against his chair.

'The late British comedian Marty Feldman performed a comedy sketch on television many years ago that I really liked. He took an – animal – to the veterinarian for an appointment, in a wicker basket. The animal was in the wicker basket, of course. Not the vet. So it remained unseen. When asked what it was, Mr Feldman said that he didn't know. He'd looked it up in the Cattle Breeders' Guide and it wasn't in there and in the Standard British Book of Birds and it wasn't in there either. Then he looked it up in the Book of Revelations, and it *was* in *there!*' Chetwynd-Hayes laughed. 'It was so very funny.'

Chetwynd-Hayes adjusted his ear piece again.

'What you now see, paying so much attention to you, is a friend of mine with a special talent. Note that I use the word "friend". He does not like the word "pet". We communicate via this remarkably adapted device'. Chetwynd-Hayes gestured at the ear piece. 'It was he who retrieved the partial remains of three of my friends who were enjoying a late night "sup" in the basement of The Monster Club when your underling burned it to oblivion. Each of these bottles, do you see, contains some small part of Manfred, the werevamp, Theobold the zombie and Eramus the vampire – the latter, as I mentioned, being my promoter and benefactor. You profess not to have an interest in "horror" Mr Pearce, but I'm sure that even you will have at least some awareness of the devastating effect of a silver bullet on a werewolf or a stake through the heart of a vampire? Neither applicable in the scenario under discussion, but we all know from the movies that the anger of a torch wielding mob of frightened peasants and the burning of castles can have a very deleterious effect on supernatural entities of all denominations. As indeed, was the case for my three friends in question.'

Pearce moved slightly.

The thing that looked like a dog stepped out of the bag in his direction and growled.

Pearce froze.

'I'm tempted to ask if you've ever seen a Hammer horror film from 1965 called *Dracula, Prince of Darkness* starring my friend Christopher Lee as the Count. But I fear my enthusiasm to explain what happens next is colouring my awareness of your ignorance in this genre'. Chetwynd-Hayes sighed in disappointment. 'That's the second Hammer Dracula film – the Count having been crumbled into ash at the end of the first. In the 1965 sequel, those ashes are collected, placed in a coffin and the Count's manservant – Klove – cuts the throat of a human visitor to the castle. The blood mixes with the ashes and Dracula is reconstituted once more. Literally, rising from the ashes. The part of Klove was played by a wonderfully lugubrious actor called Phillip Latham. It's a part that I would love to have played myself, and I did make my feelings known to Hammer at the time. But the powers that be didn't take up my offer. Very disappointing. Just like the film version of *The Monster Club* years later where my character was...'

The thing that looked like a dog made a *gruffling* sound and Pearce responded with a noise that sounded like a squeak. Chetwynd -Hayes' hearing aid responded with a one-note whistle, and he said: 'What?'

The thing that looked like a dog *gruffled* at him again.

'Oh, yes – sorry. My friend wants me to stop digressing and get on with it. The point? Oh yes, the point is – whether the screenwriter was aware of this or not, the resurrection in that Dracula sequel involving the ashes and the blood actually has some important basis in truth! Well, within the rejuvenation process, I mean. I'm sure that was accidental on Hammer's part. And the point here, Mr Pearce, is that you have two options available to you.'

Chetwynd-Hayes cleared his throat and raised a finger.

'First option – you can provide a small sample of your own blood for each of these bottles. Voluntarily. I can provide you with a small scalpel or a syringe for that purpose.'

Pearce's mouth opened, but no sound came out.

'Or,' Chetwynd-Hayes continued, raising a second finger. 'Two – I can arrange to have those samples taken against your will. Involuntarily. At least in the first option, you will have an element of control in the process. And it has to be your blood, I'm afraid – since you were the instigator of the arson incident. That's all part of the "mystical" process, you see. Part of the – spell? Your accomplice – the chap who started the fire? We couldn't use his blood, you see. It wouldn't have the same effect. Did I mention that we found him, and dealt with him? No? He didn't believe any of this, either. He certainly believed everything at the end though, didn't he?'

The thing that looked like a dog *gruffled* again.

'Once we have your – voluntary deposits – we'll do what needs to be done and be on our way. Believe it or not, no vengeance for your appalling act will be visited upon you by the club members. A vote was taken. By the Committee Club. Would it surprise you to learn that many members – to whom horrible behaviour is something to be commended – were actually impressed by your horrible act? Extraordinary, isn't it? However – should you reject this first option, then I'm afraid we will have to exact the second course of action. That would be very much more unpleasant and the consequences considerably more severe.'

Chetwynd-Hayes put his hands back in his lap, looked at the thing that looked like a dog, smiled with real affection and then looked back with expectant, raised eyebrows at the glass bottles on the desk.

Pearce ran his hands through his hair, then down across his face as if in surrender. And then, stepping quickly back to the desk he pulled open the top drawer and grabbed the old Webley service revolver that he'd kept in there, oiled and fully loaded, ever since someone had tried to rob his office several years ago.

The gun went off with the sound of thunder even before he'd had a chance to aim properly, the bullet carving a splintered track across the table, narrowly missing the bottles and passing so close to Chetwynd-Hayes' hearing aid that it resulted in a high pitched reverberation from the device that sounded like a snapped bedspring. As cordite smoke filled the air, obscuring vision, Pearce fired the five remaining shots directly at the thing that looked like a dog, blundered past his chair and headed for the door.

At the very moment that Pearce flung open the door – and recoiled from the sepulchral figure in tattered sheets that stood there – the thing that looked like a dog was upon him from behind. Unaffected by the five bullets that had passed through it, the thing hit Pearce squarely between the shoulder blades and brought him down heavily on the office carpet.

'Oh dear,' said Chetwynd-Hayes, adjusting his hearing aid as Pearce's screams mingled with the savage growling of the thing that savaged like a dog.

The ghoul shambled into the room, followed by the humgoo and the werewolf – all members of The Monster Club – and all known personally to Chetwynd-Hayes.

'It looks like the second option, after all.'

Afterwards, when the bottles had been filled – unnecessarily so, since only the smallest of samples would have sufficed – the ghoul, the humgoo and the werewolf retired to an ante-room to dispose of what remained on the carpet in the manner accustomed to creatures of their kind. The thing that looked like a dog gave the messy carpet a particularly thorough licking, until it was astonishingly clean.

During that time, Chetwynd-Hayes lit the necessary candles, checking that there was still requisite time available for the ritual before sunrise, and added the final necessary ingredients to each of the three bottles while intoning invocations which had been so carefully provided by experts in such matters (who were also revered members of The Monster Club).

Red smoke and foam bubbled from the glasses in what might have been considered an overly theatrical manner in any film version of Chetwynd-Hayes' own work, to which he responded with a rueful smile.

The smoke filled the office, but did not irritate his lungs. The smell was, if anything, less unpleasant than some of the furniture stores that he'd worked in before his writing career. When it cleared abruptly, the bottles were empty and spotlessly clean. The thing that looked like a dog sat happily on the spotlessly clean carpet, wagging something that could only loosely be described as a "tail".

A figure began to form in the room, hazy at first but attaining solidity in a very short time.

'Hello Manfred,' beamed Chetwynd-Hayes. 'It's literally good to see you.'

The werevamp smiled widely, revealing sharp and yellowed fangs, throwing wide his arms in welcome as if giving a hirsute imitation of Al Jolson performing a song.

A second figure began to materialise next to him.

When the process was complete, and the tall cadaverous figure fully formed, Chetwynd-Hayes declared: 'Theobold! You're looking very... well. If you know what I mean.'

Theobold bowed as the three Monster Club members who had completed their task of removing all trace of the latter day Mr Pearce re-entered the room and began to applaud.

A single and final figure began to appear in a billowing haze of purple mist, accompanied this time by the sound of an unfurling cape, or the flutter of a giant bat's wing. The haze suddenly whirled into itself and vanished, revealing a tall and distinguished figure who stepped forward with a smile of delight on his face.

'Ronald.'

The voice sounded uncannily like the voice of the horror actor Vincent Price.

'You've brought us back. You are really *so* kind.'

Chetwynd-Hayes beamed a large smile and held his arms wide.

'Eramus, my friend. Welcome!'

'It's good to *be* back.'

'We have a new location for The Monster Club, said Chetwynd-Hayes. I think you'll like it very much. But in the meantime...'

He smiled again, and inclined his neck to one side.

The opposite side of his neck, of course, to where the hearing aid was located.

'You must be famished. Please feel free to sup.'

'So, *so* kind, said Erasmus.'

MY NECROMANCE WITH CHETWYND-HAYES' FONTANA BOOK OF GREAT GHOST STORIES

By

Robert Pohle

RATHER THAN SAY that I lived in London in the 1970s and 1980s, it would be truer to say that I haunted London... and that now London haunts me.

Certainly I haunted the bookstores in the city back then. And among the most haunting of my phantom memories from those days are my searches for the anthologies in that magical series of *The Fontana Book of Great Ghost Stories* edited by R. Chetwynd-Hayes.

It's not just the books themselves that haunt me, but the places I searched for them, and the company I kept when I found them. It's not just a matter of bibliography for me, but of bibliophilia... even ghostophilia. Both romantic and necromantic.

My memory ghosts can reappear with startling suddenness at any time, in any circumstance. When I watch British movies or TV shows from that epoch, my wraiths wing back wistfully from my long-ago there and then. Just now, a TV showing of the outlandish 1969 film *The Bed Sitting Room*, set in a post-apocalyptic London of the future, recalls to me the city of my past.

While watching a scene in which Rita Tushingham wanders through a bleak tube station, memories rattle back like a train from a dark tunnel. The tube station reminds me of the time I was robbed in one, and then given all my money back by a surprisingly sympathetic bunch of street toughs – below-street toughs, I suppose, since they haunted such buried places. They had found so little money on me that they simply gave it back, and we parted friends.

I was in that tube station in the lonely wee hours because I was traveling home from seeing a London girlfriend... one who comes

THE 9TH FONTANA BOOK OF GREAT
GHOST STORIES

Tales from 'beyond the veil' by Edith Wharton, Rudyard Kipling,
Judith Merril and others – selected by R. Chetwynd-Hayes

into this story because she and I haunted London bookstores together looking for fantasy books like those of R. Chetwynd-Hayes.

And when I see the weird, quirky bird that Tushingham plays in that film – in a mini-skirt, of course – I remember more than a few girls. They were mostly expatriate Americans like me, actually, but they liked to dress like Swinging Londoners. Or at least how they imagined Swinging Londoners ought to dress. One of them, as I said, was quirky and bookish enough to share my literary interests.

When I see one of the scenes in that film with a row of nasty, decaying volumes on a rickety shelf, I think of so many old fantasy books in old London bookstores, and especially of *Great Ghost Stories*. I don't need to resort to ghostly memory only, in this particular case, because I still have every single one of them. The girl has long departed but the books linger, a tangible presence on my shelves.

It is a half century since the start of the 1970s, when she and I arrived in London. We were seekers, in all senses, seeking after so many things in life. Younger readers might need to be reminded that in those days there was no internet for buying books. If you liked obscure, out-of-print titles you had to trudge around on foot from door to door. It must be emphasized that London in those days made the trudging a joy, and the journey was radiant with wonders.

There were wonderful, numinous little specialist places with names like *Dark They Were And Golden-Eyed...* and there were also the big multi-story (in every sense) edifices like Foyle's, which spilled into two buildings full and over-full of everything from current paperbacks to yellowing treasures. Some of these shops seemed more like H.G. Wells' *Magic Shop*, fugitive places appearing only to eyes that were seeking, rather than to casual passers-by.

I recall that the most venerable places still had many used books on the shelves which had prices scrawled in them in the old money, 2/6 (two shillings and sixpence) for instance, instead of 30p (thirty new pence). Great bargains were to be had, with remote corners harbouring musty titles which looked as if they had been there for centuries.

Among the mustiest (and most pleasantly nasty) were Sir Charles Birkin's anonymously edited, pseudonymously authored and mononymously titled anthologies of the 1930s – *Creeps, Horrors, Terrors,* and so on. Could it be that Birkin's *Shudders* (1932) and *Shivers* (1933) had an impact on the young Chetwynd-Hayes when they were published, which bore unholy fruit a half century later when Chetwynd-Hayes published his own *Shudders and Shivers* (1988)?

One hesitates, as a connoisseur of great writing, to admit that one has ever judged books by their covers... but it is undoubtedly true that what drew me first to the *Great Ghost Stories* series were the covers – I still think that, overall, these are simply the most insidiously haunting, evocative covers ever, for any paperback series. Some of them still make me uneasy.

Next, one noticed the name of Robert Aickman as the original editor, and knew that one was going to be leaving the mundane world to slip sideways at a slight angle into a subtly otherwordly realm. It was a world that might not have the explicitly visceral shocks that one found in the Birkin books or Herbert van Thal's *Pan Book of Horror Stories* series... but it changed the way in which you saw and experienced everyday unreality. The question arose, just what *is* a ghost? What isn't?

At that point, in 1971, the Aickman-edited Fontanas had been coming out for five years, so there were plenty of ragged, well-thumbed copies of them to be ferreted out from used bookstores for prices about the same as a cheese sandwich... and of course they were regularly coming out new as well.

R. Chetwynd-Hayes memorably took over the Fontana series editorship from Aickman with *The Ninth Fontana Book of Great Ghost Stories* in 1973. Chetwynd-Hayes had already edited kindred Fontana anthologies in their *Tales of Terror* series: *Cornish Tales of Terror* (1970), *Scottish Tales of Terror* [as by "Angus Campbell"] and *Welsh Tales of Terror* (1973). But *The Fontana Book(s) of Great Ghost Stories* were something else altogether, the crème de la crème of the ghost anthologies.

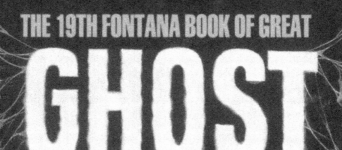

THE 19TH FONTANA BOOK OF GREAT

GHOST

—— STORIES ——

By famous writers including Washington
Irving and Guy de Maupassant, and also
by great new writers — edited by
R. Chetwynd-Hayes

As Aickman had done, Chetwynd-Hayes made of this series something very special. These are not just collections of stories by myriads of authors, but in a tangible way they are personal utterances of the editors.

With *The Ninth Fontana Book of Great Ghost Stories*, Chetwynd-Hayes began his practice of not only contributing to each volume an Introduction but also including among his story selections one of his own unique tales, in this case '*The Liberated Tiger*'. Once we had been introduced to him, those of us who had been following the series devotedly knew that we were in the custody of a safe helmsman... a safe one if you enjoyed being terrified on the voyage.

In the Introduction to *The Ninth Fontana Book*, Chetwynd-Hayes began memorably by describing himself as 'a professional horror-monger,' but noting sorrowfully that 'I wish that I could say truthfully that I had seen a ghost.' Since he went on to cast shades of ambiguity upon the claims of those who had alleged to have seen ghosts, and also upon the claims of those who said that ghosts could *not* exist, he left us in the perfect state of intellectual half-light to enjoy the world into which he was about to usher us.

He stated that 'My own contribution, "*The Liberated Tiger*", was, as indeed are all my stories, written blind. In other words, I took up my ballpoint pen and began to write. I had no idea how it would end until the last page but one.'

What days those were, when great writers wrote by personal calligraphy on tangible paper! Such beautifully balanced, musical sentences, too: just setting the single word "was" between two commas, let us know that we were in the hands of a master.

In fact, Chetwynd-Hayes now proceeded to make the Fontana series very much his own. Aickman had done the first eight, but Chetwynd-Hayes now did a dozen, and pushed the boundaries of just what a ghost story was, or could be, more and more with each succeeding volume.

For *The Tenth Fontana Book of Great Ghost Stories* in 1974, he produced another illuminating and luminous Introduction. 'Experience has taught me that people like three ingredients in a collection of ghost stories. Fear, to make them shudder; pathos, to make them shed the occasional tear and humour, to dilute the other two. But of course the greatest of these must be fear.'

His own tale this time was '*Non-paying Passengers*'. 'What can I say? It's true – every word of it. Honestly. If you don't believe me, stand on Platform 16 at Waterloo Station during the evening rush hour and look out for the – more than one – odd passenger that climbs aboard the five-forty-five train for Shepperton. You'll be surprised – to say the least.'

And we *were* surprised. Try it yourself, reader. If you can't get to Waterloo, you can read the story. And you should.

The Eleventh Fontana Book of Great Ghost Stories came in 1975. Beginning his Intro with the dictum that 'ghosts haunt the most unlikely places and objects,' Chetwynd-Hayes further explored the phantasmic geography even beyond the reach of Waterloo Station. 'So – having read about ghosts that lurk in houses, submarines, streets, holes-in-the-floor, churches, time, gardens, inns, mirrors, scarfs, chess-sets, brains, trains, ground, and egos – don't bother to climb under the bed.

'There's bound to be one there too.'

Need the reader be assured that indeed ghosts dwelling in every one of those places can be found in *The Eleventh Fontana Book of Great Ghost Stories*? Chetwynd-Hayes's own story this time, '*Matthew and Luke*', is the one that deals with the haunted ego: as he says, 'It makes for a change.'

1976 brought the *The Twelfth Fontana Book of Great Ghost Stories*, more change, and more exploration of the possible places for hauntings. 'I have often thought that there ought to be more ghosts – of one kind or another – on the sea than the land,' Chetwynd-Hayes begins. 'After all, there is more of it, and water could be a perfect conductor for the peculiar vibrations that appear to be necessary for psychic phenomena. Ships are but floating houses, that over a period of time must become saturated with emotional atmosphere which – under certain circumstances – may be able to crystallize as a time-image.'

THE 14TH FONTANA BOOK OF GREAT
GHOST STORIES

Sinister tales of the occult by L. P. Hartley, Robert E.
Howard, Daniel Defoe and others – selected by
R. Chetwynd-Hayes

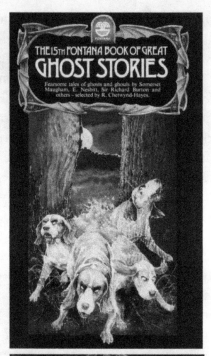

THE 15TH FONTANA BOOK OF GREAT
GHOST STORIES

Fearsome tales of ghosts and ghouls by Somerset
Maugham, E. Nesbit, Sir Richard Burton and
others – selected by R. Chetwynd-Hayes.

THE 16TH FONTANA BOOK OF GREAT
GHOST
STORIES

Haunting stories by
M. R. James, Marjorie Bowen,
Pamela Hansford Johnson and others –
selected by R. Chetwynd-Hayes

THE 17TH FONTANA BOOK OF GREAT
GHOST
STORIES

By famous writers including STEPHEN KING,
AGATHA CHRISTIE, JEROME K. JEROME –
edited by R. CHETWYND-HAYES

Discussing Barbara Joan Eyre's contribution to the volume, '*That Summer*', Chetwynd-Hayes spins his own spell with phrases like 'the murmur of sun-drugged sea' and 'the gentle sigh of a sluggish breeze,' conjuring up a scene with Haiku-like numinous terseness. One struggles to resist the temptation to quote each of his story introductions, but cannot forbear to quote the one to his own '*Cold Fingers*': 'My ghosts are always nasty. Sometimes in fact really vile... Which only demonstrates what an awful mind I must have.

'Well – I will not wish you happy reading, because that is not my intention...'

'75 and '76 also saw Chetwynd-Hayes's other Fontana anthologies *Tales of Terror from Outer Space* and *Gaslight Tales of Terror*. Then the lucky thirteenth in *The Fontana Book of Great Ghost Stories* series in 1977 found Chetwynd-Hayes wondering why we all 'and I do mean all – are so interested in ghosts? Maybe it is a subconscious need to have some confirmation that there is an afterlife; that we continue to exist, in no matter what form, once this brief earthly journey comes to an end. Undoubtedly there would be certain advantages in being a ghost...'

There were certainly advantages both certain and uncertain in reading the stories he selected this time... maybe even more in reading his comments about them. Discussing 'adventures on the astral plane during sleeping hours' in his remarks on one piece, Chetwynd-Hayes confides in us that he himself once 'retired to bed, determined to find out if there was anything in the theory or not. Suddenly I found myself staring down at my own sleeping body. I was so frightened, I instantly woke up, drenched in perspiration, my heart thumping like an overworked steam engine.'

You must read the rest yourself, reader, as you must Chetwynd-Hayes's own 'very humble offering' this time, '*My Dear Wife*', 'a story with a moral: always make sure you have got rid of one love before taking on a new one. Otherwise life – and death – can become very complicated.'

The complexities of life and death continued to perplex in 1978's fourteenth offering. 'Many authors confuse horror with pleasurable fear and I find that some editors are in a like quandary,' Chetwynd-Hayes fretted. '... I have only just kept within my own guidelines, but such is the arrogance of editors, I make no apology for doing so.' Of one story, he says that it 'is not so much terrifying as disturbing,' and of another that 'Dissatisfaction with this world might engender an increasing curiosity as to the shadow-clad inhabitants of the next.' Of his own 'The Sad Ghost', Chetwynd-Hayes wonders if the ghost is 'a gormless idiot who only comes to his senses on the last page.

'May black demons watch around your bed,' Chetwynd-Hayes blesses us troublingly as he departs.

When he returned with the fifteenth in 1979, Chetwynd-Hayes's ghosts were hardly gormless. Formless, some of them, maybe, but realer than real. 'I am of the opinion that to write a successful ghost story, the author must believe in the existence of ghosts,' he wrote. 'I do – although I have yet to experience any form of psychic phenomenon myself – and cannot understand why anyone should harbour doubts. Surely it is inconceivable that such a complicated being as an intelligent man or woman ceases to be once the chains of corporeal life have fallen away. And if we are granted a state of continuous memory, then it must follow that regrets... might compel certain of us to linger...'

His own story in this fifteenth was 'The Hanging Tree'. 'Yes, I wrote that,' Chetwynd-Hayes affirmed. 'A few people may recognize the setting, but I hasten to add that this is the only authentic part about it.' But of course it was all authentic, in the deeper sense.

The Sixteenth Fontana Book of Great Ghost Stories in 1980 further explored the nature of the beast. 'To have a full chilling effect a ghost should be heard and not seen. Possibly this is the reason that the radio is such a perfect medium for the ghost story, because the listener is only permitted to hear approaching footsteps, creaking doors, a disembodied sigh – and his imagination does the rest. To actually meet a ghost face to face must be an anticlimax...'

It wasn't, of course, and least of all in Chetwynd-Hayes's story this time, 'She Walks on Dry Land', 'which for a change I have set in the Regency period. Well – why not?'

THE 13TH FONTANA BOOK OF GREAT
GHOST STORIES

Nightmare tales of the unquiet dead by Denis
Wheatley, Guy de Maupassant, Somerset Maugham
and others – selected by R. Chetwynd-Hayes

In *She Walks on Dry Land,* one of Chetwynd-Hayes's characters asks, "Surely your lordship isn't really expecting a moaning ghost to come up from the sea?" To which the reply is made, "From such a setting one must expect anything – or nothing."

One always expected *something*, of course, when the new Fontana ghost book appeared, and in 1981 it was the seventeenth, with Chetwynd-Hayes declaring reasonably enough that 'I must surely now – with all due modesty – be entitled to classify myself as an expert in this genre.

'But – I am still not entirely certain what a ghost is... A disembodied spirit. A personality residue...I have very grave doubts about the first, as to my knowledge no one has held a conversation with a ghost... A time image is my favourite. Thought waves which have become impregnated in the woodwork, atmosphere, etc., and can be transformed into the likeness of their dead creator. I have often pondered the possibility that our descendants will be able to watch our antics on a kind of super television set. It is a sobering thought.'

But then there was his own tale this time, *'Which One?'*, which proved that rules can be broken and one might say *must* be broken. 'This makes nonsense of everything I have written in the opening paragraphs of this introduction. I ask you to accept that there is life after death and that one can hold a very lengthy conversation with a ghost.'

We had certainly been holding very lengthy conversations with Chetwynd-Hayes in these later Fontana anthologies, since his Introductions had been becoming ever lengthier and more discursive – and who was going to complain?

The Eighteenth Fontana Book of Great Ghost Stories emerged from the æther in 1982, and Chetwynd-Hayes continued his discourse on just what a ghost is, as if he had been merely interrupted by the passage of a year. He added a caveat. 'I missed one out: the fear ghost... Atmosphere, plus a generous helping of fear, will make your brain project the image it expects to see. Now, I am going to take this blood-curdling conjecture one stage further. Is it not possible that one or more people can create a fear ghost that becomes part of the surroundings and is later seen by someone who is – at first – not particularly frightened? Imagine – you may be on the receiving end of someone else's fear.'

Of his own contribution to this volume, '*The Chair*', Chetwynd-Hayes asked, 'Is it true? Could be.'

We devoted readers were most happy to be on the receiving end when *The Nineteenth Fontana Book of Great Ghost Stories* appeared in 1983. Chetwynd-Hayes was feeling reminiscent. 'It does not seem possible that almost twelve years have passed since I first agreed to take on the chore of editing the Fontana Books of Great Ghost Stories... Ghost story-addicts still demand the same mixture: a preponderance of modern plots where recognizable characters find themselves in bizarre circumstances, blended with a few oldies that have not been too over-exposed. But I find that my main problem is attracting authors who – to coin a phrase – can hide time-bleached skulls behind new faces.'

The mix was indeed the same as ever and equally indeed as different as ever. Chetwynd-Hayes opined that his own story, '*Tomorrow's Ghost*' (reprinted here from his 1981 hardback collection *Tales of Darkness*) 'is – maybe – for what it is worth – the best ghost story I have so far written.' Clavering Grange, in this tale, was also the setting of Chetwynd-Hayes's first novel *The Dark Man* – AKA: *And Love Survived* (1964), as well as appearing in his *Tales From the Other Side* (1983). In the next few years it would feature in *The King's Ghost* – AKA: *The Grange* (1985), *Tales From the Hidden World* and *The Haunted Grange* (both 1988).

For now, in 1983, 'May you never hear invisible footsteps following you down the stairs,' Chetwynd-Hayes wishes us as he vanishes.

He reappeared with *The Twentieth Fontana Book of Great Ghost Stories* in Orwell's year of 1984. Alas! Orwell was right that this was a bleak year, because it was the last one in which a new volume of the Fontana series appeared. When I returned to London in 1985, there was no new volume in the series to be searched for. Oh, plenty

THE 20th FONTANA BOOK OF GREAT

GHOST

STORIES

A collection of truly haunting stories – edited
by R. CHETWYND-HAYES

of other great British haunts and horrors continued, Herbert van Thal's series of *The Pan Book of Horror Stories* (in a few volumes of which Chetwynd-Hayes himself appeared) creaked on for a bit under the new regime of Clarence Paget... but an era, an epoch, was fading away.

Chetwynd-Hayes opened *The Twentieth Fontana Book of Great Ghost Stories* with what was really a valedictory dirge. 'I sometimes like to think that long after I am dead and gone, these Fontana Books of Great Ghost Stories will become collector's items. Not impossible... I do not write for posterity, but I always have it in mind. We all haunt the future and are the stuff from which ghosts are made...'

Of his own story this time, '*My Very Best Friend*', he noted that it was 'Based loosely on incidents that took place in my own childhood...'

Chetwynd-Hayes himself was our own Very Best Friend, those of us who hunted and collected the Fontana series. It was truly our own childhood, even though we thought we were grown-ups. Now that we are old, the books of the series are still aglow and young on our shelves.

'Happy shuddering,' Chetwynd-Hayes wished us in his last words in the twentieth volume.

CONTRIBUTORS

FRED ADAMS, Jr is an American novelist (*Hitwolf*, *Six-Gun Terrors*) who has spent his life in love with the English language, English literature, and the good old English ghost story. He particularly enjoys the creepy craftsmanship of R. Chetwynd-Hayes for his ability to evoke in the reader a frisson alongside a nervous laugh.

'*Chetwynd-Hayes had the rare ability to put new wine in an old bottle, modern ideas in a time-honoured genre, and create entertaining gems of supernatural literature.*'

DAVE BRZESKI is a fan who was unwise enough to get involved in the creative side of the book business when he began contributing reviews to the British Fantasy Society website in 2011. Since then he has branched out into editing for various publishers, including Pro Se Productions in the US. He was immensely proud to have his name on the front cover of *The Spirit of the Place and Other Strange Tales: The Complete Short Stories of Elizabeth Walter*, from Shadow Publishing. Since then he has co-edited, with John Linwood Grant, the magazine, *Occult Detective Quarterly* and its companion anthology *Occult Detective Quarterly Presents* for Ulthar Press.

'*I spent no more than an hour, probably less, in Ron's company at several Fantasycons, beginning in 1986. He really made an impression. Cliché, or not I can state with some certainty that he was genuinely the nicest old gentleman one could ever hope to meet. He was always very pleased to sign copies of books for fans. On one occasion, I don't remember exactly which, he told me he'd flown to the convention (London to Birmingham) simply because he'd never been in an aeroplane before. Sadly, I'd dropped out of the convention scene for almost 20 years and so missed his final convention appearance at the World Fantasy Convention in London in 1997, where he was deservedly one of the Guests of Honour.*'

SIMON CLARK is the author of many novels and short stories, including *Blood Crazy*, *Vampyrrhic*, *Darkness Demands*, *Stranger*, *Bastion* and *Inspector Abberline and The Just King*. Simon adapted his award-winning *The Night of the Triffids* as a full-cast audio drama for Big Finish, which was subsequently broadcast as a five-part series by BBC Radio 4 Extra. As an anthology editor, he is also responsible for *The Mammoth Book of Sherlock Holmes Abroad* and

Sherlock Holmes' School for Detection.
    'I discovered Ronald Chetwynd-Hayes in my teens, and was utterly captivated. For me, one of the quintessential Chetwynd-Hayes stories is "The Resurrectionist" where a young man falls in love with a girl who died fifty years ago, and his obsession drives him to open her grave. It features Ron's trademark underdog/oddball character on a mission (usually a self-destructive mission), and though this is an undeniably dark and morbid tale Ron's vivid descriptions employ words that flash and sparkle from the page. Later, I was privileged to meet Ron at conventions, drink a beer in his excellent company, and listen to him read stories aloud in such an entertaining way, his eyes always twinkling with impish glee.'

ADRIAN COLE has been a published author since the 1970s, when his sword and planet saga, *The Dream Lords* first came out from Zebra (US). Its three volumes are due to be reprinted by Pulp Hero Press in the near future, along with a new, fourth volume, *Dream Lords Legacy*.
    Cole has worked in heroic fantasy, horror, science fiction, Mythos and all the various crossovers in between, and has had some two dozen novels published, including the four volume *Omaran Saga*, the *Voidal* trilogy, two Young Adult novels, and the science fiction work, *The Shadow Academy*. He has also had a number of collections published, including *Tough Guys* and the soon to see print, *Dark Ships Passing*, which pulls together his various Sword and Sorcery stories across the years.
    In 2015 he won the British Fantasy Award for the Best Collection with *Nick Nightmare Investigates* (Alchemy Press) and this is due to be reprinted in the near future, together with two more collections, *Nightmare Cocktails* and *Nightmare Creatures* (all from Pulp Hero Press).
    Also in the works are an Elak of Atlantis collection, which continues the adventures of Henry Kuttner's character, and a Mythos collection.
    'I have been a long time fan of Ron Chetwynd-Hayes' work, enjoying the quirky, humorous style of the writer and his ability to tell a good yarn, a skill not found often enough these days. 'Shadmocks Only Whistle' is my tribute to Ron, written in a style that, perhaps, the old master would have appreciated. My abiding memory of Ron is sitting with him in a London pub, back in the 1980s, when Ron delivered to my wife and I the entire closing speech from Things to Come, *the classic H G Wells movie, a speech that clearly moved and motivated him.'*

PETE 'CARDINAL' COX has had his various writings published in the small-press for around thirty-five years. Posts held include poet-in-residence of a Victorian cemetery (for three years) and for the Dracula Society (for two years). Out of the latter grew his one-man 'spooken word' show *High Stakes* that has been widely performed including at Worldcon75 in Helsinki and the Dublin 2019 Worldcon.

For the Cardinal, Ron Chetwynd-Hayes (who Cox considers himself honoured to have briefly met at the World Fantasy Convention in 1997) represents one of the stout hearts of British horror, whose astute editing of anthologies introduced the Cardinal to many fine writers, and that the unjustified neglect that Chetwynd-Hayes' own novels and short-stories suffer is little short of a crime.

THERESA DERWIN writes Dark Urban Fantasy and Horror and has over forty anthology appearances.

Having retired from the civil service in 2011 on medical grounds, she decided to pursue a writing career.

She's had three collections published; *Monsters Anonymous* (Anarchy Books 2012), *Season's Creepings* and *Wolf at The Door'*. She edited *Weird Ales* (2016) creating volumes 2 and 3 in 2017. Forthcoming books are *Once Upon a Feather*, publisher TBC, then *God's Vengeance* from Crystal Lake Publishing.

'*Why I love Ron: When 'Monsters Anonymous' came out, Joel Lane told me it was raw, but that I was like "an R. Chetwynd-Hayes for the Facebook generation." I was of course, ecstatic and very flattered. I'd been raised on Hammer and Universal horror films, but when I watched* The Monster Club, *I knew I was home. Monsters, comedy, horror and chilling endings. The Humgoo and the Shadmock, became the monsters to inspire my writing.*'

PAULINE E. DUNGATE is a writer, reviewer and poet. She travels to far flung places and has a tendency to set stories there. At home she counts butterflies for Butterfly conservation and spends time in the garden when not playing with her photographs. A prolific reader since the era of *The Pan Book of Horror Stories*, she has a vivid memory of R. Chetwynd-Hayes' The Monster Club.

It seemed appropriate to set her story against that backdrop.

JOHN LINWOOD GRANT is a pro writer/editor from Yorkshire, with some forty plus stories published in a wide range of magazines and anthologies over the last three years, including *Lackington's Magazine*, *Vastarien*, *Weirdbook* and others. His story '*His Heart Shall Speak No More*' was picked for *Best New Horror 29* (PS Publishing 2019), his '*The Jessamine Touch*' was in the Lambda award winning anthology *His Seed*, and his short story collection, *A Persistence of Geraniums*, came out from Ulthar Press in 2019. His latest novel *The Assassin's Coin* is available from IFD. He is editor, of the magazine *Occult Detective Quarterly* (with Dave Brzeski) and various anthologies, including the recent *Hell's Empire*. News of his projects can be found on his popular website greydogtales.com. He first encountered R. Chetwynd-Hayes in tatty paperback collections when young, and then watched *The Monster Club* when it was first released, which cemented his affection for a very British author.

STEPHEN LAWS is an award-winning horror novelist, whose work has been published all over the world. His novels include *Ghost Train, Spectre, The Wyrm, The Frighteners, Darkfall, Gideon* (AKA *Fear Me*), *Macabre, Daemonic, Somewhere South Of Midnight, Chasm* and *Ferocity*. His short stories can be found in the collection *The Midnight Man*.

'Ronald Chetwynd-Hayes – 'Britain's Prince of Chill' – was a horror writer whom I've been reading, it seems, all my life. I still love his macabre style and always looked forward to his short stories and novels.

He was also an editor/compiler of an excellent series of horror anthologies over the years, having taken over the editorship of The Fontana Book of Great Ghost Stories *after the departure of editor Robert Aickman.* Cornish Tales of Terror, Scottish Tales of Terror *and* Welsh Tales of Terror *followed (among many others). They're collections that I'd very much recommend, my particular favourite being 'Tales of Terror from Outer Space' which contains two of my all-time favourite fantasy/horror tales by other hands, but I'm not going to tell you which ones they are. So there.*

Frankly, I loved Ron's tales – and when I was asked to be a Guest of Honour at the British Fantasy Society Convention in Birmingham way back in 1989, and also discovered that Ronald Chetwynd-Hayes would be attending as a guest of honour and panellist, I grabbed the opportunity to tell him so, face to face. He was unwell then, I think, and his hearing was severely impaired; but he soldiered on, and I still have fond memories of that meeting.

He passed away in 2001, but it's always pleased me that since then, with the sterling support of such genre editors as Stephen Jones and others, his name has been kept alive for appreciators of Ron's work, old and new – engaging and encouraging new generations of fans and writers alike. Dave Brzeski is one such "appreciator", and the collection of original stories by other writers that is now before you, inspired by and in tribute to Ronald Chetwynd-Hayes, is something to which I have been delighted to contribute. My story – 'Fire Damage' – is not only a tribute to Ron's book The Monster Club, *but also the subsequent film made by Amicus and starring Vincent Price. It's a story that can (hopefully) be read on a number of levels since it references not only the book, but also the film and some inside references to the making of the latter. It also features Ron himself in the story as I remember him and in affectionate memory, takes his hearing difficulty and empowers it with a supernatural "twist" that I hope would have appealed to him.*

Another aspect of Ron's work that I loved was his macabre yet quirky sense of humour, and it's this also that I've tried to replicate. For what it's worth, and given what I've just said, I'd like to end this mini-tribute with something that might seem like a non sequitur. And it's this –

I really learned from him the power of a well-placed semicolon.

Honestly.

I'm not joking.

Or am I?

To readers of this collection – I hope you enjoy 'Fire Damage'.

To Ronald Chetwynd-Hayes – My ongoing admiration for a writer who is still pleasing fans of horror From Beyond The Grave.'

WILLIAM MEIKLE is a Scottish writer, now living in Canada, with over thirty novels published in the genre press and more than 300 short story credits in thirteen countries. He has books available from a variety of publishers including Dark Regions Press and Severed Press and his work has appeared in a large number of professional anthologies and magazines. He lives in Newfoundland with whales, bald eagles and icebergs for company. His story in this volume is a tribute to Ron, his way with a comeuppance, his wit, and his insights into the murkier depths of the human condition.

MARION PITMAN writes all sorts of fiction, most of it short, much of it supernatural. Recent short stories have appeared in *Occult Detective Quarterly* and *Hell's Empire* (Ulthar Press), and her first collection, *Music in the Bone*, is available from Alchemy Press. She also writes poetry, and will sing if you are not careful. She grew up reading M R James, Dorothy L Sayers and Algernon Blackwood among others, which explains a lot. She had a second-hand bookshop before someone burnt it down, and Ron used to come in from time to time, usually looking for one of his own books of which he no longer had a copy (occasionally she was able to supply one).

The invitation to contribute to this collection was an honour which she was glad to accept.

JIM PITTS was born in January 1950 in Blackburn, Lancashire, in the north west of England. He started illustrating in 1970, with submissions to David Sutton's Shadow Press magazine, *The HPL Bibliotheca*, and Jon Harvey's *Balthus*. Over the next nearly fifty years Pitts' work has seen publication extensively in Europe and America in various semi-professional and professional magazines. He worked with the artists Martin McKenna and Dave Carson, on a collaboration to illustrate Stephen Jones's collection of Mythos stories *Shadows Over Innsmouth* (Fedogan and Bremer). Jones later went on to ask him to contribute some black and white interior illustrations for the forthcoming R. Chetwynd-Hayes collection *Looking For Something to Suck and Other Vampire Stories* (Fedogan and Bremer). Jim Pitts met Ron just once when Stephen Jones was putting the latter book together. A recent high point was the publication by Parallel Universe Publications of *The Fantastical Art of Jim Pitts*, a large collection of Pitts' work looking back over his long career. Jim Pitts still resides in Blackburn, and retired from the brewing industry in 2014. He spends his retirement still dabbling at his drawing board and easel, watching films and TV, reading, and keeping in touch with friends (including the occasional Convention).

ROBERT POHLE has appeared in over 30 books as either sole author or contributor, beginning with *Sherlock Holmes on the Screen* in 1977.

In his contribution to the present volume he remembers with affectionate melancholy his residence in London in the 1970s when he avidly collected *The Fontana Book of Great Ghost Stories* series edited by R. Chetwynd-Hayes. Ron's memorable dicta in those books about the creation of fantasy fiction influenced everything to which Pohle subsequently put his hand, up to his appearance in *Occult Detective Quarterly Presents*, edited by John Linwood Grant and Dave Brzeski in 2018.

Like more than a few ex-Londoners of his acquaintance, Pohle is happily retired in Florida, where he lives with his wife Maryann and near his daughter Rita and grandsons Graeme and Bret – all of whom he loves even more than the books of Chetwynd-Hayes, which is a considerable amount.

JOHN LLEWELLYN PROBERT was thirteen when he first read the stories of R. Chetwynd-Hayes. The book was THE UNBIDDEN, and that 1971 collection was a major influence on Probert's developing style as a writer. His library now contains every Chetwynd-Hayes book ever written. Probert's first book, *The Faculty of Terror*, based its portmanteau structure on Ron's *The Monster Club* and it won the Dracula Society's Children of the Night award. He has frequently mixed humour with horror in the Chetwynd-Hayes style and he won the British Fantasy Award for his macabre novella *The Nine Deaths of Dr Valentine*. Amongst Probert's many current projects is a non-fiction book about *From Beyond the Grave*, the 1973 Amicus collection of R. Chetwynd-Hayes stories culled from *The Unbidden, Cold Terror* and *The Elemental*. The title story of that latter collection introduced the world to Madame Orloff, whose latest adventure Probert is been proud to relate in this current volume.

TINA RATH has always loved dark fantasy, and hunted for anthologies of short stories to feed her addiction. The *Fontana Books of Great Ghost Stories*, edited by Robert Aikman and later by R. Chetwynd-Hayes were always particularly welcome finds. She has also been writing, and, on occasion, selling short stories since the early seventies. Her absolute first sale was to a magazine called *Catholic Fireside* (Flora Thompson, the author of the trilogy *Lark Rise to Candleford* also had stories published there, and some of the earliest sketches for that trilogy also appeared in *Catholic Fireside,* so it wasn't quite what you might think...) but her second, 'The Fetch', was to R. Chetwynd-Hayes for the *Nineteenth Book of Great Ghost Stories*, published in 1983. It was later reprinted in *Great Ghost Stories* (2004), edited by R. Chetwynd-Hayes and Stephen Jones.

'I feel very privileged to have my name associated with R. Chetwynd-Hayes and Fontana Books in my small story. I was also very happy to write one for this collection, dealing with a time In Ron's career where he worked as an extra. This is not about any particular studio, or any particular time... it is a story about stories and how they intrude, sometimes, into our reality.'

JOSH REYNOLDS is a writer, occasional editor and semi-professional monster movie enthusiast. He has been a professional author since 2007, and has had over twenty novels published in that time, as well as a wealth of shorter fiction pieces, including short stories, novellas and the occasional audio script. An up-to-date list of his published work, including licensed fiction for Games Workshop's Warhammer Fantasy and Warhammer 40,000 lines, can be found at his site, https://joshuamreynolds.co.uk/. Reynolds has long been a fan of Ron's blend of horror and humour, and considers being allowed to contribute to this anthology a high honour indeed.

I.A. WATSON writes novels and short stories when they don't make him write business reports. Since he has produced over a score of books and contributed to around forty more, he obviously still has too much time on his hands. His most recent titles were *Premium Delivery to the Centre of the Earth* (SF), *Labours of Hercules* (myth), *Vinnie De Soth, Jobbing Occultist* (urban supernatural), *Sherlock Holmes Mysteries Volume 2* (umm... mystery), and *Bulldog Drummond: On Poisoned Ground* (action adventure).

Next up is *The Legend of Robin Hood* (collecting four previous novels and some new material) and then *Sir Mumphrey Wilton and the Secrets of the Final Page* (working title; other suggestions are welcome). More details, samples, and free stories are available at http://www.chillwater.org.uk/writing/iawatsonhome.htm

Ian Watson never got to meet Ron but sincerely wishes he had.

ALSO AVAILABLE FROM
SHADOW PUBLISHING

Phantoms of Venice
Selected by David A. Sutton
ISBN 0-9539032-1-4

The Satyr's Head: Tales of Terror
Selected by David A. Sutton
ISBN 978-0-9539032-3-8

The Female of the Species And Other Terror Tales
By Richard Davis
ISBN 978-0-9539032-4-5

Frightfully Cosy And Mild Stories For Nervous Types
By Johnny Mains
ISBN 978-0-9539032-5-2

Horror! Under the Tombstone: Stories from the Deathly Realm
Selected by David A. Sutton
ISBN 978-0-9539032-6-9

The Whispering Horror
By Eddy C. Bertin
ISBN: 978-0-9539032-7-6

The Lurkers in the Abyss and Other Tales of Terror
By David A. Riley
ISBN: 978-0-9539032-9-0

Worse Things Than Spiders and Other Stories
By Samantha Lee
ISBN: 978-0-9539032-8-3

Tales of the Grotesque: A Collection of Uneasy Tales
By L. A. Lewis
Edited by Richard Dalby
ISBN: 978-0-9572962-0-6

Horror on the High Seas: Classic Weird Sea Tales
Selected by David A. Sutton
ISBN: 978-0-9572962-1-3

Creeping Crawlers
Edited by Allen Ashley
ISBN 978-0-9572962-2-0

Haunts of Horror
Edited by David A. Sutton
ISBN 978-0-9572962-3-7

Death After Death
By Edmund Glasby
ISBN 978-0-9572962-4-4

The Spirit of the Place and Other Strange Tales:
Complete Short Stories
By Elizabeth Walter
Edited by Dave Brzeski
ISBN 978-0-9572962-5-1

Such Things May Be: Collected Writings
By James Wade
Edited by Edward P. Berglund
ISBN 978-0-9572962-6-8

The Black Pilgrimage & Other Explorations
Essays on Supernatural Fiction
By Rosemary Pardoe
ISBN 978-0-9572962-7-5

Bloody Britain
By Anna Taborska
ISBN 978-0-9572962-9-9

CPSIA information can be obtained
at www.ICGtesting.com
Printed in the USA
BVHW072102180221
600365BV00005B/450

9 780957 296282